HEALING HEARTS

HEALING HEARTS

by
Donna K. Ford

2013

Credits
Editor: Ruth Sternglantz
Production Design: Stacia Seaman
Cover Design by Sheri (graphicartist2020@hotmail.com)

Acknowledgments

When I set out to write this book, I had no idea what I was getting into. Like so many others, I was inspired by the beautiful stories I had discovered as I read books by Radclyffe, and I fell in love with a world where the lesbian characters were people anyone would want to know. As I read, I became obsessed with the idea that I wanted to make a contribution to the literary world and share the passion for telling our stories as Lesbian women. From the beginning, this book was my journey into a new world where I think I found an inner strength that had been waiting to be unleashed. But this was a journey I did not take alone.

Thank you to my dear friends Keah, Sheila, Sandy, and Marie for always listening.

I offer much gratitude to my first readers Kellie and Sheila. Without their support, I am uncertain if I would have had the courage to pursue not only finishing but publishing this book. It is amazing how far a kind word can take us.

I also owe a great deal of gratitude to my editor, Ruth Sternglantz, for her patience and guidance through this wonderful journey and for helping me become a better writer and making me laugh at myself.

Many thanks to all the wonderful staff at Bold Strokes Books for supporting me and accepting my book and helping me make it so much better. And to Sheri for developing a cover that I felt captured the soul of the story.

A special thank you to Keah, who has a way of making me believe that all things are possible.

For my mom and dad. Thank you for being as proud of this book as I am and for loving me for who I am.

And to Keah, my sweetness, for believing I can do anything.

Chapter One

Christian felt the calm settle over her as she navigated the long gravel drive that would lead her to the place she hoped to finally put her grief and fear to rest. Since Cara's death, nothing in her life seemed real. She was looking forward to some peace and quiet away from everyone who questioned her isolation, pressed her to get on with life, and didn't understand her ongoing grief. As she drove, she thought over her life and realized she had never been alone like this before. She was looking forward to the fresh air and the peace that comes from solitude among strangers.

It was early April and had been an unusually warm spring following a long, cold, and wet winter. The sun was warm on Christian's arm and face as it poured in through the glass. She rolled down the window to take in the crisp morning air, and goose bumps rose on her arms as the cool air danced over her sun-warmed skin. It was cooler in East Tennessee than it had been when she'd left New Orleans the day before, but it was a pleasant change. And the quiet was a comfort from the city sounds that usually buzzed around her.

Christian smiled faintly as a loose lock of her newly cut hair tickled the side of her jaw. Reaching a hand to her face, she gently tucked the wayward strands behind her ear. Cara had loved playing with her long curls, often twisting them around her fingers and playing them across her lips. The memory made Christian sigh with longing. She had cut her hair only a week ago, trying to convince herself that change would help her move forward. She had thought that cutting her hair would make the memories fade, but she still thought of Cara each time she brushed her hair back from her face or tucked it behind her ear. She wondered somberly what Cara would think of the change.

As she drew closer to her destination, she noticed that daffodils lined the drive and grew in mounds around the giant oaks that stood sentry over the grounds, making her smile as she breathed in the welcoming air of the country and the freshness of early spring. The air was crisp and had an earthy undertone. Christian drew in a deep breath, filling her lungs. She detected a hint of sweetness that tickled her nose. She tried to place the scent but couldn't quite put her finger on it. It reminded her of lace and something wild that made her mouth water. She could almost taste it.

Christian had heard about Willow Springs from a client of her law practice and, upon further research, had learned it was a private resort for lesbians. With the promise of beautiful sunsets, rolling mountains, and pristine lakes, Willow Springs had seemed the perfect sanctuary.

The drive was a long, winding gravel path that allowed glimpses of the lodge from a distance. Flashes of the structure flickered between the intermittent trees that seemed to be standing at attention in formation. A split-rail fence lined the drive and was partially overgrown with a small twisted vine and tiny yellow flowers. Christian smiled. That had been the smell she had detected earlier—jasmine.

The lodge was a large Victorian house, renovated and expanded as a bed-and-breakfast retreat, tucked secretively into the mountains of East Tennessee. The white siding and giant red shutters were like the smiling face of a mother, welcoming the prodigal daughter home.

Christian felt her heart lighten with the warmth of the welcome, pleased with her first impression of the place that would be her home for several months. She was tired from the travel and from the weight that settled deep in her heart. She didn't pretend she would be able to forget about the accident that had claimed her lover, but perhaps she could find a way to put her own life back together.

Pulling the car around to the front entrance, Christian was met by the porter, a young woman in her twenties with golden tanned skin, her long blond hair pulled back into a ponytail. She wore tan shorts and a tight-fitting blue T-shirt that had the lodge logo embossed over her left breast. Christian took in the girl's slight athleticism and eager expression and felt some of her tension ease as she let out a breath she didn't realize she had been holding.

The girl smiled cheerfully as she greeted Christian at the door of her car as it came to a stop. She offered Christian her hand as she opened the door.

"Welcome to Willow Springs, you must be Ms. Sutter," the woman said more as a statement than a question. "We've been expecting you."

Tucking the stray hair behind her ear again, Christian reached out and took the offered hand. Christian welcomed the warmth of the girl's hand as her fingers curled around her own with a firm strength that offered both comfort and welcome. Christian smiled up at her as she stood, thankful for her kindness. "Yes," she replied, "but you can call me Christian."

As they circled to the back of the car, the young woman took the bags from the trunk and ceremoniously offered her other arm. "May I escort you?" Her smile was genuine and her eyes were like blue diamonds, sparkling in the sun.

Christian studied the eager young face, feeling somewhat self-conscious from the attention. "What's your name? I can't exactly accept your arm when I don't even know your name," she said playfully.

"Hannah," the girl replied. "Please, it would be my honor."

"Well, Hannah," Christian said taking her arm, "I believe the honor is all mine, thank you." Christian was thankful for the support, as her strength faltered and her legs threatened to give way.

The front entrance to the lodge was a long porch that stretched the length of the original home, with wide plank steps leading up to large French doors. As they entered the lodge, Christian paused for a moment to take in the front room. It was beautiful. There was no traditional front desk. Instead, guests were greeted in a formal living room, with a library, an open bar, and a fireplace that begged to be worshiped.

There was so much to take in: a baby grand piano, the rich dark wood of the bar, two elegant formal sofas set facing each other, the large fireplace centered on the far wall. Christian could imagine the scores of women who had sat in this room, basking in the warmth of the fire, sharing stories about their lives, and she was suddenly short of breath as a wave of loneliness washed over her. Hannah led her just inside the door to a small desk that looked like it belonged in someone's study. Most of her arrangements had been made over the phone, and it only took a few moments for Christian to sign the needed forms and get checked in. She turned to follow Hannah when she picked up Christian's bags and gestured upstairs.

"I'll show you to your room."

Christian was mesmerized as she made her way across the room. A large staircase in the center of the room branched off both right and left halfway up, mimicking the open-arm structure of the building itself. The two arms of the staircase met the grand landing at the top overlooking the large room and front entrance. As Hannah led her up the stairs, Christian felt her feet glide across the smooth hardwood floor and noted the ease of the climb as the steps were spaced at a gradual incline that made the ascent effortless. The smooth banister seemed to flow under her touch as she ran her hand along the well-worn surface. From the landing, the large windows Christian had admired on her arrival now offered a stunning view of the front gardens and the grove of oak trees that still looked like an army standing at attention.

Christian stopped at the top of the landing and studied the crown moldings that ran throughout the room.

"All the wood is hand carved," Hannah explained. "The house was originally an old farmhouse that was built around the time the TVA flooded the valley creating the lake. Of course, the original home was much smaller, just the main building here. The wings were added when the owners renovated, but they made sure to preserve as much of the wood as possible. You'll see that the local craftsmen were able to mimic the old style quite well in the new structure."

Christian met Hannah's eyes and smiled. "It's beautiful."

Reaching Christian's room, Hannah produced a small iron key and promptly unlocked the door. She opened the door and, with a sweep of her hand, motioned Christian inside and followed with the luggage. Stepping into the room, Christian's eyes took in the warm sage color of the walls, and she noticed the rich hardwood floors of the hallway continued throughout the room. At the back of the room was a queen-size bed, a small desk with a reading lamp, and a lazy chair. Christian walked around the room, stopping to check out the view, tilting her head toward the warm rays of sun that hit her skin as they filtered through the French doors that led to a small balcony overlooking the lake.

Hannah spoke softly, breaking the silence. "I am posted in the front room and entrance. If you need anything, please ring me. Breakfast begins at six a.m., lunch at eleven a.m., and dinner at five p.m. The kitchen is always open if you would prefer to eat in your room. There are marked paths around the property, horseback riding at the stables, and lots of water activities at the lake. The pool is in the back, as well as the patio. Most everyone prefers to eat on the patio at lunch so they can enjoy the sun, pool, and view. You'll find everything you need there. The staff will be happy to assist you with any of your needs."

"Thank you, Hannah."

Hannah smiled. "Please make yourself comfortable, Ms. Sutter... uh, Christian." She blushed, dropping her gaze. She placed the key on the small table by the door. "Good day, Ms. Sutter."

❖

The room was too quiet, and Christian couldn't stand to sit still a moment longer. She grabbed her key from the table and slipped into a light jacket, deciding she needed to do a little exploring. A twinge of excitement trickled through her. She was excited to get started learning her way around.

She hadn't made it far when her fatigue reminded her she wasn't quite strong enough for a serious expedition. She stepped through a set of doors in the back of the lobby into a small courtyard. An arched pergola extended from the main building, creating a sort of tunnel that led to what appeared to be an old greenhouse. The pergola was covered in old, thick vines that sprouted with new leaves and flower buds. Wisps of the last year's growth hung loosely and drifted lazily in the faint breeze. Wisteria, she guessed. Christian followed the path into the greenhouse, where she was met with an assault of color from the flowering plants and the earthy smell of soil and fertilizer.

She felt like a child who'd just discovered a hidden world enchanted with magical plants. The thought made her laugh. She let her fingers trail over the damp leaves of the plants as she passed, feeling like she had entered an enchanted world.

A rustling and a faint clicking noise caught her attention, and she followed the sound through rows of potted roses, ferns, and small shrubs. Silently she combed through the mass of plants on her way toward the unusual clicking. The maze of plants opened into an area arranged with glazed pots of all shapes and sizes. In the center was a woman, sitting on a strange stool in front of a potter's wheel. It looked ancient and was powered by the slow pushing motion of the woman's foot turning a round wheel on the floor.

Christian studied the intensity in the woman's face as she studied her work, unaware she was being watched. Although her face was partially turned away, everything from her posture to the set of her jaw suggested she was a woman on the verge of creating something born from her soul. All her energy was focused in that one instrument. The clay turned with the wheel, and the slightest touch of the woman's hands transformed it. Christian watched the blob of mud suddenly expand, forming a hollow in the center, when the woman pressed her thumbs gently into the clay until a vessel was born. She stretched long slender fingers along the sides of the clay, and again, the form was transformed, pulled upward into a tall vase. Ripples flowed along the sides of the vase with just the slightest touch of her finger.

The whole scene was intense, and Christian found herself watching the woman more than the clay. She wore a dark rubber apron over her clothes that protected her from the sling of the water and slip. The apron was spattered with light brown specks of clay and water. Her arms were bare from the elbows down, where her long-sleeved T-shirt had been pushed up, bunching at her biceps. On the back of her shirt, the name *Alex* was stenciled in bold black letters above the number thirteen. There was strength in her broad shoulders and well-muscled arms, but there was also something tender about the way she worked the clay. Her touch was guiding and commanding, but gentle and intuitive.

Calm settled over Christian as she watched the woman's hands caress the ever-changing form in her grasp. Christian swayed with the rhythm of the spinning wheel, with its rasping and clicking, as if she was being molded beneath the sensual guiding hands. Warmth spread through her, and she caught her breath. Startled by her response, Christian glanced around, reorienting herself to her surroundings.

Silently she stepped back among the lush foliage of the plants, fighting the urge to run. Instead she let the image of the woman fade from her vision slowly as she stepped among the flowers.

Christian could still hear the rhythmic sound of the wheel as she closed the greenhouse door and tried to gather her breath. She was confused by the stir of sensations bubbling beneath her skin but felt more alive than she had in months. The thought made her smile.

❖

The next morning, Christian sat at the window of her room watching the sunrise. The pinks blending into orange, and then red, reflected off the lake back to the heavens. She listened to the sounds of life awakening around her as the other patrons and the staff began to stir.

She had set up her books and computer at the desk and contemplated whether she would brave the outside world today. She hadn't left the room since her adventure to the greenhouse the evening before. Now, contemplating even trying to be with other people, a sudden fear knotted her stomach and she struggled to push the feeling away. She hadn't come here to hide in her room, but the thought of facing other people suddenly seemed too much to bear.

At nine o'clock she heard a knock at her door. Frowning, confused by the interruption, she pushed away from the desk. As she answered the door, she was met by the glow of Hannah's smile.

"Good morning. I noticed you didn't come down for breakfast, so I brought you some fruit, juice, and some banana bread." She carried the tray into the room, setting it on the small table that held the coffeemaker and the teapot. "I hope you slept well."

Christian could feel Hannah assessing her state of disarray as her eyes quickly traveled down Christian's body and across the room. She felt a little embarrassed by her appearance. She was wearing an old pair of faded blue sweats and a thin white tank top that showed her too-thin frame, and she hadn't even bothered to comb her hair.

"I had a very pleasant night," Christian lied. "Thank you. You're very thoughtful." Christian saw Hannah's continued assessment and fought to quiet her unease. But as she looked into Hannah's eyes she saw only caring. There was no pity, and Christian suddenly felt grateful for the tenderness.

"I hope you'll consider joining the group for lunch. Alex is firing up the grill and her burgers are the best. I hope you'll try them. She only cooks for us once a month, and it's always a real treat."

"Alex?" Christian said with surprise, remembering the woman in the greenhouse and the name printed on the back of her shirt.

"Yes. She's an artist who lives nearby. She teaches a pottery class sometimes and helps out around the grounds. She's an amazing cook too."

Christian's curiosity was piqued. This had to be the same woman she had seen in the greenhouse. "In that case, how can I resist? I'll see you at lunch. And thank you for the breakfast. I guess I let time get away from me."

"It happens." Hannah shrugged. "Call if you need anything," she said as she exited the room.

"I will, thank you again, Hannah."

❖

Christian stepped onto the patio at noon. Several women sat at a table next to the pool, drinking brightly colored drinks and laughing. She searched the group, trying to find the most comfortable place to blend in but not be noticed, so she could take some time to watch the other women and settle into her surroundings. Most people who knew her as a take-no-prisoners attorney couldn't believe how shy she could be in social situations. It had always been difficult for her to meet new people. And today was no exception. Her instinct was to fade into the woodwork. She chided herself again, knowing she needed to step outside her comfort zone and try, but she just wasn't ready yet.

"You came." Hannah beamed as she seemed to step out of nowhere to appear next to Christian, startling her and yet making her feel instantly more at ease. "Let me take you to a table. Alex is just putting another round on the grill. You're just in time."

Christian looked over Hannah's shoulder toward an elevated deck where savory smoke billowed from a large grill. She recognized the tall lean figure leaning over the dancing flames as the woman she had seen in the greenhouse. Instantly it seemed as if every hair on her body was standing on end, and her pulse beat a steady cadence against her throat. The sensation was unexpected, and Christian tried to push the feeling aside, quickly looking away.

Hannah took Christian's hand and led her to a quiet table that provided a view of the grounds leading to the lake. "Can I get you something to drink?"

"An ice water please, and a glass of Chardonnay would be wonderful, thank you." She didn't usually drink in the middle of the day, but she wanted something to help her calm the cluster of emotions raging inside her. She hadn't been interested in any woman since Cara's death. Her body might be ready, but her mind and heart were not, and she felt ridiculous swooning over a woman she had never even met.

"Would you like something to eat?" Hannah asked.

Christian could hear the anxious tone in Hannah's voice and wondered why this young woman was being so caring of her. She found herself uncharacteristically wanting to please Hannah—at the very least, she didn't want to present any further reason for the worry she saw in the girl's eyes. "I'll have the chef's special," she answered, smiling. "I can't resist such a glowing recommendation. I am sure it will be wonderful."

Hannah almost skipped away.

The funny thing was, Hannah was right. Lunch was fantastic. The smell of charred meat made Christian's mouth water, awakening her hunger. She hadn't had an appetite in months and found herself devouring the burger and fresh vegetables Hannah had returned with. This was what she needed. Christian savored each bite of her burger and the crisp flavors of lemon and asparagus. With the last hint still lingering on her tongue, she leaned her head back to take in the kiss of the sun, feeling stronger already. She took her wineglass in her hand and stretched out to lose herself in the warmth of the sun.

"Hello, do you mind if I join you?" a voice said, making Christian jerk, her reverie interrupted.

The woman standing before her smiled. "I'm sorry to startle

you. You just looked so alone over here, I felt compelled to thrust my company upon you."

Christian chuckled. "Please, join me then."

"Thank you," the woman said as she plopped down in the chair next to Christian with a dramatic sigh. "Elaine Barber," she said, extending her hand.

"Christian Sutter," Christian replied, clasping Elaine's hand and saluting her with her glass.

They sat facing the water for a while, taking in the warm spring sun. Breaking the silence, Elaine spoke. "I never tire of this view. Is this your first time at Willow Springs? I haven't seen you here before."

"It's only my first day, actually," Christian replied, sheepishly trying to avoid making eye contact. She found herself wanting to bolt up and run back to the solitude of her room. She might have come to Willow Springs with the intention of starting a new life, but she was finding that, after months of solitude, it was difficult for her to engage in the simplest social exchange. "Splendid," Elaine said. "You're in for a treat. This makes my third stay here, and I grow fonder of the place each time I visit. The grounds are beautiful, of course, and the staff...well, let's just say there are women here after my own heart. For instance, Julie at the stables is a god with the horses. When I ride or go through some of her exercises, I feel like a queen. There's just something about the girl that makes me all warm in the middle, if you know what I mean." Elaine smiled at this revelation and flashed Christian a wink.

Christian found herself suddenly curious and noted perhaps she would have to visit the stables. Not wanting to give away her interest, she decided to divert the conversation. Her thoughts had instantly drifted to Alex. In the short time she had been at Willow Springs, she had already experienced more warm, fuzzy feelings than she was comfortable with. She was here to get herself together, not to fill her head with fantasies about women.

"The lake looks beautiful, I think I might like going out on the water," she said, contemplating the sun glistening on the water as a family of ducks made their way across the lower lawn. The grounds leading to the lake were well manicured with a texture that made

Christian want to feel the cool, soft blades of grass against her bare feet. From the patio, the ground followed a gentle slope leading to the water's edge, giving the illusion that one could simply step out onto the water as if stepping onto glass.

Nodding her agreement, Elaine added, "They have all sorts of access to the lake—kayaks, boats, fishing, swimming. I'm sure you will find what you like. There are also these lovely picnic areas and benches along the shore that offer a more intimate view if you just want to sit as we are now." She smiled, nodding her head and waving her hand over them, punctuating her meaning.

Christian was amused by the gesture and felt herself warming to the kindness.

"Look at the time," Elaine announced, promptly rising from her chair. "I must go. I have a massage in twenty minutes, and I like to freshen up before seeing Abigail. She is simply delicious," she said gently, biting her lower lip, a gesture Christian found oddly out of place with the commanding confidence Elaine had shown.

"How about joining me for lunch tomorrow around noon?" Elaine asked as she stood before Christian, forcing her to look at her.

Christian stared blankly at Elaine, the question catching her off guard. For a brief moment, she felt the familiar panic grip her chest. Gathering herself, she managed a reply before she could think of an excuse. "That sounds lovely, thank you."

"Splendid," Elaine replied. "I will see you tomorrow, then." And she turned and seemed to glide across the patio, her flowing red hair billowing around her shoulders.

It wasn't until Elaine was leaving that Christian truly took her in. Although she had noted general information about Elaine, she had been too preoccupied with her social awkwardness and intrusive thoughts about Alex to truly take the time to make a clear assessment of Elaine. She was about forty years old, with auburn hair that fell just past her shoulders. She wore black linen slacks and sandals and a loose-fitting cream shirt. Her build was average, but the way she moved spoke of grace and confidence.

Christian thought over the interaction and was pleased by the exchange and felt comforted. No one knew her here. She didn't have to worry about uncomfortable questions about her accident or her health or about Cara. This was why she had come. She could relax and have a casual lunch with someone without the feelings of guilt and betrayal that she felt when she was around her old friends. Christian sighed in relief and sat back in her chair, feeling she was off to a good start.

CHAPTER TWO

Unable to sleep, Christian wandered the path that circled the lake. The sun was rising, and she welcomed the hint of warmth as she wrapped herself tighter in her jacket. The air was chilled—she hadn't planned for the coolness of being by the water. Finding a bench in the thicket of trees facing the rising sun, she decided to sit and watch the birth of the new day. Birds were singing in the trees around her, voicing their excitement for the spring and the morning sun. She had always loved springtime. It just seemed filled with hope and new beginnings.

A pang of guilt pierced her chest at the thought of what it would take to start a new life. "I miss you so much," she whispered into the air. "Can you forgive me for staying behind when you could not?" Tears filled her eyes as the memories threatened to take her breath. She felt the light dim as consciousness began to slip away. She had not been able to think of Cara since the accident without losing herself. For months she had shut out the world, the guilt and hurt filling her to the point that she felt she no longer belonged in the world.

Just as she was about to succumb to the darkness, someone stepped out of the clearing, and she could hear singing, the sound and the sudden interruption pulling her back from the brink. A tall woman with broad shoulders and short dark hair stood at the edge of the water. She wore running tights, tennis shoes, and a light formfitting jacket, all in black. The only contrast was the pale glow of her skin. Christian stared in disbelief. It was Alex.

Christian watched as Alex stretched and stood looking out over the water, watching the final moments of the sunrise. Her song seemed so natural out here. As pure as the song of the birds. Alex completed her song, bowed to the sun, and turned and began to run along the path. Christian watched until she was out of sight, the sound of her voice still singing in Christian's mind.

All her earlier thoughts of the past had been swept away the moment Alex stepped into the clearing. Everything about Alex captivated Christian, leaving her breathless with yearning. She didn't understand why she was so drawn to Alex, but each time she saw her, she wanted to be close to her. She wasn't sure what these feelings meant and they scared her. But they felt good too.

❖

Elaine was already at the table on the patio when Christian arrived. She looked splendid in a silk Asian-style pantsuit. Anyone else would have seemed overdressed, but the look was perfect for Elaine. Catching sight of Christian, she waved her over. Once at the table, Christian noticed with concern the hint of bluish circles under Elaine's eyes.

Elaine picked up her sunglasses and put them on, the dark lenses covering the pain in her eyes. "I am so glad you came. I've had the most dreadful morning and I need the company."

"Are you all right?" Christian asked, taking a chair.

Elaine hesitated a moment. "It's nothing. Just difficulty sleeping. It makes me cranky."

This was something Christian understood. She hadn't slept well in months and was certain her face and skin showed her fatigue as much as Elaine's did.

As if Elaine had read her mind, she looked Christian over, and when she spoke, her voice softened. "How was your evening? If I had to wager, I'd say you have your own night haunts to contend with."

Not wanting to explain, Christian simply didn't answer, choosing instead to fix her gaze on the water.

"I see," Elaine said. "Well, if we aren't going to bare our souls, we might as well gossip."

Christian shot a questioning glance at Elaine.

Elaine cleared her throat and continued. "I do believe our young

Hannah has found a new friend. I saw her leave last evening with a very attractive young woman. They seemed quite taken with one another."

Thankful for the change of subject, Christian smiled. "Seriously, Elaine, surely we aren't reduced to peeping, are we?" she said playfully.

"Peeping? I was simply sitting in the lounge having a drink while reading. Can I help it if the girl is irresistible? I'm surprised it's taken this long for a woman to sweep her off her feet."

Christian thought of the sweet young woman and the tenderness she had shown her since she had arrived, and she found herself somewhat uneasy when she thought of young Hannah with another woman. She didn't want her to experience the pain of loss that often came with love. Silently scolding herself, Christian felt uncertain why she suddenly felt protective of Hannah. She remembered herself at Hannah's age, and the beginnings of a smile played at the corners of her mouth. She could remember young love. She envied that innocence. And, despite the pain she had experienced, she would not want to give up a single moment of the love she had shared. Hannah deserved to experience love and all the wonders that came with it too.

Trying not to give herself away, Christian turned her attention to Elaine. "Is there anyone you *don't* find attractive?" she asked, chiding. She liked the playful banter and didn't want to return to more painful topics.

Elaine scoffed. "Who said anything about attraction? I'm simply taking notice of the beauty of the female form. Perhaps it wouldn't hurt if you did a little looking around yourself."

Speechless, Christian turned away. She felt a flush rise as she suddenly thought of seeing Alex that morning by the lake. She could almost hear the sound of her voice singing through her memory. The song had been playful, and the melody had continued playing in her mind. Alex had been a vision standing there, facing the rising sun as if it had arrived just to see her. She had embraced the day, and it had seemed to embrace her in return. Christian had wanted to touch her. She wanted…

"Christian…Christian?"

Christian heard Elaine's voice questioning, her concern almost frantic as she placed a cool hand on Christian's arm. Taking in a sharp breath of air as if she had been holding it, Christian tried to hide the shaking in her hands. "I'm fine Elaine, really. I must have gotten lost in my thoughts."

"You looked as if you were about to faint." Elaine's voice was tremulous, and Christian couldn't help but feel touched by her concern.

"I'm fine," Christian said, trying to sound convincing as she took Elaine's hand, giving it a little squeeze. "I'm just a bit tired, that's all." She hoped Elaine couldn't feel the slight tremble that still shook her.

Elaine didn't question her further and seemed to respect her secrets. Christian changed the subject. Gossip really was the safest. She pointed out a group of women sitting together that she had seen the day before. "They're having a very good time," she said, inclining her head toward the group.

"Ah." Elaine chuckled. "You've noticed the Haverty sisters." Elaine smiled and sketched a wave toward the group of women.

"The who?" Christian asked, wanting Elaine to tell her more.

Elaine smiled. "They call themselves the Haverty sisters, although there is no relation. They've been friends since college. I think they find strength in their numbers. They've been coming here since Cynthia, the silver-haired one, had breast cancer about five years ago. Since then, they've weathered many storms together."

Elaine's voice had become soft and reverent. Turning to the left, she pointed to a couple huddled together on a blanket on the lawn. "See those two there? That's Anna and Kate. They come here every year to celebrate their anniversary. Sweet couple," she added thoughtfully.

"Sounds like you know everyone's story," Christian said, glancing conspiratorially at Elaine.

Raising an eyebrow and peering over her sunglasses, Elaine studied Christian. "Like I said, I've been coming here for a while. I guess I've made my share of friends. Like us, for example, two women enjoying each other's company, talking about casual sorts of things, and before you know it, an affinity begins to grow and, just like that, we become friends."

Christian shifted uncomfortably in her chair as she felt Elaine's gaze on her. She suddenly felt vulnerable and guarded her emotions, not wanting Elaine to know her secrets.

As if sensing Christian's discomfort, Elaine changed the subject once again. "Have you had a chance to do any exploring of your own?"

Grateful for the shift, but still feeling guarded, Christian thought for a moment before answering. "Nothing more than a walk by the lake," she said with a faint smile as the thought of Alex again presented itself. "I find I tire easily, still. It's been a long time since I've been out anywhere." She felt suddenly shocked to have revealed so much of herself with this simple statement.

"The fresh air will do you good. You mentioned yesterday an interest in the lake."

Thankful Elaine hadn't pushed for more details, Christian smiled and went with the casual conversation, but she sensed Elaine was keenly aware of her distance and reluctance to talk about her personal life. But as she considered the way Elaine had guided the conversation, Christian became acutely aware that Elaine was also avoiding. She had said something about night haunts, and Christian recalled the darkness shading her eyes. She recognized that pain, and her heart suddenly wept for her new friend.

❖

Christian's morning walks became a daily routine. She had been coming here for a week, drawn to the lake in the hope of seeing Alex sing to the sunrise. This morning, Alex had arrived earlier than usual and sat looking over the water. Her voice was hushed, and the melody of her song was mournful and filled Christian with longing.

Although she couldn't hear the words, the tone of Alex's voice brought tears to Christian's eyes, and she found herself weeping with the sunrise. Somehow, she found peace with this stranger who didn't even know she was there. Today Christian felt a connection with Alex, who seemed to sing the pain for which Christian had been unable to find words.

As she was filled with the comfort of Alex's voice singing in the distance, she felt love fill her once again, and this time, the darkness did not come.

Movement caught her eye as Alex stood. Christian watched as

she bent and placed something in the water, faint ripples playing across the surface from the disturbance. Christian couldn't see the object but made out the delicate flower Alex now extended and dropped into the water.

Mesmerized, Christian watched as Alex wiped her eyes with the back of her hand and took her bow to the sun. This time, as she turned to leave, her steps were heavy and slow. Christian's heart beat against her chest, her own pain mirroring the weight settling upon Alex's shoulders.

She sat motionless as Alex paused, then turned toward her. Christian caught her breath as Alex looked up and saw her sitting there watching. She hadn't meant to intrude. She felt torn between her own grief and the sudden desire to wrap her arms around Alex and console her, to stop the pain and protect Alex from her sadness.

As if sensing Christian's understanding, Alex nodded once and turned quietly and walked away. Christian felt a sudden desire to go to her. She wanted to tell her she understood. But she knew she shouldn't intrude. There had been something mournful in the song and the way Alex carried her body had been different from all the other mornings, and Christian knew as if by instinct that Alex needed to be alone. But she craved some connection with this mysterious woman who consumed her thoughts and seemed to understand her pain. There seemed to be so much beauty surrounding Alex, and Christian wondered what could have caused her so much sorrow.

CHAPTER THREE

Alex sat on her porch, watching the sun play across the lake. It was warm, and she was happy to be able to sit outside again. Sipping her beer, she watched the small kayak slowly make its way around the cove. As she watched, she became aware of the woman in the boat, who seemed mesmerized by the rocks and growth along the bank. Alex thought she looked right, there on the water, like a flower blown in on the breeze. She warmed as she found herself smiling at this simple thought. She took in the woman, her auburn hair tucked behind her ears as it curled around to trace her jawline. The faint kiss of sun had only begun to darken her delicate skin, and she seemed to meld into the natural beauty around her.

After some time, the boat turned and headed toward the little dock Alex kept down by the lake, and she found herself growing anxious about someone being so close. This was her safe place, her sanctuary. No one had ever been here in the two years she had made it her home. Getting to her feet, she made her way down the pebble path that led to the water. She watched as the boat glided up to the shore.

The woman looked flushed from her effort and the warmth of the sun on her face. She wore sunglasses that hid her eyes, but Alex took in the sharp cut of the woman's cheekbones and jawline, thinking her too thin for her strong shoulders.

With a deep breath, Alex reluctantly steeled herself to do her best to be social. As she stepped from the shelter of the trees, she gasped as the woman slipped as she stepped from her boat, hitting her head on the dock and falling into the water.

Jolting into a run, Alex jumped off the end of the dock and wrapped her arms around the motionless body. Heart racing, she took the woman into her arms, carrying her up the muddy bank and onto the dock. As she searched for signs of breath, she frantically called out, "Are you okay? Can you hear me?"

The woman moaned as her eyes flickered and opened, peering up at Alex, lost and confused. "Cara?"

Alex's heart fluttered, and she felt her face redden as her hands gently held the woman's face and she looked into the most beautiful green eyes she had ever seen. "Are you okay?" Alex asked with fear thick in her voice. The woman didn't answer. "I'm going to take you up to the house. You hit your head pretty good." Getting to her knees, Alex lifted the woman, gently sliding an arm behind her shoulders and the other behind her knees. Effortlessly, she lifted her into her arms, clutching her to her chest, relieved to feel her breath hot on her neck as her head pressed gently against Alex's shoulder. An arm lay lazily around Alex's shoulders and the other lay against her chest. Alex was surprised by how light she was. Holding her firmly, she made her way up the path to her home.

❖

Christian began to wake up, stirring softly, becoming aware of the warmth surrounding her and the gentle caress of music. She let go of a sigh as she thought of Alex, singing to the sunrise each morning. Suddenly the singing stopped. Confused, Christian opened her eyes. A woman sat beside her, concern creasing her forehead as she frowned.

"Feeling better?" the woman asked gently.

Christian startled. "Where am I? What happened?"

"You slipped down by my dock and banged your head pretty good. You're in my cabin."

"Okay," Christian said hesitantly, reaching a hand to her head, only now recognizing the persistent throb beating against her skull. "Alex?" Christian asked, recognizing her rescuer, and more than a little confused.

"Yeah, that's right," Alex said, leaning back with a look of surprise on her face.

"How long have I been here?" Christian could feel the embarrassment beginning to color her face.

Smiling slightly, Alex placed a palm to Christian's forehead and then her cheek. Christian felt her face warm from the heat of Alex's touch.

"You're right, I'm Alex, Alex Moore," she said, "and I guess you've been here about two hours now."

Panicked, Christian started to sit up, only then realizing she was naked under the blankets tucked neatly around her. Her eyes flashed to Alex as her hand grasped the edges of the blanket. *Holy shit, where are my clothes?* This was not how she had envisioned meeting Alex. She could only imagine what Alex must be thinking of her. How could she be such a flake? This could not be happening.

"I'm sorry, but I had to remove your clothes," Alex explained. "They were cold and wet from your fall into the lake. I was afraid you would get sick from the cold."

"Oh," Christian stammered, her brow furrowing. "Thank you. My name is Christian," she said, trying to figure out what to do next.

"I know," Alex said, matter-of-factly. "I recognized the logo on the kayak as one from Willow Springs. I called to let them know what had happened and that I had you here with me. They told me your name since you were the only guest out in one of the boats."

Christian was relieved someone knew where she was, but she still did not know what to do.

"If you're feeling better, once your clothes dry, I'll be happy to take you back up to the lodge," Alex continued.

It was then Christian realized that talking was Alex's way of trying to comfort her. It was working. Christian watched her move about the room as she talked, taking in her short hair, broad shoulders, lean muscles, and most of all her striking ice-blue eyes. "Oh my God," she whispered as a pulse began to thrum in her center. And suddenly she felt a bit like Alice, tumbling down the rabbit hole. She wasn't sure what was happening to her. Sure, she had watched Alex from a distance, but nothing had prepared her for this.

As if sensing Christian's discomfort, Alex came and sat next to her again, a worried look on her face. "What is it?" she asked.

"Nothing, I just realized I've seen you before. I didn't mean to intrude, but I've seen you down by the lake in the mornings. Haven't I?" she said, more a statement than a question, not wanting to sound like she had been stalking Alex. She could feel the heat she pulled from Alex's body as Alex's thigh pressed against her side through the blanket.

Thoughtfully, Alex said, "I go to the lake every morning, yes. I remember seeing you there, although I wouldn't have known it was you."

"I recognized your voice," Christian said in a whisper. "You were singing when I woke up." Christian apologized again. "I'm sorry. I'm just trying to get my bearings. I didn't mean to intrude."

Every emotion she had experienced while observing Alex from a distance came flooding back. She let her eyes linger over the strong, lean hands she had watched create the vase on the potter's wheel, and she imagined those hands touching her, lingering on her skin like a cool breeze. She watched the movements of Alex's body as she talked, wondering how someone could have so much grace with so much strength. There was no denying her attraction to Alex and the thought planted the seed of panic. She didn't even know Alex. She wasn't ready for feelings like this. Christian shifted uncomfortably, pulling the blanket up to her chin as if the plush fabric could shelter her from her own desires.

The expression on Alex's face softened as she smiled down at Christian. "Listen, I can't imagine it feels very comfortable to wake up in a strange place with a strange woman, to find you have no clothes. I have some dry things you can slip into that may help you feel a little less exposed."

Sighing in relief, Christian smiled back, finding that the brief closeness had left her skin hot. She almost gasped from the sudden lack of contact. "That would be great, thank you."

"No problem," Alex said, patting Christian's hand softly. "I'll be right back."

Christian listened to the footsteps pad softly across the floor as Alex left the room. Alone now, she began to take in her surroundings. She was on a brown leather sofa, the leather worn from use, allowing it to meld to the weight of her body as if it were cradling her. She was facing a beautiful fireplace, made of gray stacked stone, that roared with the life of a new fire. The mantel was a large roughhewn timber that looked like it had once been a mighty oak. It stretched the width of the fireplace and matched the exposed rafters overhead. For the first time, Christian noted the temperature and guessed Alex had started the fire to help warm her and to prevent further shock, since the room was warmer than would normally be comfortable. She found it soothing.

Above the fireplace hung a painting of a striking blond woman dressed in what appeared to be a black evening gown. The fabric draped across her shoulders and was open down her back, revealing creamy smooth skin, the slight lift of a shoulder blade, and the curve of her spine leading down to the gentle swell of her hips. She sat with her back to the artist with her head turned slightly over her right shoulder as if looking back at someone. She appeared to be holding something to her chest, and the gentle curve of her lips emphasized the sparkle in her blue eyes, their gaze playful and sensual. As Christian gazed at the portrait, warmth flooded her body, wrapping her in a feeling of welcome. She wondered who the woman was. She was obviously important to Alex to have earned such a bold position in the room. The thought struck her that Alex might have a partner, and she grew even more self-conscious about her attraction to her.

Christian started as Alex came back into the room, holding out a pair of sweatpants and a long-sleeved T-shirt. Christian saw Alex's brow furrow slightly when she saw her looking at the painting.

"They may be a little big on you, but they should do."

"Thank you," Christian said, suddenly aware of the shift in Alex, as a strange discomfort flashed in her eyes and her body tensed.

Alex shifted from foot to foot. "I'll just go back to the...other room to give you some privacy," she finally managed.

Christian felt her face grow warm, realizing Alex had already seen her naked. She felt exposed and vulnerable, both afraid and excited at the thought of what it must have taken for Alex to get her here, and of Alex's strong hands undressing her, touching her. Her head felt like it would burst as the pressure intensified behind her eyes. She groaned and massaged her temples, wondering how things had gotten so messed up. She couldn't imagine what Alex must think of her. She must look ridiculous. How had this happened?

The clothes were loose on her, which was a small comfort, since she didn't have a bra and her nipples had hardened at the thought of Alex touching her. The soft cotton brushing against her swollen breasts only intensified the reaction. Christian crossed her arms over her chest to hide herself. She had to get a grip.

❖

Alex trembled as she stood grasping the edge of the sink in the bathroom. "Keep it together," she said repeatedly to herself. "She's okay. It's not like before. She's okay."

Alex flashed back to seeing Christian hit the dock and her lifeless body floating in the water. "She's okay," she repeated.

Something about Christian had drawn her to the dock, had made her want to reach out when she saw her kayak on the water. When she had pulled Christian out of the water and Christian had looked up at her for that brief moment when their eyes met, Alex had felt like she was holding an angel. She had touched the cool skin of Christian's face, brushing the wet strands of hair from her cheek. Something had shifted inside Alex at that moment, a softening of her defenses, and a longing for tenderness. When she had undressed Christian, she had tried to divert her eyes as much as possible from the soft swell of breasts, the firm flat stomach, and the small triangle of neatly trimmed hair between her legs. But she couldn't help but think of how beautiful Christian was, and how fragile she'd seemed.

Alex felt an innate desire to protect Christian. She'd listened to Christian's breathing for at least the first hour, her stomach clenched in knots. She had feared the injury might have been more serious than it appeared, and she'd struggled with what she should do. When Christian had begun to mumble in her sleep, Alex had finally convinced herself that Christian was okay.

She struggled to understand this feeling of connection to a woman she had never met before. She had only experienced a similar emotion once in her life, and it was difficult for her to imagine it was happening again now.

❖

Having finally dressed, Christian began to look around the room. Alex had been gone for a while, and she found her curiosity getting the better of her. The front room of the cabin was open, with high ceilings and exposed timbers, and the exterior wall was mostly glass that allowed the sunlight to pour into the room. A large porch with a view overlooking the lake ran the length of the house. Christian could see the small dock, with her kayak pulled up onto the grass.

She tried to remember what had happened and suddenly felt foolish to have been so careless. She'd thought the spells were getting better, but she shouldn't have pushed herself. Studying the length of yard from the dock to the house and the small winding path that joined the two, she wondered how Alex had managed to get her to the house.

As she thought of Alex, she remembered strong arms holding her tightly. She remembered feeling safe and surrendering to that strength as she was wrapped in protective arms. Shaking her head slightly to rid herself of the feeling of needing someone, she turned to find Alex standing in the doorway, watching her.

Christian smiled. "You carried me, didn't you?"

Softly, as if understanding her thoughts, Alex nodded, never taking her eyes from Christian's.

"I don't know what to say. Thank you. I'm terribly sorry to have caused so much trouble," Christian said nervously. She wished the sweats had pockets so she could hide her trembling hands.

Alex strode over to her. "I'm just glad I was there to help. You still seem a little shaky," she said as she took Christian's hand. "Please sit down. Can I make you dinner? It might help if you had something to eat."

Christian looked down at their entwined hands, feeling the gentle pressure of the long lean fingers caressing her own. The touch was warm and tender, and Christian felt her body begin to melt. The power of the sensation surprised her, and she pulled her hand away.

"No…really," Christian said. "I shouldn't impose on you any further."

Studying Christian for a moment, Alex casually stepped away. "Well," she said, "I haven't eaten yet and I'm hungry. I'd like the company if you'll stay a while longer." Her face was smooth and confident, as if she knew Christian wouldn't be able to refuse the offer for fear of offending her.

Christian didn't want to be rude, so she agreed. "Okay," she acquiesced, "but only if you allow me to help you."

Smiling, Alex nodded. "Right this way. I hope you like steak. I was planning to grill."

"That sounds perfect," Christian said, watching Alex glide across the room in front of her. Her eyes played down the length of Alex's beautiful, strong body, taking in the taut lean muscles of her shoulders and how her back tapered to thin hips and the round firm curve of her butt. Christian felt the muscles in her stomach tighten, and she froze in midstep, shocked by the sensation of wanting another woman. She pushed the feeling away, resolving not to focus on the physical prowess of her host. Her life was confusing enough without complicating things with this strange infatuation with Alex. She was supposed to be figuring out who she wanted to be now, what she wanted to do with her life. This was just another way of avoiding what she really needed to be doing. So what if she found Alex attractive? She was attractive. She was having a normal physical response, that was all. It didn't mean anything.

At least, that was what she tried to tell herself.

The meal was fantastic, and Christian found herself very relaxed as they sat on the porch listening to the mockingbirds rejoice. She imagined their song was a celebration of the wonderful day she and Alex had had. They had talked nonstop as they cooked and ate, and Christian felt comforted in the presence of this stranger. She drifted off as this realization settled in her thoughts. She hadn't spent time with anyone in months, aside from the brief lunches with Elaine. She had forgotten what it was like to *enjoy* not being alone. For the longest time, she had wanted to be alone. She had needed that time to find herself to figure out how to move out of the past. She had gotten so complacent, she hadn't realized when being alone had become lonely. The realization now was a bit of a surprise, and she didn't know what she wanted to do about it.

Noticing the shift in the silence, Alex turned to Christian. "What? What were you thinking just now?"

Christian studied Alex for a moment, taking in the sincerity of her voice and the gentle question in her eyes. Feeling no threat, Christian answered, "I was thinking of how safe, how comfortable it feels being here…with you." She dropped her gaze, suddenly feeling shy and embarrassed, then added, "I haven't felt comfortable around anyone in a very long time. It feels nice."

Alex hesitated and then made a choice. Never taking her eyes from Christian, she said, "I know what you mean." Christian's expression was doubtful, so Alex added, "I've lived out here for the past two years. You're the first person to be here in all that time."

"Really?" Christian asked. "Don't you get lonely?"

Alex dropped her voice as she turned to face the water. "Yes and no," she replied. "Alone isn't always lonely."

"What makes you want to be alone, then?"

A long silence stretched between them as Alex thought about her answer. Finally, she let out a deep sigh and closed her eyes. Her shoulders slumped under the weight of her grief. She felt compelled to tell Christian about her past. It was the first time she had wanted to share her story with anyone.

"My partner died. I found it difficult to be around people…after. It seemed easier to deal with everything if I just stayed to myself. I was tired of the questions, the sympathy, the *pity* from everyone." Alex struggled to hold back the pain that threatened to choke her.

"How long ago," Christian asked, her voice strained.

"Three years, two months, and six days ago," Alex answered. Her voice was flat as she recalled each moment of that grief.

Christian's hands clenched the arms of her chair and tears welled in her eyes. "She's the woman in the painting, isn't she?"

Nodding once, Alex said faintly, "Yes."

"She's beautiful," Christian continued in a whisper. "I lost Cara eighteen months and four days ago."

Alex looked at Christian and saw her own pain mirrored in Christian's expression. She closed her eyes and wept.

"It was a car accident. I survived. She didn't," Christian said.

Nodding, Alex reached across and took Christian's hand. It had been so long since she had talked about Sophia, but the pain still wrapped around her heart like barbed wire. She needed to touch Christian to know she was real. Feeling the tender touch, she knew Christian shared her pain, and she wanted to help her.

"I've never talked about what happened," Christian said, her voice deepening. "I don't have any family, and Cara's family didn't approve of our relationship."

Alex squeezed Christian's hand. She could hear how difficult it was for Christian to talk about what had happened. Her voice was hoarse and dry, and Alex felt her own throat thicken with unspoken emotion.

"I feel guilty. We were supposed to grow old together. I promised I would never leave her." Christian swallowed, the sound punctuating her silence before she continued. "It isn't fair that I lived and Cara didn't." Tears streamed down her face now, the guilt and hurt of months spilling out.

"No, it isn't fair," Alex said softly. "It isn't fair that they died. But you said it was a car accident. It doesn't sound like there was anything you could have done. You didn't leave her. It wasn't a *choice* you made." Alex felt bile rise in her throat and she clenched her teeth.

"What happened to you, Alex?"

Alex sighed. She had come this far, so she decided to answer. "Sophia had been sick. A brain aneurism. They were doing what they could, but it was inoperable. She insisted I go to work that day. I left her alone in the apartment. I didn't think I would be gone long, but when I returned, it was too late. She was gone. I left her and she died alone."

"Oh, Alex. I'm so sorry."

"It was a long time ago. Like I said, it isn't fair that they died. I miss Sophia every day, but it isn't like it was in the beginning. I won't say it gets better, but it gets easier. Eventually you stop thinking about the end so much and learn to focus on the good memories. You have to learn to remember the love or the loss will drive you mad."

❖

Alex watched Christian sleep. She had cried herself out on Alex's shoulder after describing the accident that had killed her lover. Christian jerked in her sleep from time to time, as if in some kind of unseen struggle. Alex stroked her hair and whispered that she was safe, encouraging her to rest.

Alex looked to the painting over the fireplace as her own tears fell. She understood Christian's pain. The face looking back at her smiled as if she knew something Alex didn't. She imagined she could hear Sophia's voice, as she had so many times before. *It's okay, baby.* Now, looking down at Christian, she realized that for the first time in three years, she didn't feel alone. "Thank you," she whispered.

CHAPTER FOUR

Elaine sat in the darkness outside the lodge, watching the lights turn on and off in the rooms above. She sighed heavily, knowing that she wouldn't be able to sleep, and if she did, the nightmares would come. Shuddering at the thought, she drew a knee up and wrapped her hands around her leg.

She watched as a silver Mini Cooper pulled up to the front entrance and a young woman got out. She looked to be in her early twenties and had a carefree air that reminded Elaine what it was like to have the eagerness of young love. The front door of the lodge opened, and Hannah stepped outside, throwing her arms around the young woman's neck and kissing her soundly. Elaine watched as the two women took each other in, and Hannah slid her hands around the woman's waist and hooked her thumbs in the waistband of her jeans.

Elaine smiled at the gesture and was happy to see Hannah with someone. She had met Hannah during her first stay at Willow Springs three years ago. Hannah had been little more than a child then, but now…she had become a strong and beautiful young woman.

Elaine thought back to her own love, and she longed for the gentle touch of her lover's fingers on her skin. She ached to feel that she was no longer alone. But the fear that gripped her said no. A blinding red light flashed through her thoughts, and she shuddered as she gripped her leg tightly and stifled the scream that threatened to escape her.

She sat alone in the darkness holding her breath, her hands trembling as she watched Hannah and her lover walk to their car and drive away.

❖

It was just past sunrise when Christian woke with her head in Alex's lap. Alex was lying with her head against the corner of the sofa and her legs propped on the coffee table that stood between the couch and the fireplace. Her breathing was deep and restful, and her hand twitched slightly as it lay protectively across Christian's chest.

Christian starred up at Alex, amazed at her beauty and shocked by the fact that she had awoken for the second time on Alex's sofa without knowing how she had gotten there.

As if feeling Christian watching her, Alex opened her eyes and looked down at Christian as she tightened her embrace.

"Sorry," Christian said guiltily as she sat up. "I guess I fell asleep."

"You had a tough day. You needed the rest," Alex said gently.

"Actually," Christian said, stretching, "I think that's the most sleep I've had in months. It feels incredible." Then she paused, seeing the tired look in Alex's eyes. "You, however, must feel terrible. You couldn't have been comfortable sitting like that all night."

Smiling softly as she worked the stiffness from her legs, Alex said, "It was nice to feel needed, and I guess it was nice not to be alone. I'm glad you were here."

After breakfast, Christian decided to paddle back to Willow Springs. Alex offered to drive her in her Jeep, but Christian was feeling good and wanted the peace of the lake to help her process everything that had happened. Alex still looked worried, but Christian assured her she was okay.

Christian had the urge to put her arms around Alex as she thanked her again, but instead, she took a step back, uncomfortable with the intensity of the feeling. Their time together had been intense, and the intimacy that had formed between them was unsettling now that she was rested and thinking more clearly. She needed to put distance between them so she could clear her mind, and getting back in her kayak was the best way to do that. Finally, she settled for taking Alex's hand as they said good-bye. She was acutely aware of the warmth of Alex's hand, and her heart beat faster when she caught Alex's intense gaze on her. She pulled away quickly. She didn't want these feelings. It was too much.

The water was smooth as glass as the boat skirted across the surface with very little effort. The air was crisp and the coolness soothing as Christian filled her lungs with deep cleansing breaths. She thought about Alex and the gentle way she had taken her into her home and listened to her pain. Being with her had been easy. The memory of waking up in Alex's arms sent a tingle down her body, making her smile. An equally disquieted feeling immediately followed, and she sighed. She had made Alex into a dream figure over the past weeks, watching her from afar. Allowing Alex to soothe her, confiding in her, was beyond her imaginings. But this wasn't real. She didn't really know anything about Alex. She shook her head to dislodge any further images of Alex from her mind. She had to stop kidding herself and focus on what was real.

Looking ahead, she could see the dock at Willow Springs and a figure standing, looking out over the water, waving her in. It was Hannah. Smiling broadly, Hannah steadied the boat and took Christian's hand to help her onto shore. Christian shook her head in disbelief. "How did you know to be here?"

Hannah chuckled. "Alex called and said you were paddling in. She seemed a little worried and asked me to see that you made it in okay."

The peaceful feeling filled Christian again. "Of course she did," she said with a smile. Everything she had seen so far told her it was Alex's nature to care for others, but it wasn't like she had to have her hand held.

❖

Alex felt a weight settle over her as she stood in her studio. It had been two hours since she had watched Christian paddle across the lake, finally disappearing from sight. She hadn't been able to concentrate on her work and now felt frustrated. She had always been able to lose herself in her work, but now she couldn't quiet her worry. What was she doing getting so worked up over this? Christian had seemed perfectly fine when she left. There was no reason to imagine she would come to any harm. She stood slumped over her workbench and shoved her fists into her pants pockets. The vision of Christian falling played over in her mind, but it wasn't the image of Christian's vulnerability that stirred her now, it was the nagging sense of loss she had felt since Christian had left. The silence in her cabin seemed stale, and she missed the sound of Christian's voice and the way the air seemed to vibrate from her presence in the room. She jumped when the phone rang, grabbing for it before it could finish the first ring.

"Yes. This is Alex," she said hastily.

"Hello, Alex," the sweet voice said over the line.

Alex's heart calmed the instant she recognized Christian's voice and she felt some of the tension fall from her shoulders. Trying to hide her anxiety, she asked, "How was your trip back? Are you feeling okay?"

"Yes," Christian said, "I'm fine, thanks to you."

Alex imagined the voice as soothing as a touch on her skin. She listened to the sound of Christian's breathing through the phone, and it was as if she could feel the hot breath brushing the skin of her neck as she remembered carrying Christian's limp body from the dock.

"I wanted to call you myself to reassure you there are no worries. Young Hannah was waiting at the dock as I arrived. She insisted we call before going back to the lodge," Christian explained.

"Thank you," Alex said, allowing a sigh to escape as she gripped the phone, wanting to reach through the distance and touch Christian for proof that she was okay. "I'm glad you're safe. I hope you'll come back out to the cabin sometime. I really enjoyed your company," Alex said, holding her breath.

"I'd like that," Christian answered.

Alex held onto the phone even after she heard the line disconnect. She leaned her palm on the surface of her workbench to steady herself from the sudden feeling of loss that overcame her when Christian's voice was gone.

CHAPTER FIVE

Elaine sat in the plush leather chair, staring at Dr. Cook. "Helen, do we have to keep going through this? I refuse to take medication. I have to find another way to deal with this." Elaine knew she was being stubborn, but she didn't believe medication was the answer to her problem. She needed to feel in control of what was happening to her. She felt like such a hypocrite when she thought of all the times she had asked her own clients to consider medication to calm feelings of anxiety, depression, and problems with sleep. But this was different. She hadn't verbalized as much, but she feared that medication would make her less alert to what was happening to her and around her. She was afraid if she was less than hypervigilant, she would miss something that could cost her her life. She had been back in counseling for months, trying to break down the mental barriers that blocked her from remembering what had happened to her.

She didn't drop her gaze as Dr. Cook studied her. She sat with her back straight and her shoulders squared as if daring Dr. Cook to challenge her.

"Elaine, I would like to try a new approach to the problem. I'd like you to consider hypnotherapy as part of our addressing your trauma. As you know, hypnotherapy will not reduce your control over what you experience but will allow you a state of relaxation that may make it possible for you to work through aspects of the shooting that your mind is afraid to remember."

"Well, I didn't see that one coming," Elaine said, this time not trying to hide her discomfort.

"Elaine, I can see this makes you uncomfortable," Dr. Cook

interjected. "But, please, just give it some thought. We can practice with some milder forms of exploration before we address the shooting, so you can become more comfortable with the process."

After a brief silence, Elaine agreed to think about it.

"How have you been sleeping?" Dr. Cook inquired. "Have you had any more dreams?"

Elaine sighed heavily. "Just the same one as always. I'm in my office, preparing for my next client, when there's a knock at the door. I look to the clock, realizing it's too early for my next appointment. I open the door, and there's a blinding flash of red light. I never saw who it was before, but now a little girl stands in the door. Her skin is pale and her hair is dirty. Her clothes are ripped and she has blood on her hands. I don't see what causes the flash, but I feel the searing-hot pain in my chest. I no longer wake up screaming or looking for the blood, but the fear is paralyzing."

"Let's talk about the little girl. Do you recognize her?"

Elaine paused. She felt her body grow cold at the memory, and a lump began to form in her throat, making it hard for her to swallow. "Yes. It's Missy Carlton. The missing girl I was helping the authorities try to locate."

A slight frown creased Dr. Cook's brow. "What did you hear when you opened the door? Did she say anything to you?"

"I don't remember any sounds. She just stares at me. Her eyes are dead."

"What do you feel when you see her?"

"My insides go cold. I want to tell her I'm sorry. I want her to know I tried to find her." Elaine's throat grew tight as she struggled to hold back her revulsion as she saw the girl in her memory.

"You just went tense all over, Elaine. Tell me what's happening right now."

Elaine sat forward and gripped the edge of her seat as panic began to wash over her. "She's disgusted with me. She's angry that I didn't save her." Tears filled Elaine's eyes as she thought of the child suffering under the torture of Eric Flask.

Using the only tool of defense left to her, Elaine rationalized her position. "I tried everything. It wasn't my fault she died. He was a sick, murdering bastard, and he reveled in toying with us, knowing he wouldn't reveal her location in time to save her."

"You sound angry, Elaine."

"Damn right, I'm angry," Elaine shot back at Dr. Cook. "He knew exactly what he was doing. I should have been quicker at figuring him out. I should have…" Elaine let her head drop in her hands and sobbed.

Dr. Cook waited, giving Elaine time to feel her pain. "You have every right to be angry, Elaine."

When Elaine took a deep breath and looked up to face Dr. Cook, she felt more in control. Dr. Cook's validation of her feelings had helped ease her emotions. She was angry, she was tired, and she was so very afraid, but she needed to stay in control.

"You said you should have been quicker, you should have…what? It sounds like you're blaming yourself, Elaine. Tell me about that."

Starring blankly at the wall behind Dr. Cook, Elaine thought about the little girl. She had been found dumped in a trash bin. "I was the primary profiler on this case. This little girl was relying on me to save her. I didn't."

"You were shot two weeks before Missy Carlton was murdered, Elaine. How was getting shot your fault?" Dr. Cook's voice was soft and held the hint that this was not really a question but meant to challenge the irrationality of Elaine's thought.

Elaine thought about the statement for a few moments and tried to remember. All she could see was the blinding red light.

❖

Christian hung up the phone and turned to Hannah, who stood waiting by the door. She was still a little embarrassed by all the attention she was getting but knew she had brought it on herself. She would have to be more careful.

"Can I walk you back to the lodge?" Hannah asked once Christian had finished her call.

"Thank you, Hannah, I'd love the company. And thank you for coming for me."

Offering her arm as she had done the first time they had met, Hannah smiled. "My pleasure."

Christian paused a moment studying Hannah as she offered her arm. The feeling of peace still calmed her, and she reached out and took Hannah's hand instead, twining their fingers together. "Do you mind?" she asked. "I feel a strange need to feel connected to someone right now. I haven't felt that in a very long time, and I'm afraid it will slip away," she said, her voice a whisper.

Beaming, Hannah squeezed Christian's hand. "I don't mind," she said, turning to lead them back to the lodge.

Christian felt Hannah's hand close around hers and noticed the feeling was different than when she had clasped Alex's hand earlier. Hannah's hand was gentle and helpful but seemed foreign to her. Alex's hand had felt strong and warm in a way that made her feel like she was protected and caressed at the same time, like she belonged there.

Christian took a deep breath. Her new infatuation with Alex was beginning to irritate her. She didn't *belong* with anyone. She had just been tired and out of sorts—there was nothing else going on between them.

After a few moments, Hannah broke the silence. "Alex seemed very concerned about you. Are you sure you're all right?"

Christian could tell by the tightness of Hannah's jaw that she was asking more than her words revealed. "Yes, quite. I was very lucky Alex was there, or I might not have been. I'm sorry I worried everyone. Alex took very good care of me."

Hannah looked thoughtful as Christian explained what had happened. Her eyes seemed to darken for a moment, and then she was her cheerful self again.

Christian decided to press further. "Do you know Alex well?" she asked, trying to hide the faint stirring in her voice.

"I guess I know her as well as anyone at Willow Springs. She's very private. She's lived here for a couple of years and has always been a part of Willow Springs. She helps with the grounds, teaches a class now and then, and she's a great cook. I don't know anything of her personal life, except she's some kind of artist. She has a workshop or something at her house and rarely leaves. She has supplies and stuff delivered here and picks them up herself, and no one ever goes out to her house." Hannah's brow furrowed. "What was it like?" she asked. "Being at her place?"

"It was very nice," Christian responded. "It's very peaceful out there." Christian remained silent for a while, thinking about Hannah's experience of Alex. She had found Alex painfully open, very caring, and, yes...she was a great cook.

Christian felt Hannah's hand protectively squeeze hers as she studied each step along the path. "How about you, Hannah? Tell me about you."

Hannah's face flushed at the question, seeming surprised to find the attention turned onto her. "Well...I'm in my junior year at the university, studying business management. I've worked and lived here at Willow Springs for three and a half years. I learned about Willow Springs from a runaway shelter in the city when I was staying there."

"Runaway shelter?" Christian said a little too forcefully, unable to hide the surprise in her voice as she stopped to face Hannah.

Squaring her shoulders Hannah said flatly. "I grew up in a small town that didn't like people who were...different. I ran away when I was seventeen. I had already been taking college courses and had enough credits to graduate high school, so I put in for early graduation and left, to be on my own. I took what money I had saved from my part-time job and took a bus to the city. The shelter was the only safe place I could find. They helped me enroll in school, and one of the counselors told me about Willow Springs. She made some calls for me and...well, here I am."

Drawing in her breath as she studied Hannah, Christian felt like she was seeing her for the first time. "That was incredibly brave of you," she said as she reached out and brushed a strand of hair from Hannah's cheek. "You're a very special young woman. I hope you have someone in your life to tell you that every day."

Hannah's blush deepened with the comment. But then a proud smile brightened her eyes. "I met a woman about three months ago. She's special, I think."

"Good," Christian said, feeling it right that Hannah have someone to love her. "Maybe I'll meet her sometime," Christian said, putting her arm around Hannah's shoulder and pulling her to her.

Hannah chuckled. "That would be nice."

❖

Once back in her room, Christian showered and readied for lunch. She found the silence of the room stale and still longed to be around others. It was as if she had been locked away in a dark place, and now that she had seen the sun, she couldn't bear to face the darkness again. Her thoughts drifted to Alex and sitting with her and talking about Cara. She had long feared sharing what had happened with anyone. She had thought that if she said the words out loud, it would make the truth too unbearable. *My Cara is gone*, she thought. But now, for the first time, she realized that the love they shared was still with her.

Thinking of young Hannah and her journey to find the freedom to love, Christian felt blessed to have had those years with Cara. She thought about what Alex had said about moving on with life, that eventually she would begin to hold on to the good memories. The thought made her feel hopeful. She drew a breath…then another. She pocketed her key and left the silence of the room behind.

CHAPTER SIX

Elaine sat at the far end of the patio at their usual table. Her head was thrown back, and she held a drink in her hand. The light fabric of her slacks and camisole rippled across her skin as the breeze caressed her body. She raised her hand and shielded her eyes as Christian's shadow fell over her.

"Well, well...look who returns. I heard you had a bit of a scare yesterday," Elaine teased playfully.

Christian bent and swiftly kissed Elaine on the cheek. "Stop it, you," she said, pinching Elaine's chin. As she pulled away, she saw the pale hue of Elaine's skin and the dark shadows clouding her eyes hadn't improved. She felt a wave of concern for her new friend. "How are you?" she said a bit more seriously.

"No, no," Elaine said, pulling Christian onto the chair beside her. "You must tell me all about your little adventure with Alex. She's a tough one, you know. I can't remember her ever not being at Willow Springs, but I simply don't know anything about her. Well, aside from the fact that she's gorgeous, of course."

Christian chuckled at the inquisition and settled onto the lounge with Elaine, resting her head on Elaine's shoulder. She felt Elaine stiffen slightly at the contact, but Christian was tired of pretending she didn't need anyone, and she could see that Elaine could use the comfort of a friend too. After an uncomfortable moment, she began second-guessing this impulsive move and thought, perhaps, she might be overstepping her bounds a little bit. Then Christian felt the breath slip from Elaine as she relaxed against her.

"I'll tell you all about it," Christian said, pulling Elaine's arm around her shoulder. "But don't think for a minute I don't see that something is wrong. When you're ready, I hope you'll talk to me about it."

Elaine was still and quiet for what seemed like forever. Christian could feel her uneven breath on her hair. After a while, Elaine whispered, "I'll try."

Christian squeezed Elaine's hand and started her story. She noticed she talked faster as she became excited, and she became more demonstrative with her hands when she described the cabin and talked about her long conversations with Alex, about how much they'd enjoyed cooking together. Despite her resistance, she felt happy just thinking about Alex.

"Oh my, Christian Sutter, you are smitten!" Elaine exclaimed, giving Christian's shoulder a playful squeeze.

"Don't be silly, Elaine," Christian said, unable to hide her smile. "I think I'm too old to be *smitten* with anyone." She grew defensive, knowing Elaine was too close to the truth. "We talked and I enjoyed her company, that's all. I'm not interested in anything else."

Elaine laughed, a beautiful laugh that Christian found somewhat contagious. Turning her head up to look at Elaine, Christian's heart warmed to see a hint of pink in Elaine's cheeks.

Elaine put up a placating hand to stop Christian. "I'm not talking about schoolgirl crushes. I just mean that you two found a connection that has brightened your spirits. You may not know what to do with these feelings yet, but they sure look good on you."

Relenting, Christian smiled. "I've found, over the past few weeks, more than one new connection that lifts my spirits," she said, patting Elaine's hand. "Look at us, for example—you make me laugh and not take myself so seriously all the time. And it's been a long time since I felt like I could be a friend to anyone. Something about you just makes it easy. I like you."

Elaine's eyes closed briefly, and a look of gratitude crossed her face. "Me too," she said, squeezing Christian's hand. "Your friendship is important to me too. I know I kid around a lot, but I really do want you to be happy." She sighed. "It isn't easy for me to share things about myself, but I'll try. It just may take a while."

Christian smiled, satisfied. "Whenever you're ready."

❖

One a.m. The clock stared mockingly at Christian. Although tired, she found herself afraid to sleep. Since returning to her room, it was as if the silence were closing in on her. The feelings of calm and comfort she had felt with Alex had transformed into guilt and confusion. *What was I thinking? How could I have let myself get so close to Alex?* She had allowed herself to be vulnerable with Alex and had allowed her to comfort her. She couldn't deny the attraction, but her body seemed to be leading her in one direction and her head in another. Physically, she was feeling stronger, and she had started looking forward to spending time with Elaine and getting to know the other guests at Willow Springs. She was happy to find she could laugh and enjoy people again. She was learning to be comfortable with herself again. But she didn't want to let her need for company and friendship confuse her feelings for Alex. It was unusual for her to have such a physical reaction to anyone, but what disturbed her more was the way she was aware of Alex, the way she looked for her, hoping to catch a glimpse or a random moment of connection with her.

Giving up on sleep and desperately wanting to quiet the storm raging in her mind, Christian got up and crossed the room to her computer. She needed a distraction, something to fill the void until she could be outside again. When she was outside walking the grounds or exploring the lake, she was better able to focus. When she was surrounded by the flowers and trees and the warmth of the sun, she felt the possibilities that were still out there for her. But once night fell and she closed herself off in her room, the darkness seemed heavy and lonely. She turned on her computer, hoping to find something to fill the sleepless hours. She stared at the screen blankly. She had been trying to start a new book but found her efforts fruitless. Every time she sat down to write, her mind became overwhelmed with turmoil. Cara supported her writing, and all her imagination, passion, and inspiration had died with her.

Christian felt the pain of missing Cara begin to well up within her. *No! I can't do this again.* Instead, she began to busy herself by looking through news headlines, checking her advocacy posts, and avoiding her e-mail. She thought of Elaine and her secrecy and wondered if she could—or should—look for information about her. Deciding that general information couldn't hurt, she Googled Elaine Barber. As expected, the search returned multiple pages of information she knew would be useless. A memory came to her of her first meeting with Elaine, and she recalled Elaine mentioning she had been coming to Willow Springs for the past three years.

Christian thought of her own reasons for choosing Willow Springs and recalled the information packet still in her messenger bag. Pulling the packet out, she flipped to the Specialties section. Aside from being an all-lesbian facility, Willow Springs specialized in therapeutic services to address a wide range of physical and emotional problems.

Christian narrowed her search to information going back more than three years. The first three hits caught her eye.

FBI BAFFLED IN ELAINE BARBER SHOOTING
PROMINENT FBI PSYCHOLOGIST / PROFILER ELAINE BARBER SHOT
ELAINE BARBER NAMED TO HEAD SERIAL KILLER INVESTIGATION

"Oh my God!" Christian said out loud as her hand flew to cover her mouth as if it could somehow protect her from the words staring back at her.

Her thoughts were reeling. Was this really about Elaine? The timeline fit, but this was more than the general information she had expected to find. She stepped away from the computer to pace the floor. Of course some of Elaine's behavior made more sense now. Her use of humor and her focus on other people were defense mechanisms to deflect attention away from herself. She had briefly mentioned difficulty sleeping, and Christian had seen the darkness circling Elaine's eyes.

Poor Elaine. Christian couldn't imagine the fear and pain she must be dealing with, but now that she knew some of Elaine's past, how could she help her?

Christian remembered the way Elaine had made her feel welcome and accepted without expectations or intrusions, and she had her answer. She would just be her friend and meet her where she was. Taking a deep breath, Christian felt at peace with her answer. A friend. Yes. It was time she learned how to be a friend again. She had spent the last eighteen months wallowing in her own self-pity, not thinking of the people in her life who were also hurting, who *she* was hurting. She hadn't been a friend to herself or anyone else. She knew what it was like to become trapped in a moment when life was ripped apart and to feel unable to put the pieces back together again, and she wanted to help Elaine find her way back.

Christian fell onto the bed, trying to make sense of what she had just learned and all she had experienced since coming to Willow Springs. Christian knew something was changing in her, and although she was frightened of what this might mean, she knew she had to find a way to allow change to happen. As if taken back in time, to when life was perfect, Christian could see Cara sitting on the balcony of their flat, a glass of red wine in her hand. The sun was setting, Cara's favorite time of day. *Look, Chris, the light show is starting. It happens so fast. The most glorious things in the world just happen so fast.*

Christian smiled. Since coming to Willow Springs, she had felt as if life were suddenly moving too fast. Maybe it was just that she was finally moving again, finally beginning to live again.

It was light out when Christian woke, the lingering touch of Cara's lips still playing on her skin. It had been months since she had dreamed of anything but the accident. She clasped a hand to her chest. The pain was there, as always, but now for the first time, she had been able to feel Cara's love again. And that made her smile. She felt grateful for the memories. Her life had been meaningful, and she was beginning to understand that although her life had been irrevocably changed, it was not over.

CHAPTER SEVEN

Alex ran the familiar path around the lake. It had rained during the night, and the earth was soft beneath her feet. Each breath filled her with the woodsy smells of pine trees, wildflowers, and honeysuckle and the crisp cleanness that always followed the rain.

Her legs felt strong and sure as she pounded the path. She had risen early and had watched the light begin to glow in her garden as the first hints of morning light filtered into the sky. The tulips were in bloom and the pansies were like fields of smiling faces. She loved her garden. It was a good spring, and it made her feel strong. But this morning she had felt alone as she looked out over all the things she loved.

She had been content living here and spending her days focused on her work. Now she felt something was missing. For years, all she had felt was pain. Sophia had been so full of life and adventure. Once she was gone, Alex had pushed everyone away. Love meant pain. Then Christian had come along and all that had changed. It had been five days since she had met Christian and something in her world had shifted.

The thought of reaching out to someone was terrifying. *I can't risk it*, she thought as her feet pounded the packed earth. *It didn't mean anything, it was just a moment shared.* But as hard as she tried to convince herself that she could forget about Christian, a part of her didn't believe it. In the days since meeting Christian, she had been tempted to call her and had resisted the urge to make up random reasons to visit Willow Springs in the hope of seeing her. But each time she had convinced herself she was being foolish. Christian had her own issues to work through, and she hadn't made any attempt to reach out to Alex. But, still, she couldn't stop thinking about her.

After crossing the ridge of the old swinging bridge, she cut down the hill to the water's edge. It was a path she traveled most days, and she traversed the rocks and tree roots with ease. As she came to the clearing, she stopped and dropped her hands to her knees to catch her breath. When her breathing became steadier, she drew in a deep breath and began to sing. Today she sang of promise and allowed the feeling to fill her to her soul. She made her way through the clearing to stare out over the water and watched as the sun rose above the tallest tips of the trees. She felt the air warm as the sun kissed her skin and made the rain-drenched evergreens sparkle with tiny points of light.

"Good morning, love," she whispered. Alex always felt close to Sophia as the sun rose. Sunrise reminded her of waking in the morning with Sophia in her arms. Sophia always woke smiling and eager to start a new day. "What will today bring us, Sophia?"

The sun had fully risen now, and the day was beginning to press down upon her. Alex took her bow and turned to finish her run when a thought stopped her and she lifted her head, looking all around her. *You are the woman by the lake.* She searched the edges of the clearing, her gaze finally resting on the small wooden bench just along the row of trees at the trailhead leading to Willow Springs.

She saw the figure of the woman sitting quietly, gazing back at her. Alex smiled and stepped forward to cross the clearing, raising her hand slightly in greeting.

"Good morning," Alex said as she approached Christian, smiling broadly.

"Good morning, Alex."

"It's good to see you. How have you been feeling?" Alex asked, noticing that her palms were beginning to sweat, and her heart beat so loudly she feared Christian would be able to hear.

Christian scanned the long, lean body of the woman in front of her. Not able to hide her assessment from Alex, she said, "I'm very well, thank you, and I must say, you look very refreshed this morning."

"Thanks." Alex grinned. "Mind if I sit down?" she asked. "I don't want to intrude or anything."

"Please," Christian said, patting her hand on the bench next to her. "I'd love the company."

"You're up early," Alex noted.

"I woke early with the sound of the rain, and I thought it might be a good sunrise. I wasn't sure you would be here after the rain," Christian said, admitting she had been looking for Alex. She shifted uneasily with the realization that she had come to the lake hoping to see Alex again. She had worked hard over the past few days to put Alex out of her mind, focusing her energy on experimental hobbies, long walks, and spending time with Elaine. But each morning she had wandered to the lake with the faint hope that Alex would be there.

"Actually, it's been a great morning to run. Everything seems so fresh and new. The woods seem more alive. It's very energizing."

Christian took in the calm, smooth face and the glint in Alex's eyes as she talked. Christian warmed as she realized she was happy to see Alex. "I know what you mean. I've been sitting here, trying to take it all in, and feeling a bit surreal. It's almost as if nothing can touch me when I'm here."

Smiling, Alex turned her body sideways on the bench so she was fully facing Christian, the gesture closing the space between them so her knee rested against Christian's thigh. "I haven't seen you on the lake lately. I thought perhaps you had left Willow Springs. Has everything been going well?"

Christian warmed at the slight touch and consciously willed herself not to pull away. There couldn't be any harm in just talking. "Oh yes. I've been exploring more and more of the lake, actually. Well... to be honest...I've been avoiding your place. I didn't want to intrude on your privacy. You must have thought me crazy after everything that happened. I'm sorry—I shouldn't have pushed my problems on you like that."

Alex touched Christian's shoulder. "You are always welcome. As a matter of fact, I was hoping to convince you to come to dinner with me. If you're up for it, I have something I want to show you."

This time Christian did pull away from Alex's touch. "I don't think that would be a good idea," Christian said, dropping her eyes.

"Why not?" Alex sounded hurt.

Christian struggled with an explanation. "I just think it's best...I don't want to give you the wrong impression—"

"Impression of *what*?" Alex interrupted. "I know how confusing it feels to allow yourself to be vulnerable with someone and not know how to deal with the guilt that comes afterward. I don't have any expectations. The time I spent with you was the first time I allowed myself to be close to anyone since Sophia. I have the same feelings you do. But I don't want to live the rest of my life closed up in my cabin and never feel connected to anyone again." Alex took Christian's hand, tightening her grip when she felt Christian try to pull away. "Please, Christian. Don't run away."

Christian's insides turned to jelly. Every time she was with Alex, she found herself craving the closeness of her company, and that was the problem. The intensity of her feelings when she was with Alex was overwhelming. Self-consciously, she bit her lower lip and tried to gather her resolve. The warmth of Alex's hand held her firmly, the pleading in Alex's eyes making her bones melt. She couldn't say no. "When did you have in mind?" Christian asked hesitantly.

"How about tonight?" Alex said, her voice suddenly cheerful.

Christian laughed, surprised by the sudden enthusiasm. "You're relentless," Christian said, conflicted between the urge to run away and the desire to press herself closer to the warmth of Alex's body. "Not tonight. I've promised to have dinner with Elaine tonight."

"Elaine?"

"Yes, she's a good friend. We met my first day at Willow Springs."

"Tomorrow, then," Alex pressed.

"I'll have to think about it." She needed a little time to prepare herself for being alone with Alex again and time to think about what to do about her feelings. Alex's persistence was making her feel anxious, and she was having second thoughts about agreeing to dinner.

"You're avoiding me again. It's only dinner. If you want, I can meet you at the lodge."

"No," Christian said forcefully. "Perhaps next week. I really need to go now." Christian stood, but as she tried to pull her hand free, Alex again tightened her grip, forcing Christian to meet her eyes.

"I'm sorry if I made you uncomfortable. I won't bother you again." Alex sounded hurt. "Let me know if you change your mind." Alex's fingers slipped from Christian's, and she stepped aside and began to walk away.

Christian felt her heart clench at the loss of Alex's touch and the obvious hurt she had seen in her eyes. *Damn.* Christian cursed herself as she frantically tried to figure out what to do.

"Alex." Christian's voice held pleading. Stretching out her hand, she took Alex's arm before she could step out of reach. "I'm sorry. I'm being a coward. I don't mean to hurt you."

Alex stopped, her head bowed.

"I want to see you. But the way I feel when I'm with you…"

Alex stepped closer to Christian. "You don't have to be afraid of me. We can help each other," Alex whispered, her lips so close, Christian could feel the heat of her breath brush her skin. "But you have to stop running. I'm just as scared as you are."

It hadn't occurred to her that Alex might be feeling as scared as she was, and she softened with the understanding of how difficult the admission must have been for Alex. When Christian didn't pull away, Alex lifted her hand and ran a finger along Christian's jawline. Christian felt Alex's arm slide around her waist. "Don't," Christian said without conviction.

"You don't mean that," Alex said, leaning in so their foreheads touched.

Christian moved her hands to Alex's chest and pressed as if to push her away, but there was no force in her gesture. Despite her protests, she wanted Alex to touch her. She knew she was crossing a line, but she couldn't find the strength to pull away. Alex felt too good against her, and she didn't want that feeling to stop. If she let this continue, she knew she wouldn't be able to stop wanting her. "Alex—"

Before Christian could say another word, Alex pressed her lips gently to hers. It was a tentative kiss, a kiss that asked permission, a kiss that shook of fear and longing.

Christian's eyes closed, and she melted under the gentle touch. Heat flooded her body as she pushed into the kiss, and her hands brushed the skin of Alex's neck. She felt Alex's hand on her face guiding her further into her as tender lips explored her mouth. With one final brush of lips, Alex pulled away. "I will call you, if that is okay."

Christian's breath shook. She closed her eyes tightly, trying to bring herself back to earth. "Okay," she said breathlessly. She felt like she was losing her mind. One minute, she wanted to run as far away from Alex as she could, and the next, she felt as if she wouldn't be able to breathe if Alex didn't touch her. Her stomach churned. She had no idea what to do.

Alex smiled warmly at Christian as she took her hand and kissed the tips of her fingers. And without another word, Alex turned and walked away, leaving Christian staring after her.

❖

Elaine sat on the balcony of her room, watching the sun rise over the lake and feeling the last lingering dread left over from her dreams slowly fade with the dawn. The water shimmered like diamonds as she watched the world wake up from the long dark night. She was lonely this morning and found herself wishing for things she knew she could no longer have.

Her thoughts drifted to Hannah and her young lover. She envied that innocence and the ability to abandon reason and follow love. She had turned her back on such childish fantasies long ago. She still loved with all her being but knew that being close to people only meant pain. She had spent her career chasing after those who used getting close to someone as a means of getting what they wanted, which too often meant the death of those willing to trust.

Eric Flask had been one of those people. She had studied his past, his family life, his relationships, and the twisted ways he earned the trust of others so he could inflict his sick torture on the innocent. He had killed six girls across three states that she knew of, and each murder had been the same. Although she was aware of the abuse Flask had endured as a child and could rationalize how he'd developed into this specific monster, she would never be able to understand his behavior.

Shuddering from the memory, Elaine tried to clear her mind of the troubling thoughts of death. She reached for the forgotten cup of coffee waiting on the table beside her. Touching it to her lips, she found it still warm and took in a long swallow, the bitter liquid warming her as it flowed across her tongue. Taking a deep breath and letting it go, Elaine stood to go shower and get ready for her day. She paused as she looked over the lawn below and saw a slow-moving figure step from the wooded path and make her way back to the lodge.

Elaine's thoughts were interrupted as she recognized Christian by the dark curl of her short hair and the way she moved. Elaine studied Christian, taking in her lean body and the power in her gait, as she slowly meandered along the grounds.

Elaine had known women like Christian before. Women who drew attention just by entering a room, but not wanting the attention their strength drew from people. Thinking about the conflict, Elaine thought there was more to Christian. She carried an obvious pain that never left her eyes, even when Elaine made her laugh. Behind the veil of pain, there was gentleness in Christian that Elaine recognized as something innately good. Christian was the kind of woman who saw the good in people, and her compassion was like the embrace of a mother comforting a child. Watching her now, Elaine wondered what would bring Christian out at such an early hour. The loneliness she had tempered with the sunrise pressed again on her heart, and Elaine suddenly wanted to be close to Christian. She didn't know why, but she wanted to be there walking with Christian, holding her hand and sharing her silence. Perhaps it was the gentle way Christian had offered her friendship that made it easy for her to accept the comfort she had so long denied herself. Christian offered caring and tenderness without judgment or expectation, and at that moment, Elaine needed that comfort.

❖

Christian ran her fingers along the prickly spines of a blue spruce. Although stiff, the spines tickled her and she smiled. She had walked back along the path lost in her thoughts and confused by the emotions raging within her since being with Alex. She had *kissed* Alex. She knew she had to learn to stop living in the past. Was it possible she could have a second chance? Or were she and Alex just enthralled with the deep understanding they offered each other? She wondered if it was wrong of her to want to find out. She was undeniably drawn to Alex in a way she had only experienced one other time in her life, and losing that had almost killed her. Could she risk another pain so deep?

The scuffling sound of someone walking on the loose pebbles drew her attention, and she turned to see Elaine moving gracefully toward her. Something in Elaine's posture made Christian feel sad.

"Hi," Elaine said as she came up to Christian.

"Hi." Christian smiled weakly at Elaine and held out her hand.

Elaine stepped up to her and took the offered hand, closing her eyes for a moment. She looked tired, and her posture was unusually slumped as if she were carrying a heavy weight. Christian turned so she was facing Elaine and gently stepped into her, wrapping her arms tenderly around Elaine's shoulders and pulling her close. She felt Elaine shudder as she gave herself to the embrace and laid her head against Christian's shoulder. Christian wondered what could be causing Elaine such visible pain. She wanted to try to get Elaine to talk to her, but something told her that the more she pried, the more Elaine would close off. So she did the only thing she knew to do: she held her and comforted her, waiting for Elaine to tell her what she needed.

Time seemed to stand still as Christian stood there holding Elaine. All the conflicted emotions that had ravaged her mind only moments before vanished, and all that mattered now was the comfort she offered a friend.

Feeling Elaine pull away, Christian loosened her hold, allowing her hands to slide down the length of Elaine's arms to grasp her hands. She felt the smooth cotton of the pullover brush between her fingers and realized this was the first time she had seen Elaine so casually dressed. This morning, she wore loose cotton pants and athletic shoes paired with the slim-fitting cotton top. Her hair was pulled back and she wore no hint of makeup. Her red hair seemed darker, pulled back on her head in disarray, and Christian noticed for the first time Elaine's natural beauty and athleticism.

Christian marveled that she had never noticed this strength in Elaine before. She had always been drawn to her feminine poise, and seeing this side of Elaine now left Christian intrigued by the layers of complexity she was beginning to unravel as she allowed the intimacy between them to grow. There was no fear with Elaine, only simple comfort. There was none of the physical tension she had felt earlier with Alex. Christian accepted what she was feeling for Alex was attraction and desire and she couldn't kid herself into thinking her feelings were anything less. But with Elaine she didn't have the same struggle with her emotions. With Elaine, she was safe.

Elaine squeezed Christian's hand gently and as their eyes met she asked, "Can I walk with you for a while?"

"Of course," Christian said, leaning in and slipping an arm through Elaine's and resting her head against her shoulder. "I'd be very glad for the company. Your timing is perfect. I'm a little out of sorts this morning, and I could use a friend."

Walking the loose stone path, Christian and Elaine found themselves in a beautiful rose garden that had been hidden from view by a row of boxwood trees. In the center of the garden was a fountain, surrounded by stone planters and benches. In the far corner of the garden, they found cushioned lounge chairs with small tables.

Elaine looked around, her gaze gliding over the wall of roses. "I can't believe I've never been here before," she said. "I thought I knew all the gardens at Willow Springs. I don't even recall this being on the visitors' map."

Christian smiled at the brief moment of joy she saw in Elaine's eyes. "Maybe it's supposed to be one of those secret gardens you read about. I don't think I've ever seen so many roses. I suppose if everyone knew about it, it would lose some of the quiet charm."

"I suppose," Elaine said thoughtfully as she held a rose bloom delicately in her hands and fingered the velvet petals.

Christian slid her fingers into Elaine's hand, "Come sit with me for a while. I'm feeling a little tired."

Elaine studied Christian's face, suddenly concerned. "Are you feeling all right?"

"Just tired. I didn't sleep much last night, and I think the walk has taken more out of me than I expected."

Elaine spotted a hammock tucked away in a bend surrounded by large yellow climbing roses. "How about over there?" she said, pointing.

"Hmm...Yes, that would be wonderful."

Christian climbed into the large hammock. "Come on," she said as Elaine stood watching. "Lie down with me for a while. I just want to rest, and I don't want to be alone," Christian pleaded gently when Elaine hesitated. "Besides, you look exhausted."

Elaine looked into Christian's eyes and saw her anguish and felt her own loneliness well from within. She was so tired and she felt safe here with Christian. Steadying the hammock, she climbed in. She felt Christian's arms slide around her as her back came to rest against Christian's chest. They fit together with a familiar comfort, and Elaine felt thankful for the warmth of Christian's body pressed against her. It was strange to allow herself to be close to someone like this. Normally, she wouldn't have dreamed of allowing herself to be so vulnerable, but she was so tired and there had never been any sexual tension between her and Christian. It was nice to feel simply comforted.

"Thank you," Christian whispered, her breath brushing the stray strands of hair along Elaine's ear.

The gentle sway of the hammock was soothing. Elaine took in the feel of Christian's arms wrapped lightly around her, and she brushed her fingers over the delicate skin of Christian's hand. She closed her eyes and focused her attention on the rise and fall of Christian's breathing, remembering a time long ago and imagining someone else's arms holding her. Someone she still longed for. Slowly, Elaine began to drift, and her body relaxed into the safety of Christian's arms.

❖

The sun was beginning to feel warm on her skin as Christian stirred. She lingered in the memory of waking with Alex holding her. Her eyes flashed open as the feeling of the woman lying next to her registered in her thoughts. Seeing the red hair and pale skin, her brow furrowed. *Elaine?* Christian felt momentarily confused before remembering the walk that morning and lying down with Elaine to rest. A smile edged the corners of her mouth as she took in the rumpled red hair of the still-sleeping woman cradled in her arms.

The sun was almost uncomfortably warm, and Christian wondered how long they had been asleep. She felt Elaine stir as a breeze played in her hair.

"You're awake," Christian whispered.

Elaine turned to face Christian, who moved to her side to allow the shift.

Christian spoke before Elaine could say anything. "Thank you, Elaine. Thank you for staying with me and allowing this closeness." Christian's voice was tender.

Somehow Christian knew that if she didn't say the right thing, Elaine would retreat back into herself. "Sometimes I feel so lost," Christian started to explain. "I needed this closeness so I don't begin to believe that I am untouchable, unlovable, and invisible. Thank you," she said again.

Elaine sighed. "I should be thanking you," she said as she touched a hand lightly to Christian's arm. "Before today I couldn't imagine allowing anyone to hold me as you just did. I can't thank you enough for this brief respite." Elaine's eyes darkened.

"Elaine," Christian said, drawing Elaine's face up so their eyes met, "I don't know what you've been through, but I know we are both hurt and lonely. For some reason, when I'm with you, I don't feel like running away anymore. We don't have to talk about anything if you don't want to, but we can at least offer each other this one tenderness."

Elaine's eyes were glassy from unshed tears. "Yes," she said burrowing her head beneath Christian's chin. "Thank you," she whispered.

CHAPTER EIGHT

Three days had passed since Alex had kissed Christian by the lake. She'd replayed that moment over in her mind, scolding herself for pushing Christian too hard, fearing she'd gone too far. So, despite her promise to call, she hadn't tried to contact Christian—she wanted to give her time and space. But today was the monthly cookout at Willow Springs, and she couldn't help but hope she would see Christian while she was there.

Alex stepped onto the patio and made her way to the outdoor kitchen. She smiled as she saw Hannah already making preparations for lunch. Hannah had cut up the zucchini and squash and had a basket of onions peeled and quartered. She knew Hannah liked to be hands-on with most things going on at Willow Springs and imagined Hannah running her own place someday.

"Hey," Alex said as she stepped up behind Hannah, "the kitchen looks good. You sure you need me here? Looks to me like you have things covered pretty well."

Hannah laughed. "Yeah, do you want to get me lynched? These women all know you're the one doing the cooking. I'm not going to be the one to disappoint them. Besides, maybe this will give you a chance to talk to Christian."

Alex was shocked by the mention of Christian, and she suddenly felt defensive. She didn't like other people knowing anything about her personal life, and she wasn't ready to deal with—didn't even *understand*—her feelings for Christian. Trying to sound casual, Alex asked flatly, "What do you mean?"

"Oh, nothing. I just thought you might want to catch up. That was a really nice thing you did for her the day she fell. She was really lucky you were there."

"I guess so," Alex said cautiously. Then, still curious, Alex added, "Has she been okay? Did I misjudge her injury or something?" Even though she had seen Christian herself only days earlier and had seen for herself that Christian was okay, fear, hot and searing, filled her belly, making her feel sick. What if she had made a mistake, and Christian had been more seriously injured than she'd thought?

"No, no, no. Christian was fine. Really, Alex, are *you* okay? Have I said something wrong?"

Alex shook her head. She was relieved that Christian was really okay. "No, nothing like that. I guess I'm just a little taken off guard. I'm not used to talking about...well...about people," Alex admitted.

Hannah kept piling skewers of vegetables onto a tray as they talked. "Okay. I get it. I won't push. I just thought you two clicked, or something."

Alex thought about that. They had clicked, as Hannah put it. She hadn't been able to put Christian out of her head since they'd kissed at the lake. Despite all her excuses not to call Christian, she had wanted to see her, talk to her, just to have any connection with her. Having Hannah call her out like this set Alex on edge and made her feel like a schoolgirl.

Putting the first of the pineapple-chicken kebabs on the grill, Alex busied herself with the lunch preparations. "I need to go get the other tray from the main kitchen. I'll be right back. Do you mind putting on the first tray of vegetables for me?"

"No problem."

Alex was still preoccupied with her thoughts when she rounded the corner of the patio and almost ran into two women entering the dining area. "Oh, so sorry," Alex said, trying to gather herself, then stopped in her tracks as she recognized Christian, who was holding the hand of a beautiful redhead Alex had seen around Willow Springs from time to time. Alex looked to Christian, trying to understand what she was seeing. As she tried to understand, jealousy, sudden and fierce, ran through her body like fire, and she tensed.

Christian was elated to see Alex, but the joy was quickly quenched when she saw a succession of surprise, hurt, and something akin to anger flow across Alex's face. Christian moved forward, placing a hand on Alex's arm. "Hello, Alex. Are you all right? We didn't mean to startle you."

A muscle tensed in Alex's jaw. "No, I'm fine. I guess I wasn't watching where I was going. I'm sorry."

Christian had let go of Elaine's hand and now stood between the two women, one hand on Alex's arm and the other gesturing toward Elaine. She was unsettled by Alex's reaction but had been unable to resist the urge to be close to her. "Alex, this is my friend Elaine Barber. Elaine, this is Alex Moore."

"Ah yes, Alex. It's a pleasure to finally meet you. I've been an admirer of yours for quite some time—at least your cooking, anyway. I understand you were quite the hero, saving Christian the way you did." Elaine had extended her hand to Alex, who stood staring at her.

Alex hesitated, then said, "It's a pleasure to meet you, Ms. Barber." She shook Elaine's offered hand.

"Please, call me Elaine." Christian looked from Alex to Elaine, hoping Elaine would give her a moment alone with Alex.

As if on cue, Elaine said, "I think I'll go find us a table and give you two some time to talk. It was truly a pleasure meeting you, Alex. I do hope to see you again."

"Thanks, Elaine," Christian said, smiling faintly.

After watching Elaine leave, Christian turned to Alex, who remained stone still, staring at her. "Alex, are you sure you are all right?"

Rubbing her hand down her face and then through her hair, Alex shook her head. "I didn't realize you were involved with anyone. I'm sorry, I—"

"What?" Christian interrupted. "Involved? What are you talking about?"

"Well, you and Ms. Barber. I didn't realize you were—"

Christian couldn't hold back a gasp of surprise. "Oh, Alex. No. You misunderstood. Elaine and I are just friends. She's a very special friend, but there's nothing more between us." She suddenly understood the hurt and anger she had seen on Alex's face. Then her own anger began to rise as she recognized Alex's jealousy.

"Oh God! I'm sorry, Christian. I had no right." Alex had turned red in the face and shifted from foot to foot as if trying to find a place to run.

Finally meeting Christian's gaze she said meekly, "I really made a fool of myself, didn't I?"

"Maybe a little bit." Christian shook her head, trying to stifle her own frustration and confusion over what had happened. She didn't like having to explain herself. What right did Alex have to be jealous? They weren't dating. But she had to admit there was something going on between them that she couldn't explain. Perhaps she was being a little hard on Alex. "It was an honest mistake. No harm done." Despite her own discomfort in having to explain herself, Christian wanted to comfort Alex. She had seen the hurt in Alex's eyes, and she hated feeling she had done anything to put it there. Maybe she wasn't the only one confused by what was happening between them.

"I really need to get to the kitchen." Before pulling away Alex lifted her eyes to meet Christian's. "I'm sorry. I don't know what came over me. Please forgive me."

Christian smiled and brushed her fingers along Alex's hand. "We can talk more about this later. Don't worry about it." Then, looking across the patio and seeing Elaine, Christian had a second thought. "If you get a chance later, would you mind stopping by our table for a while?"

Alex looked toward the table where Elaine was waiting. "Yes. I'll come by. I need to apologize for my behavior. That's the least I can do."

"Thank you." Christian leaned over and kissed Alex lightly on the cheek. "I'll look forward to seeing you later, then." Still smiling, Christian stepped away to join Elaine.

❖

Elaine tried to hide her grin as Christian seated herself across the table. "Well, that was interesting," she said, her voice chiding. "What was that all about?"

"It was nothing, just a misunderstanding."

"Misunderstanding? That seems to be just the tip of the iceberg. I thought the poor girl wanted to throttle me." Elaine was laughing now—she couldn't help but feel amused by Christian's growing discomfort. She had heard the excitement in Christian's voice when she spoke of Alex; she had seen the way her eyes lit up and the way she moved her body closer to Alex when they ran into her. It was obvious that Christian had feelings for Alex, and by Alex's reaction, those feelings were mutual.

"She thought you and I were a couple," Christian explained. "Since I hadn't mentioned being with anyone, she was surprised, that's all."

"Hmm," Elaine said faintly, pausing a moment to think that over. "Would you being with someone have been a bad thing?" Elaine asked, studying Christian's response, seeing her brow furrow and her shoulders tense. Noting the discomfort, Elaine quickly added, "I mean, why would it upset Alex? Is there something between you two?"

Christian frowned and looked thoughtful. Elaine studied the way Christian toyed with the hem of her blouse and the way her eyes darted nervously, not focusing on anything. Christian was obviously uncomfortable acknowledging her feelings for Alex.

Elaine reached across the table and took Christian's hand. "Now I've upset you. I shouldn't have teased you. Don't worry—things are okay between us. But why don't you tell me what's going on with you and Alex."

Christian bit her lower lip nervously. "I'm so confused all the time. I'm really not sure how I feel about Alex. I'm not sure I want to feel anything. But then sometimes…sometimes I want to feel everything." Christian sighed. "I know that doesn't make any sense."

Elaine smiled and patted Christian's hand. "I don't think it's supposed to make sense right now. But don't worry, you'll figure it out."

CHAPTER NINE

Elaine sat with her spine rigidly pressed against the back of the sofa in Dr. Cook's office. She had requested an early appointment, but now that she was here, she was anxious and uncertain.

"What brings you in today, Elaine? You've never requested an early session before. What's happened?" Dr. Cook sat across from Elaine with her legs crossed at the knee and her hands resting loosely on the arms of her chair. Elaine knew everything about her posture was designed to induce calm. Her tone of voice, her relaxed pose, her compassionate expression, even the cadence of her breathing were all purposefully controlled to present a peaceful air of safety.

Elaine sat staring at her hands as they lay limp in her lap. Slowly, she drew in a deep breath and exhaled. "I've met a woman at the retreat where I'm staying." Elaine hesitated. "She and I have become good friends, and I've found that when I am with her I don't feel the fear that's normally with me." Again she paused, and Dr. Cook waited in silence for her to continue. "Since we've been spending time together, something in me is changing. At first, it was a need to feel connected, to feel like I was a part of something again. But, recently, I've been living in dread, like I'm waiting for something bad."

"Go on." Dr. Cook encouraged. "Your dreams have changed."

For the first time since entering the office, Elaine looked up at Dr. Cook. She took another deep breath and continued, her voice breaking with her first words. "Now when I dream of the shooting, she's there with me. Just after the bright light, she takes my hand and calls my name. For a while I didn't think much of it, but now the dreams have changed again." Elaine's shoulders slumped, and she clenched her hands into fists.

"Okay, just take your time. Tell me how the dreams have changed."

Elaine fought back the tears.

"Why don't we start by talking a little about your new friend? Tell me about the woman you've met."

A smile quirked the corner of Elaine's mouth as she thought of Christian. "Her name is Christian Sutter. I met her about a month or so ago. She doesn't ask questions, she just seems to understand without having to know my story. She helps me feel safe. She doesn't know anything about my history, and when we talk, I don't have to think about the past."

"What's making you uncomfortable about this relationship?"

"The past few days, when I dream of the shooting…" Elaine paused as her body shook with fear. "Now when I dream, it's as if I'm *watching* and no longer a participant in the dream. Christian has taken my place, and when the door opens"—Elaine sucked in a deep breath—"it's Christian who is shot and lying on the floor, not me."

"You seem to care a great deal about Christian," Dr. Cook said gently. "Tell me what you're feeling right now, Elaine."

"I'm afraid," she whispered. "I'm afraid that my getting close to Christian will get her hurt." She knew the person who had shot her was still out there somewhere, and despite the odds, there was a risk that her life was still in danger. That meant that anyone close to her could be a target as well.

"Have you felt this way before?" Dr. Cook asked.

Elaine's head flew up and her tone was suddenly fierce. "What?"

"Who have you protected in the past, Elaine?"

"Don't," Elaine said sharply. She didn't want to think about Chacey. Of everything she had given up, she couldn't bear to think about what it had taken for her to leave her lover.

"This has obviously brought up some feelings that you have been repressing. I know you're afraid. But you're safe here. It's time to let go, Elaine. Who are you protecting?"

"No one," Elaine said, hearing her voice flat and distant, hardened, as she fought back the memories of the life she had given up.

"How have things been between you and Christian since the dreams changed?"

Elaine flinched and then refocused. "I haven't seen her in the past week."

"What's changed to prevent you from seeing her?"

"I've been busy." Elaine could feel her heart beating hard in her chest as she thought about the dreams, and she couldn't bear to see Christian lying there on the floor, bleeding. She knew the only way to keep Christian safe was to distance herself from her, so she had been avoiding her friend.

"If I remember correctly, this is the first time you've mentioned a friend in any capacity since beginning your counseling with me. You said she makes you feel safe. She sounds very special."

Elaine closed her eyes, trying to figure out how to get out of this. She had come to the session frantic, but now she didn't want to face the truth. She knew the dream wasn't about Christian, but she wasn't willing to talk about the truth, either.

"She is special. I guess I've been overreacting a bit. You're right. I think I panicked, thinking I had to protect her. It sounds more like I'm using her safety to shield myself in the dreams." Elaine chuckled, hoping to convince Dr. Cook of her explanation. "I can't believe I couldn't see it before now." She was certain Dr. Cook could see through her diversion and waited for her to confront her. She could feel the doctor's eyes assessing her, and she tried to control her breathing and body language to mask her feelings.

"I'm glad you feel better," Dr. Cook said with a faint smile. "I think we can use this to help us find the feeling of safety you've needed to progress with the hypnotherapy. Let's keep your regularly scheduled appointment, and we can pick up then."

Elaine let out the breath she had been holding, thankful that Dr. Cook wasn't going to push her on the issue. "Okay," she said in acquiescence. "Thank you for seeing me, Helen."

"Of course," Dr. Cook said as Elaine stood and made her way to the door. "I'll see you Thursday."

Elaine inclined her head in a nod as she slowly shut the door behind her.

❖

Elaine drove around for two hours after leaving Dr. Cook's office. The session had made her nostalgic about her past, and she had been reminiscing about her relationship with Chacey. The memories made her feel lonely and disconnected, and she longed for the life she had given up years ago. As she pulled to the front of the lodge, she saw Christian and Hannah standing on the landing watching her approach. Although anxious at the prospect of explaining her recent withdrawal, Elaine was happy to see them. She was deeply comforted that someone had missed her and was waiting to welcome her home.

Hannah was the first to step forward. She opened the car door and assisted Elaine from the car. As she took the keys to drive the car to the parking area, she whispered in Elaine's ear, "She's been worried about you. She's checked in on you every day for the past week."

"Thank you," Elaine said, drawing in a deep breath and turning to face Christian.

Christian didn't wait for explanations. As soon as Elaine stepped forward closing the distance between them, Christian put her arms around her shoulders and hugged her. "I've missed you," Christian said.

Elaine's resolve melted away as she felt Christian's arms close around her, holding her. Slowly, she wrapped her own arms around Christian's waist and hugged her back. "I'm sorry. I've missed you too."

Christian took Elaine's face in both hands and peered into her eyes. "You look tired." Christian brushed her thumb along the ridge of Elaine's cheekbone. Elaine knew she was tracing the dark circles that shaded her eyes. "Have you eaten anything today?" Christian asked.

Elaine was grateful for Christian's nurturing and smiled, the warmth of Christian's touch filling her. She had been alone and denied her need for connection with others for so long that she was now overwhelmed with relief and tenderness for this woman who insisted on being her friend. "No."

"Well then, let's go see what we can do about that." Christian slid her hand down Elaine's shoulder, took her hand, and led her to the patio.

They dined on a fruit-and-cheese plate while drinking mimosas. The conversation was light and playful, despite the questions that lingered. Elaine knew Christian would want to talk about her absence, and she tried to ready her explanations. But, to her surprise, Christian didn't pry. She just sat with her and ate with her. Yet Elaine knew the time had come for her to tell Christian the truth. She needed to tell her. The thought of explaining her past was terrifying, but she was tired of carrying this secret, and she trusted Christian.

After lunch they made their way back to their secret garden. Christian wrapped an arm through Elaine's and pulled her close as they walked. They finally settled onto a small cushioned bench, tucked peacefully into a corner just in sight of the fountain. The smell of the roses was sweet, and the fragrance washed over them on the breeze.

Christian spoke first. "Did I do something to upset you, Elaine? Is that why you've avoided me all week?"

Elaine heard the hurt in Christian's voice. "No. You've been wonderful. I just needed some time to work through some things."

"What things?" Christian's voice was still and hesitant. Elaine could hear fear lingering on her words like a shadow. Elaine could see no way around this except the truth. Her hands began to tremble as she tried to put the pain and fear of years into words. Christian had been a friend to her. Someone she trusted. Now she had to trust her with her truth.

"A few years ago, I was shot while working at my office. I never have been able to recall the face of the person who did it, and the police have been unable to solve the crime. I have these nightmares that make it difficult for me to sleep. The fear that this person might come after me again is paralyzing. I have shut everyone I love out of my life for the past three years, trying to protect them."

Christian laid her hand on Elaine's. Her touch was warm and comforting and encouraged Elaine to continue. "The time I've spent with you these past few weeks has been the closest I've been to anyone in all that time. I got scared. I don't want anyone to hurt you, so I did what I always do—I ran away."

Christian's eyes were tender when she spoke. "No one is going to hurt me. No one is going to hurt you. We're safe here, Elaine. I can't imagine what you've been through. I can see why you would be afraid, but I won't leave you."

"Thank you," Elaine whispered as she squeezed Christian's fingers. "That's why I continue to come to Willow Springs each year. When the fear becomes too much for me to bear, I come here, where I feel safe."

"You must get terribly lonely. You said you pushed everyone you cared for away. Who did you push away?"

Elaine hadn't expected this question. She tried to push back the pain she had denied for so long. "There was a woman in my life then. She was everything to me. But, after the shooting, I couldn't bear the thought of anyone harming her. So I sent her away. I couldn't risk..." Her voice trailed off in a choked whisper.

Christian moved closer and wrapped her arms around Elaine, holding her tightly. All of Elaine's defenses shattered in that instant as she embraced the tenderness. A flood of emotions began to poor out, through a stream of tears that streaked her cheeks.

Christian stroked Elaine's hair and held her as she cried. "I'm here," she whispered. "I'm here."

After a few moments, when the tears had stopped, Elaine turned and curled her body into Christian, allowing herself to be held and needing to feel Christian's gentle touch and warmth. She felt oddly peaceful after telling her story and allowing herself to cry. She'd turned a corner. She couldn't pretend she didn't need people anymore, and she knew she had to start being honest with herself if she was ever going to get her life back. She would push forward with the hypnotherapy. Accepting that she did not have to be alone, she was ready to face her fears. "Thank you," Elaine said as she pushed her arm behind Christian, wrapping it around her thin waist.

In return she felt Christian's arms tighten around her.

Christian left Elaine shortly after dinner and retired to her room after Elaine reassured her she was okay and was going to bed early. She thought of all the pain Elaine had endured alone and the sacrifices she had made to protect those she loved. She thought of her own life and how she had spent the last year pushing her friends away and shutting herself off from the world. She was protecting no one, and she realized she had been selfish in her grief.

Hours passed, and Christian lay on her bed, drifting somewhere between waking and sleep. Her restlessness was like a thorn slowly grating and digging into her consciousness, making her toss uncomfortably from side to side. An open bottle of Merlot sat on the table beside the bed. She had hoped a glass of wine would help her sleep but had found the thoughts swirling around in her head too unruly to allow her to rest. A faint tapping came from somewhere, pulling her from her stupor. She listened for a moment, her brow furrowed. There it was again. She swung her legs to the side of the bed, crossed the room to the door, and opened it to find Elaine standing awkwardly in front of her.

Elaine looked stricken and afraid. "Can I come in?" Her voice was low and rough.

Without thinking twice, Christian took Elaine's arm and pulled her inside. "Of course. Are you all right?"

"I couldn't sleep. I just can't bear to be alone. I'm sorry if I woke you."

"No," Christian soothed. "I was pretty much awake. Can I get you a glass of wine or something?"

"No. I just…well, I don't really know what I'm doing here. I just couldn't be alone."

"You can stay here with me. It's all right. Come on," she said as she pulled Elaine farther into the room toward the bed. She pulled back the covers and turned to Elaine. "Lie down. You can sleep here tonight. It'll be like the day in the garden. You're safe. I'll watch over you."

Elaine looked stricken. She stared at Christian and didn't move.

Christian took her hand and guided her to sit on the bed, then gently placed her hands on Elaine's shoulders, encouraging her to recline.

Christian pointed to the lazy chair by the balcony door. "I'll be over there if you need anything."

"Thank you," Elaine whispered.

Christian watched her struggle in her sleep, her body shaking occasionally as if she were running or struggling with something. Eventually, Elaine's breathing calmed, but she whimpered softly from time to time. Her body stilled, and Christian hoped she had chased away the nightmares.

CHAPTER TEN

The next morning, Christian awoke early, her body stiff from her night of sleep in the lazy chair. She had watched Elaine until she was certain she was sleeping peacefully before finally allowing herself to drift off. Elaine awoke shortly after Christian and returned to her room after thanking Christian for staying with her through the night.

Christian decided to take out one of the kayaks and spend some time gathering her own thoughts about what she had learned and experienced over the past few weeks. She was troubled by what she now knew about Elaine, but mostly, she needed to put her own feelings into perspective.

The boat glided effortlessly across the water. The sun was warm, and the cool water was a welcome contrast to the heat. Christian ran her hand through the water, drawing the coolness to her face and wetting her hair. The water was refreshing as it cascaded across her face and down her neck, washing the heat from her skin and the tension from her soul.

She had come to Willow Springs to find peace with her life and the loss of the woman she loved. Now she found herself intimately connected to two women, both dealing with their own fears and hurts.

She still missed Cara. But lately she found she had been filled with thoughts of Alex and Elaine and the new relationships that had become so important to her. Elaine, with all her complexity and pain, whom she desperately wanted to comfort and protect. Elaine had gotten to her with her laughter and playfulness, and through her vulnerability, she made Christian feel needed.

Then there was Alex. The mysterious woman who had rescued her from herself and awakened feelings she thought she would never know again. Just the thought of Alex evoked such strong emotions that she felt like screaming. Christian's body cried out for Alex, but it was so much more than just sexual energy she felt when she was with her. Being with Alex was like tasting a forbidden fruit, a flavor unlike any other that she would ever find anywhere else. She knew she had been unfair to Alex. She had been avoiding her for days now, so she could figure out her feelings or allow the infatuation to pass. After experiencing Alex's jealousy, she had decided it was unfair for her to see Alex until she understood her feelings and what had been happening between them. She had thought that the time away would help her forget her feelings and she could move on, but move on to what?

If she had learned anything through Cara's death and listening to the pain that Elaine had suffered, it was that no one had time to waste.

Christian was overwhelmed by the loneliness of her life, and she had come to the lake to sort out her feelings. The water always made her feel that, for a little while, she could step outside her life and make the world stop for a moment. On the water, she felt peace.

She hadn't set out in any particular direction and was surprised but not disappointed when she looked up to see the familiar dock and footpath leading to Alex's cabin. She smiled as she thought of Alex and the day and night she had spent at the cabin. Her stomach quivered slightly and she felt her heart rate speed up as she paddled toward the dock. As she approached, she saw a form take shape. It wasn't until she was right up close that she realized it was Alex, lying on the dock, basking in the sun. She lay on her stomach with her head turned away from Christian's position on the water, and her arms were stretched out over her head.

Christian's stomach tightened as she realized Alex was naked. She hadn't been prepared for the vision before her. Her eyes roamed the length of the strong, beautiful body. Alex's defined shoulder muscles, her sculpted arms, cradling her head. Her back dipped down at her waist and her round buttocks rose in scrumptious mounds, blending into well-muscled, lean thighs.

Christian surged with arousal. Her gaze was locked on the

beautiful form before her, and her groin pulsed in time with the beat of her heart.

She remembered what it had been like for her to wake up on the sofa in the cabin, knowing Alex had seen her naked and she had had no control. She panicked and tried to reverse the path of her boat. The paddle slipped and smacked the water as she tried to correct her course.

Christian knew she'd failed to make a clean getaway when Alex called out, "Hey, where are you going?" The surprise in her voice was clear.

"I'm sorry. I didn't mean to intrude."

"Don't be silly," Alex said. "Come back."

"You can't be serious. I can't."

"Why not, you already came all this way." Alex was propped up on her elbows, and her breasts were barely obscured.

"But…you're naked!" Christian felt her face burn with the heat of her embarrassment as she said the words, still trying not to look at Alex. She felt foolish for showing up without an invitation or at least giving Alex a warning that she was coming. She didn't know what to make of Alex's apparent lack of concern at being caught sunbathing in the nude. She couldn't believe Alex was so calm. Obviously, Alex wasn't as physically affected as she was.

"Oh," Alex said, sitting up. "Give me a minute. Just don't leave." She hurriedly gathered her shorts and her T-shirt, stumbling to get dressed. She laughed. "Okay, I'm decent. Now will you please come over here?"

Reluctantly, Christian pulled the boat up to the dock and looked at Alex's smiling face. She noticed how Alex's skin was beginning to tan from the exposure to the sun and felt the sudden desire to run her fingers across the muscles of Alex's arms. Accepting her attraction for Alex had only made her desire for physical contact stronger, and she struggled to control the storm brewing inside her. She had to get a grip. It was one thing to admit she was physically attracted to Alex, it was something altogether different to do anything about it.

"It's good to see you," Alex said, still smiling. "What brings you out?"

"I don't really know. I was just enjoying the lake, and the next thing I knew, here I was. I'm sorry about sneaking up on you like that."

"Don't worry about it. I guess that makes us even."

Christian was confused. "What do you mean?"

"Well," Alex said as she reached over the dock, taking hold of the bow of the boat and pulling Christian closer, "I saw you naked that first night, without you knowing about it, when I had to strip off your clothes. Now you've seen me naked without my knowing you were there. That makes us even." Her look was devilish as she smiled down at Christian.

Christian scoffed. "I hardly think this is the same thing."

"Okay. What do I have to do to make it up to you?"

Christian struggled to remain composed as they joked. Alex was so close. All she wanted to do was reach up and touch her. She could remember the feel of Alex's lips on hers, and her body cried out for more. "I hardly think that's necessary."

"Maybe not, but it would be fun. And it would give me an excuse to see you again." Alex held firmly to the handle on the end of the boat. "I'll tell you what. How about letting me cook you dinner?"

"Sorry. I really can't—I already made plans with Elaine."

Alex looked thoughtful for a moment. "Yeah. I'm still sorry about how I acted the day she and I met. I don't know what came over me."

"Tell me about what happened. What made you so upset?"

Christian saw the color in Alex's cheeks brighten. Alex looked away and sighed heavily. "I'd been thinking about you, about kissing you. I was caught off guard when I ran into you, and when I saw you holding Elaine's hand, I jumped to conclusions. I got jealous, I guess."

Christian frowned, remembering her reaction to Alex. "Why were you jealous?"

Alex looked at Christian as if the answer was obvious. "I wanted to be the one you wanted to be with. I had put myself out there, I had asked you to dinner, and you said no. I told myself you weren't ready. But when I saw you with Elaine, I thought you just didn't want to be with me."

The words stung Christian like a slap. She hadn't meant to hurt Alex. She hadn't meant to hurt anyone. She had to do better than this push-pull dance she and Alex were in. "I'm sorry."

"Me too. I'm not usually a jealous person. I shouldn't have jumped to conclusions like that."

Christian's heart grew heavy as the smile faded from Alex's face, and she wanted nothing more at that moment than to have Alex smile again. "Back to your offer of dinner—what are you doing tomorrow?"

Alex's eyes flashed as she jerked her head up, her expression hopeful. "Nothing really, tomorrow would be great."

"Are you sure?" Christian asked, suddenly anxious. She couldn't believe she was asking Alex out on a date. No, not a date. She just wanted to spend time with Alex so she could figure out what she was feeling. Her stomach quivered with excitement. So what if it *was* a date?

Alex nodded. "Very sure," she said, her eyes glinting in the sun. "How about I pick you up at the lodge, say around eleven?"

"That's hardly dinner," Christian said, beginning to feel a little cautious. Alex had a way of grabbing hold of a moment and running with it. She already felt as if she were standing on the edge of a cliff, and she didn't want to feel pushed.

Alex laughed. "I'm sorry. I didn't mean to come across as overzealous. I'm just not sure if you'll give me this chance again, and I thought we could make a day of it."

Seeing the sincerity in Alex's expression, Christian relaxed. "Well...okay. But can we make it a little later? I have some things to take care of first. I could meet you at one o'clock."

"That'll be great." Alex waited a moment and decided to take a chance. "Would you like to come up for a bit now? You can't be very comfortable sitting in that kayak. I can get you something to drink—I have a few things out here in the cooler. Or I could go inside and get you something to eat."

"Thanks, no. I really should be getting back. And I'll let you get back to your sunbathing." Alex felt her cheeks grow warm, but she enjoyed Christian's grin. "I'll see you tomorrow, then."

"Tomorrow." She held Christian's gaze for a moment before giving her boat a gentle push to send her back out onto the lake. "Be safe out there."

As she watched Christian paddle off, the memory of her smile warmed her. She could see Christian's uncertainty, but she thought she had seen something else in her gaze too, the subtle hint of desire. Alex clenched her teeth as a shudder of want ran through her. Her mind spun as she put together plans for her day with Christian. Tomorrow. She might only get one chance. Tomorrow had to be perfect.

She could hardly believe what was happening to her. She hadn't wanted to share a woman's company in so long that she had forgotten what it was like to feel the first flutters of excitement and anticipation. She couldn't describe the connection she'd felt with Christian from the first moment she'd laid eyes on her, but she felt drawn to her like the flowers that lift their faces to follow the sun. It was as if a part of her was only complete when Christian was there.

She jumped up and gathered her things. There was a lot to be done before tomorrow.

CHAPTER ELEVEN

Christian faced Elaine across their usual table and waited for their food to be served before launching into her account of what had happened with Alex. Since leaving Alex on the dock, she had managed to work herself into a near frenzy thinking about her, and she was going to burst if she didn't talk about it.

Elaine laughed at her fluster as she talked nervously about her plans with Alex. "What are you worried about? She's been very caring, and you said yourself you were comfortable being with her."

Exasperated, Christian's voice was shrill. "That's what makes me so anxious. I'm not used to being comfortable. What if she thinks this is a date? I don't know what I'll do. I'm not ready to think about a woman in that way. I'm scared," Christian admitted, gesturing wildly with her hands. She couldn't stop brushing her fingertips along the dip at the base of her throat and her skin tingled at her own touch.

Elaine eyed Christian over her glass of cranberry and vodka. "You know what I think? I think the reason you're scared is because *you* think this is a date. Or perhaps you want it to be."

Christian opened her mouth to protest, gasping at the thought, but Elaine cut her off before she could interject. "Put away those expectations and just go with it. Go see what happens. Honestly, I'm afraid, at this rate, you're going to have a stroke. You decide what happens. What is there to be afraid of?"

Christian thought about the question for a moment, feeling a slight catch in her throat. She was afraid of caring for someone again. That was the last thing she wanted. Alex was already too tempting. If she was already thinking about Alex all the time, what would happen if she actually spent time with her? But maybe if she did spend time with Alex, she would realize this desire was just a fantasy. Maybe she was making too much out of this, after all. "You're right," she said with more confidence than she really felt. Drawing a deep breath and trying to regain her composure, she smiled, not wanting Elaine to guess the real reason for her fear. "I'm making too much of this. It's a simple dinner with a new friend."

Elaine nodded, her grin still playing at the corner of her mouth. "That's right, dear, just dinner with your hopelessly gorgeous new friend!"

❖

Alex arrived at the lodge at five minutes to one, pulling her black Jeep Wrangler to the front and jumping out to run up the steps leading to the entrance.

"Hi, Alex," a familiar happy voice called as she came into the lobby. "What's up? Was everything okay with the packages you ordered?"

Alex turned to meet Hannah as she crossed the room toward her. She had put in a rush order for some items from a boutique in town that she wanted for her outing with Christian and had picked them up early that morning. It wasn't unusual for her to have packages delivered to the lodge, but it was unusual for her to make more than one trip to the lodge in a given day. "Hi, Hannah," Alex returned in greeting. "Everything was fine. I'm here to pick Christian up for an outing. Do you know where she is?"

"Last I saw her, she was having lunch out on the patio, but let me ring her room. She may be there if she's expecting you."

"Thanks," Alex said, shifting back and forth on her feet, hoping Christian hadn't changed her mind. In some ways, she had been waiting for this day for ages, and based on Christian's past distance with her, she thought it very possible she might back out.

Alex jumped as a soft hand touched the back of her arm, and she heard Christian's gentle voice close to her ear. "Right on time, I see."

Turning, Alex was momentarily stunned by Christian's warm smile. She took in the casual black cotton shirt and cream-colored linen shorts that showed off Christian's lean form. Trying to ignore the jolt of pleasure that suddenly ran through to her core, Alex smiled. "I hope so. Are you ready?"

Hannah hung up the phone and stood watching the exchange. "Anything I can take care of for you, Ms. Sutter?" Hannah asked.

"No, thank you, Hannah, but I'll call if anything comes up."

Alex gestured toward the door with a casual toss of her hand. "Ready?" Alex held out her hand to Christian, hoping for even the smallest amount of contact.

Christian took Alex by the hand with a smile. "Ready."

Alex's heart raced and her feet seemed to no longer be touching the ground when Christian's hand closed around her own.

Alex drove along the dirt road leading to her cabin, pleased by the way Christian smiled as the wind swirled around her in the open air. The road leading to the cabin was little more than a trail cut through the trees and followed the hills and valleys of the terrain, making for a mini roller-coaster ride. Alex watched Christian shield her eyes from the flashes of sunlight that played across the path and danced across her face. She couldn't help but laugh when Christian shrieked as the Jeep jostled over occasional rocks and dips in the road, and she enjoyed watching the pleasure and surprise playing across Christian's face.

Christian smoothed her windblown hair back from her face as Alex finally pulled the Jeep to a stop at the water's edge, in front of her cabin. A small ski boat was tied to the dock. Christian's eyes widened with surprise. "Are we going out on that boat?"

"Yes," Alex said. The excitement in Christian's voice fueled her own. She wanted to make Christian happy, and at that moment, she couldn't think of anything more important. "If that's okay. I know you love being on the water, and I thought this might be fun." Alex looked toward Christian hopefully. Her insides churned with hope and uncertainty.

"I'd love it," Christian said, "but I'm hardly prepared to be on the water. I didn't bring any clothes or gear."

"You won't need anything," Alex reassured her. "I had everything I thought you might need delivered with my supplies." Giving her shoulders a shrug she added, "I remembered your size from cleaning your clothes, and I thought it would be more of a surprise this way."

"You ordered clothes for me?"

Hearing the uncertainty in the question, Alex gave a nervous laugh. "Yeah, I did…but not in a creepy stalker kind of way."

At this, Christian laughed too. "Sorry. You just caught me off guard, that's all."

"It's okay. Now that I think about it, I can see how strange this must seem. I assure you, I never meant to make you uncomfortable. If you'd rather do something else, I'll understand." Alex mentally kicked herself. She was trying too hard. It was difficult to know where the balance was. She hadn't been involved with anyone in a long time, and she had been with Sophia for so long it had seemed natural to do these kinds of things. She had to do better, or she might push Christian away. She promised herself to play it cool for the rest of the day and not try so hard.

Christian glanced toward the boat, then looked Alex square in the eye. "No," she said, "I trust you."

Alex felt Christian's gaze on her like an electric shock and sensed the sincerity of her words. She desperately wanted to deserve that trust. "Good. Everything is already loaded on the boat. You can change in the house, and we'll be ready to go."

❖

Alex was right. Everything Christian needed had been laid neatly on the bathroom counter. Christian sighed, taking in the array of packages, noting the inclusion of more than one swimsuit style to accommodate varying levels of comfort and exposure. It seemed Alex had thought of everything. Christian selected a modest two-piece bathing suit, a silk wrap, and a pair of flip-flops, and a pair of shorts and a sleeveless top to wear over the bathing suit. Alex was either very considerate or very controlling—and while she couldn't imagine Alex as the controlling type, everything she had seen told her Alex was very caring. Christian pondered that, surprisingly pleased that Alex would go to so much trouble for her. She slipped into the clothes, noticing how the silky fabric caressed her skin. Knowing Alex had thoughtfully selected each piece was like having Alex's hands caress her. Christian shivered at the intimacy.

Once dressed, Christian made her way back to the dock, where Alex sat, waiting. As she moved to step from the dock to the boat, Alex extended her hand.

Christian pushed down a protest as she felt herself stiffen. *I can do it.* After the accident everyone had tiptoed around her like she was a cracked piece of glass that could shatter at any moment. She didn't want Alex to think of her as someone constantly needing to be rescued. Then she saw gentleness in Alex's eyes, not pity. She took the offered hand and allowed Alex to guide her forward. As the boat shifted from the motion, Christian stumbled and found herself pulled suddenly against Alex. Reflexively, she squeezed Alex's hand and grabbed Alex by the waist to steady herself. Her body came alive where their skin met, and Christian relaxed under Alex's touch.

Suddenly very aware of herself, Christian felt shy, her face growing warm, and she pushed away from Alex's embrace. "I'm sorry. I'm not used to this," she said, admitting her fluster. "I'm a lawyer, for Christ's sake. I'm used to being in control. It's a bit, well, it's different to allow someone to help me."

Alex didn't move, her hand still gently holding Christian's arm. "I'm not very good at roles," Alex said, her face soft and her voice tender. "Helping and being helped have nothing to do with strength and weakness. It's just something we all share. I find it a strength to be trusting enough of another to know when to help and when to ask for help."

Christian studied Alex thoughtfully and realized Alex was simply stating the world as she saw it. And Christian thought of her relationship with Elaine. Trusting and being trusted. That was what she and Elaine shared. She knew that she trusted Alex too, but her feelings for Alex were on the cusp of being so much more than friendship. She had to decide if she could trust Alex with her heart. "Thank you," Christian said, smiling. "You're right."

Settling in, Alex turned the boat to the open channel of the lake. "Here we go."

Christian thought her lungs might burst from the wind and the joy. The scene was breathtaking. Clear, smooth water stretched out before them, surrounded by rolling mountains, some so tall and far in the distance that they became a line of blue haze set against the rich azure sky. *I could stay out here forever,* Christian thought as she felt the tension slip from her shoulders and melt into the wind. She could feel the clean fresh air, pulled from the water's surface, fill her lungs. Sitting in the front of the boat, she felt the world rush up to meet her. But it was more than the lake and the wind and the mountains that she wanted to cling to, it was the feeling of belonging that came with being with Alex.

Turning to look back at Alex, expertly driving the boat across the water, Christian watched the wind push the hair back from Alex's face, exposing her strong, angular features. Watching her hair dance in the wind, Christian imagined her fingers wrapped in that hair, stroking the locks back to peer into those deep blue eyes. As she watched Alex, an awareness settled over her: she felt happy here. It was a feeling of purity, a quieting of her normally restless mind. She smiled and turned away to focus again on the picture of heaven laid out before her.

The boat slowed as Alex pulled off the main current into a cove. After a few minutes, an old spillway came into view. Seeing Christian sit up with interest, Alex pointed toward the remnants of old stone walls on the hill and said, "There used to be a gristmill there on the hill, and if you cross into the stream, you can still make out the foundations and chimneys from the old buildings."

Christian's eyes grew wide and her mouth fell slightly open as if in awe of her surroundings, and Alex heard her gasp. "Wow," she murmured.

"I thought this might be the kind of thing you'd like to see," Alex said, pleased to see the glint of joy in Christian's eyes.

"It's perfect, Alex."

Alex smiled, pleased with herself. Once she had let herself relax with Christian, everything seemed to flow naturally between them. It was nice to see Christian just letting herself enjoy the moment. There was no sign of the usual pain or stress that usually clouded her expressions. Alex had watched Christian transform, as if years had faded from her eyes, and the smile that played at the corner of her mouth now hinted of playfulness. She felt herself relax with the realization that she too was beginning to let go.

They settled in with the boat and had been floating and swimming in the cool water for quite some time when Christian pointed out that Alex's shoulders were looking a little red. "You should let me put some sunscreen on your shoulders, or you're going to burn."

Giving her skin a glance, Alex grimaced. "Probably a good idea, do you mind?"

Christian smiled. "Come on, we probably need to dry out a little anyway," she said, making her way to the boat.

Alex trod her way over to Christian and the boat. Just as she was about to grab the ladder, Christian slipped, falling back into her. Without hesitation, Alex grabbed Christian, both hands gripping her waist, and Christian's weight pushed her underwater for a moment. As she surfaced, she held Christian firmly against her body and felt the muscles in Christian's back tremor as she laughed.

"Oops. Sorry," Christian said, still laughing, as she pushed Alex's hair back from her face and tried to wipe the streams of water running into her eyes with gentle strokes of her hands.

Alex held Christian, mesmerized as she felt the gentle fingers playing along her face and through her hair. Faint currents of electricity flowed across her skin with each touch of Christian's fingers. She was so close, Alex could feel her breath on her face like a cool breeze. Alex wanted to kiss her, wanted so much to taste her mouth, but she didn't want the moment to change, and Christian's laughter was all she really needed for now. Gathering herself, she laughed and released her tight grip on Christian, allowing some space between them. As Christian turned to try the ladder again, Alex gently lifted her, holding her protectively. The rush of emotions was too fast to temper, and she felt herself redden at the surging pleasure. Pulling herself onto the boat, she ducked her gaze as Christian handed her a towel.

"Thanks," Alex said, feeling the heat flaming beneath her cheeks.

"Come here," Christian said as she took a seat under the protection of the Bimini top that covered the back half of the boat.

Alex followed and sat next to Christian, turning her back so Christian could easily reach her shoulders. She felt her breath catch and her heart beat against her chest as Christian's hands played along her skin, rubbing in the sunscreen and breaking her resistance. With each stroke of Christian's hands along her shoulders, down her arms, and across her back, Alex felt as if she were being molded into an entirely different being. It was like she was the clay on the potter's wheel, and she knew what it was like to be taken from a misshapen form and remade into something new. Heat boiled beneath her skin, and she melted into Christian's touch. Her eyes closed, and her only awareness became the thrum of energy gathering inside her. She felt the wetness surge between her thighs.

Christian took in the strong back and muscular shoulders beneath her hands. Alex wore a two-piece bathing suit with a top resembling a sports bra. Christian ran her hands across Alex's shoulders and down her arms. She made sure to cover the tender area at the back of Alex's neck. She felt Alex's muscles tense as she ran her fingers under the thin straps of the bathing suit, massaging the angry red lines that marked her skin. Her heart began to race, and a growing tingling twined itself into a coil in her middle. Her hands seemed to move of their own accord as she became more and more lost in the sensation of Alex's skin.

She could feel the taut muscles roll beneath her fingertips as her breathing matched the stroke of her hands on Alex's skin. Her body swayed with the rhythm of her hands and her breathing, until she found herself swaying so close to Alex that her lips almost touched her skin.

Christian gasped, breaking the silence.

Alex jerked upright. "What is it?" she asked, turning quickly to face Christian. "Are you okay?"

"I'm fine." Christian reassured her, trying to gather herself. "I just…touching you that way…I just…I'm sorry," Christian stammered. She couldn't believe she had admitted that to Alex, but at the moment, she couldn't hide her feelings.

Alex let out a sigh as she took Christian's hand and lifted it to her lips. She kissed it gently. "Christian, I know how difficult it is to discover you still have normal human desires. But I think it's important for us to allow them. Meeting you helped *me* see that."

Christian couldn't believe what she was hearing. Alex had a way of delivering unwavering strength by naming her weaknesses. Her honesty was so tender. Before she could think otherwise, Christian reached out her hand, her fingers shaking, and placed the tips of her fingers against Alex's lips. The skin was soft and warm beneath her touch, and she wanted to feel those lips on her.

Alex kissed Christian's fingertips tenderly as they lay trembling against her lips. She leaned forward and brushed her lips across Christian's mouth as she gently stroked her cheek with her thumb. As she pulled away, she placed an arm around Christian's shoulders and pulled her into her, cradling her in her arms.

"Thank you," Christian whispered, feeling the comforting beat of Alex's heart against her cheek.

CHAPTER TWELVE

When they arrived back at the cabin, Christian showered and slipped back into the shorts and T-shirt she had been wearing when Alex picked her up earlier that day. She stepped into the kitchen to find Alex preparing dinner. She still had on shorts and stood in her bare feet. Her sunburned skin flamed an angry red against the dark blue sleeveless shirt she wore. The sight made Christian smile. There were so many things she liked about Alex, but there was something about watching her cook that was incredibly sexy.

"What?" Alex asked suspiciously, watching the way Christian was looking at her.

Smiling mischievously, Christian cocked her head to the side. "You are the most interesting set of contradictions I have ever seen in a woman."

Alex's brow furrowed. "And what does that mean?"

Stepping forward and taking a slice of cucumber from the cutting board, Christian smiled as she took a bite. "I mean you're both strong and sensitive, gentle while painfully honest, your athleticism adds a touch of masculinity, but at the same time you are elegant and graceful."

Seeing Alex blush and the lines in her brow deepen, Christian placed her palm flat against Alex's back. "I mean to say, you're beautiful," Christian said, her voice a mere whisper against Alex's ear.

Alex's hands stilled. She could feel the heat of Christian's hand, pressed against her back, warming her from within, the touch seeming to press deeper than her skin to reach inside and stroke her soul. Desire pulsed through her. For a moment, her muscles stiffened and she couldn't breathe.

"Alex?" She heard Christian's voice so close to her ear that she could feel the faint brush of her lips against her tender skin. The arousal was so fierce now, she felt her head swoon. Clearing her throat, she managed to say, "Sorry. I guess it's my turn to trust you. That was a very kind thing to say."

Christian was so near, Alex could see the play of color in her eyes. They were green, but at the center there were bursts of brown and blue. Alex could feel the vibration of Christian's body as if an electrical current connected them, and her body hummed with the desire to touch her. Leaning in slightly, she allowed her lips to brush gently over Christian's. Her skin was soft and yielding, and the taste was sweet.

Alex felt Christian's hand press firmly into her back and pushed the kiss further as she played along Christian's mouth with the tip of her tongue, savoring the brush of silken skin. This wasn't the casual exchange she had experienced from time to time these last few years, when loneliness got the best of her and she had tried to drown the silence in the arms of a woman. This time, she gave of herself, and in return felt herself wanting more.

Christian pulled back, and Alex froze, not wanting to scare her or push her away. Alex listened to Christian's breath, deep and rapid. Christian placed the palm of her hand on Alex's chest, and Alex could feel her own heart pounding against it. Christian whispered, "That was nice. I've wanted to do that all day."

Alex's eyes opened, her lids heavy with desire. "Very nice," she said, her voice husky and thick. She couldn't tell Christian that she had wanted to lose herself in that kiss, that when she was with her she didn't need for anything else. She had thought Christian was going to pull away from her again, but Christian's words only tempered her fear, for she knew she was in danger of losing her heart.

❖

After dinner, they sat talking on the porch, watching the sunset. The clouds were aflame as the setting sun bathed them in orange light. Christian couldn't count the number of sunsets she had seen in her life, and she pondered the cycle of ending and beginning. Memories trickled through her mind. Each day had been different and special in its own way. And today had been one she knew she would always remember. It was her first sunset with Alex.

She turned to see Alex watching her. "What were you thinking just now?" Alex asked.

Christian thought for a moment before answering, her mind temporarily captured by how beautiful Alex looked in the shifting light. "I was thinking about how special this sunset is."

Alex replied, "The perfect ending to the perfect day."

Christian nodded. "Yes. Something like that."

They smiled together and turned back to watch the close of the day.

"I have an idea," Christian said, breaking the silence. "Why don't you go get showered while I clean up from dinner. Then I can put something on those shoulders for you." She didn't want the day to end, and most of all, she wanted to be close to Alex again. The want had slowly grown to a need, and now she could think of nothing else but the feel of Alex's body under her hands.

"You don't have to do anything, I'll be happy to take care—"

"Please, Alex. Let me do this for you."

"Okay," Alex relented. "I'll only be a moment," she said as she stood and went into the house.

Christian finished cleaning up and went to the sofa to rest while she waited for Alex to return. It had been the most amazing day. She had been so comfortable with Alex. Their conversation came easy. She found that the more she was with Alex, the more her attraction grew. She closed her eyes and imagined the feel of Alex's lips when they'd kissed. She felt things for Alex she hadn't imagined she could feel again. Every touch was exhilarating, and Christian wanted more. She wanted Alex and the thought was both exciting and terrifying. What would it be like to be touched again?

A gentle hand on her shoulder drew her from her thoughts. Alex stood over her. "I'm awake," Christian said, "just resting." Slowly, she sat up and reached out to take the aloe Alex was holding.

"Lie down here. I can reach your shoulders better this way," Christian instructed.

As Alex lay on her stomach on the sofa, Christian ran her hands up and down the length of the lean muscles that slid beneath her touch. Christian pulled the end of Alex's shirt up and slipped her hands beneath the soft cotton fabric, working the lotion into the inflamed skin with slow, smooth strokes. Her hands shook as she absorbed the sensation of having Alex's body in her hands. She marveled at how each touch made her want to be closer to Alex, to know every part of her in a way only a lover can. The thought made her heart pound in her chest, resounding through her, making her skin vibrate. Fear still lurked at the back of her mind making her hesitate, her hands slowing as her fingers caressed Alex's shoulders. Was she ready to step out of her past? How far was she ready to go?

Alex was overwhelmed, and a moan escaped as she felt Christian's gentle fingers move across her skin. Inside her, a war was being waged. It had been years since she'd felt a woman's touch like this, since she'd let a woman touch her sensually. Christian's hands went deeper than her skin. Christian touched something deep within her that made her heart swell. With Christian it wasn't just about sex. It was so much more. And she'd thought it was something she would never desire again.

Now here she was with Christian, and the simplest touch, smile, laugh, or sigh brought her pulse hammering in her throat. And right now, much more intimate places. She moaned again, pulling up onto her elbows. "Thank you." Turning over, she found Christian's gaze full on hers like the midday sun. Christian's eyes were dark and heavy, and Alex jolted as her muscles tightened. Reaching out, she placed a hand on Christian's wrist, gently guiding Christian's hand to her chest. Placing her other hand on Christian's waist, she pulled Christian toward her until their lips met.

The kiss was tentative at first as Alex brushed the tender skin to see if Christian would allow more. Sensing no withdrawal and feeling Christian's fingers slide into her hair, Alex pressed more firmly into Christian, her tongue brushing lightly. She felt Christian's lips part, allowing her entrance. Feeling Christian's tongue brush against hers, her whole body hummed with want. Alex pressed deeper into Christian's mouth, tasting her sweetness. She swooned as Christian moaned into her mouth. She slid her hands around Christian's back and found her way beneath Christian's shirt, needing to feel the softness of her skin.

Suddenly Christian pulled back and pressed her palm to Alex's chest. "Stop," she whispered. I'm sorry...I shouldn't have..."

Christian pulled away and tried to stand. Alex caught her as she fainted.

What's happening? Alex fought the panic that sent the blood pounding in her head. She propped Christian's feet and legs on pillows on the sofa to increase the blood flow to her brain. She stroked Christian's face and pushed the hair back from her eyes. Fear twisted her stomach and rose in her throat, burning like acid. To her relief, Christian began to come around.

"Be still," Alex soothed. "You're okay." She could see the confusion in Christian's eyes as she looked up at her. She cupped Christian's face in with her hand, stroking her cheek with her thumb. "Don't worry, you're okay now." She studied Christian's face, trying to convince herself that was true.

"I'm sorry, Alex. You must think I'm crazy."

Alex knelt on the floor in front of Christian and leaned her face into her, thankful she was okay. She spoke softly, her lips brushing Christian's neck. "I think you're amazing...not crazy." Alex lifted her head and looked at Christian. "But I'd like to know what's happening to you. I doubt you fainted from being kissed."

Christian took a deep breath and nodded. "I guess I owe you an explanation."

CHAPTER THIRTEEN

Elaine sat in Dr. Cook's office, her focus centered on her breathing. Her body was relaxed. She heard Dr. Cook's voice in the distance.

"How are you feeling, Elaine?"

"Tired," Elaine answered. In her mind, Elaine followed the sound of Dr. Cook's voice, visualizing the scene she described.

"You're sitting by the pool at your home. You can hear the gentle lap…lap…lap of the water against the pool wall. You feel relaxed and calm." Dr. Cook paused a few seconds, and Elaine relaxed into the image. "What's happening around you now, Elaine?"

Elaine felt completely at ease. She lifted her hand, imagining she cradled a glass. "We're having a drink and talking about leaving the bureau."

Dr. Cook's voice remained steady. "Who is there with you?"

"Chacey." Elaine smiled at the mention of the name. She felt happy.

"You and Chacey are close?" Dr. Cook asked.

"Yes," Elaine said, still smiling.

"You're talking about leaving the FBI. Why do you want to leave the bureau?"

At the question, Elaine's shoulders tensed and she felt her brow furrow into a frown. "It's the only way we can be together."

"What are you feeling now, Elaine?" Dr. Cook responded in a calm voice.

"I'm afraid," Elaine whispered. She didn't want to lose Chacey. She would do anything, go anywhere to be with her.

Elaine listened to the sound of Dr. Cook's voice. "You're safe, Elaine. No one can hurt you here. You can feel yourself growing calm as you listen to my voice. You're feeling safe and calm." Dr. Cook repeated the message.

Elaine felt her breathing slow, matching the cadence of Dr. Cook's voice, and the tension eased in her shoulders. She was safe.

Dr. Cook's voice continued. "Think back, Elaine. Think only of the memory now. What were you afraid of when you were talking to Chacey about leaving the bureau?"

Elaine's chest rose and fell as she continued to take deep, even breaths. She remembered their plans to leave and start a new life, somewhere Chacey's ex-husband wouldn't be so close. He had been so angry when Chacey left him. Elaine hesitated before answering, remembering how violent he had been. "Charles. Charles won't like it. He'll be angry. He's been angry before. I'm afraid he'll hurt her." Elaine's voice became more forceful as her stress grew. Her breathing became more shallow and rapid.

Dr. Cook calmly placed a finger on Elaine's wrist. "You're okay, Elaine. We're in my office now, just you and me. No one can hurt you here. We're going to bring you back now. As I count forward, you will become more alert and feel safe and relaxed. One…two…three…"

Elaine was exhausted, and she rubbed her hands across her face as if the simple gesture could wipe away the memories. Her hands were shaking. She missed Chacey so much, her heart ached.

"Tell me about Chacey," Dr. Cook said.

Elaine let out a breath. "Really, Helen, I don't want to discuss this."

"She seems important to you," Dr. Cook continued.

"Fine," Elaine relented. "She was my lover. We met at the bureau. She was married. Things didn't work out."

"And who was Charles?" Dr. Cook asked.

"Her ex-husband." Elaine's body stiffened at the mention of the name and felt a vein in her forehead begin to bulge. She hated Charles for what he did to Chacey.

"What did you feel when I mentioned Charles just now? Your body went rigid," Dr. Cook noted.

Elaine tried to restrain the rage that had suddenly blinded her vision. "I'm angry with the bastard. He thought he could own Chace. He was an abusive bastard, and he had hurt her in the past, and I knew if he knew we were together, he would hurt her again. We had it all planned out. Chace put in for a transfer, and I planned to follow her after the Flask case was over."

"You were planning to leave the FBI to be with her?"

"She took a transfer a week before the shooting. I was planning to follow her once the case was over."

"What happened?"

"After I was shot, things got a little crazy. Chacey came back. She stayed with me at the hospital as much as she could. She wanted us to be together...I couldn't. After a while, I refused to let her see me." It had been so hard to turn Chacey away. The memory closed around her heart like a fist.

Dr. Cook asked, "Why do you think that is?"

Elaine blanked. She wanted to give the old excuse that the shooting and the death of the child had been too much, but this time, she didn't. She finally understood why she couldn't see Chacey, why she had been so terrified every time she visited.

Elaine shook her head, feeling defeated. "I don't know. Every time I talked to her, I felt the panic set in. I didn't want anything to happen to her. If someone could do this to me...Oh God! I couldn't bear the thought of..." Elaine choked as tears filled her eyes.

"It's been three years since the shooting, Elaine. Have there been situations since then where you've felt threatened or believed someone wanted to harm you?"

Elaine recognized Dr. Cook's attempt to challenge her rationalization for sending Chacey away. She sighed. "No. But I'd rather spend my life alone than place those I love in danger."

"What I'm hearing is that you're making choices in your life based on fear, Elaine, not *evidence* that they are truly in danger. You're trying to control everything in your world. It doesn't seem fair to those who love you that they don't have a choice in this matter."

Elaine looked at Dr. Cook. "What would you have me do? Like you said, it's been three years. Do you think Chacey would want to be a part of my life after all this time, after all I've done?"

Elaine wasn't prepared for Dr. Cook's answer. "I don't know.

That's something you have to decide if you want to find out for yourself. If not Chacey, then perhaps you can explore trust again through your new friendships. Either way, it's time to learn to live again."

❖

Elaine sat staring at the phone as if it were a wild animal that might suddenly jump up and attack her. Hesitantly, she picked up the receiver and held it in her hand, but before she could dial the number, panic gripped her chest.

Slamming the receiver back into the cradle, she flinched at the harsh sound. *I must be out of my mind. She doesn't want to speak to me. Surely, after all this time, she has moved on with her life. It's selfish of me to barge into her life again.* Gritting her teeth, Elaine picked up the phone again. *I guess I could just say hello. I could say I'm sorry for being such a fool. She can tell me it's too late, and then I can let her go in peace. It will be over.* Elaine knew she had never really let Chacey go. It was as if her life had been on pause for the last three years as she waited for the shooter to be caught. If the shooter was found, she wouldn't have to hide anymore and Chacey would be safe. But time wasn't on pause, and she knew life had moved on for Chacey. She needed to let go of the idea that they would ever be together again.

Elaine dialed the number and sat stark still as she listened to the line ring. Just as she started to hang up she heard a click and then a crisp voice said, "Hello." The voice was familiar, and Elaine could almost feel the soft breath on her cheek. Her hands trembled as she held the phone tightly to her ear.

There was a long pause as if the person was listening through the silence. Then the voice, more tender now, asked, "Elaine…is that you, honey?"

Elaine's hands shook, and she swallowed hard to choke back her tears. "Chace," was all she could say.

A heavy sigh came through the line, filled with hurt and relief. "I'm here, sweetheart."

Elaine closed her eyes tightly and tried to take a breath, the sound rasping like jagged glass. She couldn't believe this could be real. After all this time, Chacey was still reaching for her.

"Please, Elaine," Chacey begged, the desperation in her voice ringing like thunder in Elaine's heart.

Her voice a whisper, Elaine asked, "Do you remember the place we talked about spending the summer when we..." Elaine's voice trailed off. She was too afraid to continue.

"Yes." Hope filled Chacey's voice now. "I remember."

"Will you...still?" Elaine asked, not finishing her sentence, fearing it was too late.

"Always," came the reply.

CHAPTER FOURTEEN

Alex and Christian sat facing each other on the sofa, legs pulled tightly beneath them as Christian tried to explain about her head injury and the strange fainting spells.

"My therapist thinks there is an emotional connection between my feelings about losing Cara and the fainting," Christian explained. "They haven't happened as frequently since I've been staying at Willow Springs, but there does seem to be a connection to my thoughts about Cara."

"Were you thinking of Cara…earlier…when I kissed you?"

"No. I wasn't thinking of Cara. I was only thinking of you." Christian tried to remember the sequence of emotions. "I felt so alive when you touched me. Everything was moving so fast and I couldn't slow down." She had been consumed by Alex. What had started as physical desire had threatened to be so much more, and she wasn't ready for those feelings. She wasn't sure why she could open herself to physical attraction but still felt guilt at the thought of ever loving another. She wanted to be honest with Alex, but she couldn't exactly tell her she had fainted because she thought she was falling in love with her.

Alex was thoughtful for a while, then said, "I think I understand that," her own sadness soft in her voice. "Losing Sophia…I felt like my dreams died, that there would never be any happiness for me again. I went on living as if I were already dead. I was just going through the motions of life. After a couple of years, I learned that I'd always love Sophia. No one will ever change that."

Christian felt relieved that Alex understood what it was like, navigating this maze of emotions that seemed to change and turn on a whim. Sometimes she felt like she would lose her mind trying to figure out what to do next. "You're so amazing," she whispered. "Are you sure you don't think I'm crazy?"

Alex pulled her legs free and stretched before sliding closer to Christian. She pulled Christian's legs forward until they were resting on top of hers, linking their bodies together as they faced each other. Alex took both Christian's hands in hers and pulled them gently to her lips. "I don't want you to think right now. Just be here in this moment."

Her eyes never left Christian as she ran her lips tenderly over each knuckle and then kissed Christian's wrists. She placed Christian's slender hand to her face and brushed her cheek against her palm. Christian's skin tingled everywhere Alex's lips touched.

"Don't think. Just feel," Alex said before brushing her thumb across Christian's lips.

Christian held Alex's gaze and shuddered. Alex slid closer until Christian was almost in her lap. Christian gasped as Alex's strong hands embraced her, making her weak with anticipation. She felt intoxicated.

"Breathe," Alex whispered. Moving slowly, she brushed her palm against Christian's jaw and ran her thumb along the line of her lower lip, watching the fullness of the flesh darken as the blood followed the trace of her touch. In slow motion, Alex moved toward Christian until her lips pressed tenderly to the full, wanting flesh. "Breathe, Christian, just breathe," she whispered.

Then, more fully, Alex claimed Christian's mouth, feeling herself melt into her soft, swollen lips until she thought all breath was being drawn from her. She felt Christian's mouth open, probing her tongue with her own. The tickle of the tender muscle sent a rush through to her core and her stomach quivered. Alex knew, this time, she was the one standing on the edge and wondered how much she should risk.

"Oh God." Christian sighed as Alex broke the kiss.

"Still feeling okay?" Alex asked, searching Christian's face for any sign that she was going to put a stop to everything.

"Uh-huh," Christian murmured as she ran her fingers through Alex's thick black hair. This time, it was Christian who pushed forward as she claimed Alex's lips.

Alex felt dizzy and moaned, then wrapped her arms tightly around

Christian. Her body sang, everywhere. She felt Christian's fingers pull through her hair, guiding her as she tasted and explored her mouth. Christian pushed her pelvis into Alex, pushing her deep into the cushions. She pressed her thigh against Alex's legs, parting them to glide against her sex.

Alex pulled Christian's shirt from the waistband of her shorts and slid her hands under the thin fabric to brush her fingers tentatively along her back. She had to touch her. She felt the desperate need to feel Christian's skin. A moan escaped her as the familiar pulse began to build into an ache, as the blood pounded between her legs. Christian clung to Alex, returning the embrace with equal fervor.

Alex moved a hand between them and cupped Christian's face in her hands. "You're so beautiful," Alex breathed. "I want to feel you, all of you."

Christian stilled for a moment and stared into Alex's eyes. Alex thought she was going to pull away. Instead, Christian closed her eyes. "It's been so long since I wanted to be close to anyone. Your skin burns through me like fire. Touch me, Alex. Please…touch me."

The soft sound of Christian's voice asking her to touch her was more than Alex could resist. Her blood pounded in her ears as she ran her hand across Christian's chest and cupped her breast through her shirt, rubbing her thumb across the tender nipple, feeling it harden beneath her touch. Alex felt herself go wet as a surge of pleasure rushed to her groin, and she moaned.

"Feels so good," Christian said, and she began to rock her hips, pressing her thigh into Alex.

Alex pushed her hands beneath Christian's shirt and slid her fingers under the silk barrier of her bra to find her breasts. Each stroke of her fingers on the hardened nipple thundered through her own body, pushing Alex to the edge.

"Oh God, Alex, if you keep doing that I'm going to come."

Alex pulled Christian's shirt up over her head, freeing her to touch the tender skin that she craved. With a quick snap of her fingers, Christian's bra fell away, revealing firm round breasts, her nipples hard and dark, asking to be taken. Alex's lips found a tender breast and she drew it into her mouth, sucking gently as she ran her tongue across the nipple in firm strokes.

Alex pulled at the button of Christian's shorts, tugging at the fabric until the zipper slid open, sliding her hand against the thin barrier of lace. Slowly, she slipped her hand against the hot skin until her fingers brushed through soft hair and parted wet, swollen lips. Alex cupped her hand over the turgid flesh, allowing her fingers to be swallowed up by the hot, wet folds. Heat poured into her palm, and she felt Christian twitch from the sudden pressure against her clitoris.

Christian cried out, her muscles tightening around Alex's hand as the first wave of her building orgasm begged to be released. She wanted to feel Alex inside her. Rocking harder against Alex's fingers, Christian didn't want the pleasure to stop. "Please, don't stop. Please, Alex. Make me…oh God!" A pulse shot through her clitoris and raced through her, making her muscles convulse with pleasure surging, making her legs weak as her pulse hammered in her chest, echoing the pulse in her middle. Christian hadn't imagined she could feel this good.

As the last waves passed, she felt Alex shudder against her. She wrapped her arms tightly around Alex and tried to meld their bodies into one, wanting to hold on to the moment as long as she could.

"Christian?" Alex brushed her hand over Christian's hair. "Christian, are you okay?" When Christian didn't answer, Alex pushed at her shoulder trying to see her face.

Christian slowly lifted her face to peer down at Alex. She could feel tears streaking her cheeks, and she smiled wanly. Seeing the pain flash behind Alex's eyes, Christian kissed her gently, placing her hand on the side of Alex's face.

"You're crying," Alex said, the fear still evident in her voice. "Talk to me."

Christian leaned her cheek against Alex's chest and breathed deeply. "You're so wonderful. I'm sorry. I didn't mean to scare you. I thought I'd never want anyone again. I thought I'd never—"

"*Shhhh.* It's all right. You don't have to explain," Alex whispered into Christian's hair, her hands gently stroking Christian's back.

Christian felt alive again, and she didn't want to think about what being with Alex meant. She knew she didn't have those answers. At that moment, there was nothing in the world more beautiful than the woman in her arms, and that was enough for now.

❖

Elaine sat in the rose garden staring at the water, the fountain's spray kissing her skin. Fear held her motionless as she thought about her conversation with Chacey. She couldn't believe Chacey would come to her after all this time, and she felt selfish for asking her to. What would she say when she saw her again? How could she explain everything that had happened? She knew Chacey had loved her, and she had pushed her away. She'd pushed everyone away. How could she possibly put things back together again when she still didn't know any of the answers? Dr. Cook was right. She was trying to control everything, and the truth was she had no control at all. She had been lying to herself.

The past three years had been filled with fear and loneliness. Now Elaine felt tired. She was tired of the running. She was tired of walking through her life as if she were a ghost, casually observing the living as they moved through their lives around her. Until meeting Christian, she had thought that was enough. But now she felt restless. She was no longer satisfied being an observer. The shooter had meant to kill her, but she had done worse damage by shutting out her life. She had lived through the shooting, but she had robbed those she loved of the ability to comfort her, to grieve with her, or to heal with her. It was time for all that to change.

Elaine moved her hand to her chest and felt the gentle thrum. She was alive, and more than that, the love she had for Chacey still resonated there in the persistent beat of her heart. She felt a sudden thrill at the thought of seeing Chacey again. This time, she would not run. She would trust Chacey to face the darkness with her.

The scent of roses suddenly filled Elaine's senses as a breeze passed through the garden, stirring the fragrance of the flowers and lifting the weight of her fear. She looked around the garden as if seeing it for the first time. She barely remembered coming here and had no idea how long she had been sitting, contemplating her life.

Taking a deep breath, Elaine pulled the fragrant air in, filling her lungs with the smell of roses and hope. She didn't want to be alone anymore. Suddenly feeling restless, she stood, looking around as if lost and not knowing how to find her way out of the garden. She was ready to talk, and she knew just the person she needed.

❖

Alex held Christian in her arms as they stood by the Jeep. "Stay," she said, for what must have been the tenth time. She hoped that Christian would change her mind and not return to the lodge, but stay with her through the night. She wanted to feel Christian's skin against her. She wanted to hold her, feel her warmth, and smell her fragrance as she woke in the morning. Alex was afraid that if she let Christian go, it would all fade away, like a dream.

"I want to." Christian's voice was sultry and soft. "But I need to take things slow. I still have a lot to work through. I need time…to think."

Alex felt her shoulders stiffen. She let out a long, slow breath and let her arms fall to Christian's waist. "I know." Although she wanted to argue, she knew if she pushed Christian, she ran the risk of pushing her away. Maybe she had expected too much. After all, she had been going through this struggle even longer than Christian. She couldn't expect Christian to be able to resolve all her feelings just because they had shared…what? What had they shared? Alex knew what she felt, but she had no idea what it meant to Christian. She had to let Christian do this on her own time.

"Come on, I better get you back." She kissed Christian lightly on the forehead and cupped her cheek in her hand. "Since this is just the first date, I guess I should get you home at a decent hour." She smiled playfully and teased, "I'll bet Hannah is waiting up for you."

Christian laughed. "I bet you're right," she said as she pulled away from Alex's embrace and reached up to grab the roll bar and pull herself into the Jeep.

Alex felt the withdrawal like a winter breeze blowing down her back.

❖

Alex and Christian were both laughing when the Jeep came to a stop at the front entrance of Willow Springs where, as expected, Hannah promptly stepped out to meet them.

Hannah extended her hand to Christian. "Welcome back. How was your outing?"

Christian took her hand, stepped from the Jeep, and bent to kiss her cheek. "I had a wonderful time, Hannah. Thank you. We spent a beautiful day out on the lake. It was perfect."

Hannah smiled. "Is there anything else I can do for you this evening?" she asked softly. "If not, I will leave you and Alex to yourselves."

Alex noticed Hannah hadn't addressed her and had the feeling she wasn't exactly pleased with her at the moment. She wondered what she could have done to ruffle the usually pleasant girl.

Christian said, "No, Hannah, I'm fine for tonight. Thank you, as always, for looking after me."

"I'll be inside if you need me, then," Hannah said with a wry smile. "Oh, and before I forget, Ms. Barber has been asking for you this evening. She asked that you ring her when you returned if you felt up to it." Hannah stepped away and said, as if an afterthought, "Good evening, Alex."

"Good night, Hannah." Alex smiled to herself at the coolness in Hannah's voice.

When Hannah went back inside, Alex stepped around the Jeep to stand next to Christian.

Christian sighed and took her by the hand. "Thank you for everything. You really are amazing."

"It was a special day for me. I hope we can do it again soon. Tomorrow would be nice," Alex said playfully. When Christian didn't respond, she squeezed her hand gently. "Breathe, remember? That's all you have to do."

Christian smiled. Alex hoped that was enough.

CHAPTER FIFTEEN

Chacey gathered her bags and took one last look around the house, mentally ticking off a list. All electrical appliances were off, the mail had been temporarily stopped, she had an automatic timer to alternate the lights, and the cat was at her friend Joey's, next door. Chacey smiled. Joey was a good friend. Not many people were brave enough to take on that cat, but he had volunteered for the task more than once, and their friendship had survived. She didn't know what she would do without him. She looked at her watch. It had already been three hours since she'd spoken to Elaine. She couldn't believe Elaine was so close. It was only an eight-hour drive from Virginia to Tennessee.

She shuddered with anticipation. Tomorrow, she would see Elaine again. She had prayed for this day every day since Elaine had refused to see her.

Once in the car, Chacey entered the route into the GPS and sighed. She had contemplated flying but had chosen the relative privacy driving would offer. She knew Elaine was still distrustful and didn't want anyone knowing where she was staying. Besides, she had decided to break the drive over two days, to help her prepare for seeing Elaine. It had been three years since the shooting, and they had never talked about what had happened or why Elaine had closed herself off to everyone who loved her. Three years of waiting hadn't prepared her for actually seeing Elaine again, and she had a lot to think about.

Just as Chacey turned onto I-95, her phone rang. Checking the number, she hit Answer on the Bluetooth. "Hi, Karen," she said, trying to hide her annoyance. She had thought of not answering, but knew that would only make Karen more persistent in her attempts to get through.

"Well, good morning, sunshine," Karen shot back snidely. "What has you in such a cranky mood this morning?"

"Nothing, I'm just in the middle of something and I was distracted. Sorry, I didn't mean to sound short. What's up?"

"Oh, I just wanted to call and see if you were up for dinner this evening. I've been dying to try that new Moroccan place, and I thought we could take in the new exhibit at the Smithsonian."

"I'm sorry. I won't be able to have dinner tonight. I'm going to be tied up for a few days. I'll have to touch base with you when I get back into town." As soon as the words were out of her mouth, she regretted them. She hadn't prepared a cover story, and now she knew she would be subjected to Twenty Questions.

"I didn't know you were going out of town. How long will you be gone?" Karen's tone sounded wounded.

Chacey thought of how she could cover for her blunder without giving away too much information. "Just a work thing—I'm not sure how long I'll be gone."

"Okay. Where are you going in such a rush? Is there anything you need me to do at the house? And what about Miss Priss? Who's going to feed her while you're away?"

"I have everything covered. The cat's with Joey, and he'll watch the house. I don't need anything. Thanks for the offer, though." Chacey really wanted to get off the line. She had known Karen for years now, and she knew how nosey Karen could be. It was a little annoying sometimes. But Karen meant well and had been a good friend after the shooting. She'd helped Chacey get through the days when she wasn't sure Elaine would live and was there when Elaine had pushed her away. Karen knew better than anyone what she had gone through. There had been a time when Karen had made it clear she wanted to be more than just friends. And things had been tense between them for a while after she had rejected Karen's advances and explained her feelings for Elaine despite the separation between them. But they had moved beyond that, and their friendship had survived.

"Well, okay then. I guess I'll catch up with you when you get back. Call me if you need anything."

"I just need a few days to sort some things out, that's all. I'll talk to you more when I get back."

"Sure. I understand. I'll talk to you soon, then. Be safe."

"I will." She ended the call, relieved to have it behind her. Now she wouldn't feel she had to answer the next time Karen called. And there was no doubt Karen would be calling again. She was as persistent as a gnat.

Chacey stopped just outside Richmond for fuel and a few snacks. Before getting back on the road, she pulled down the visor and retrieved a well-worn photograph. She smiled as she looked at the smiling images looking back at her. She was with Elaine at the beach. Chacey could almost feel the breeze in her hair and smell the salty air. She and Elaine had been so happy when the photo was taken. They had talked about spending forever together, not knowing that only a few short months later, their world would be ripped apart. Chacey ran her thumb across the picture as if she could touch Elaine through the image. Her heart ached to see Elaine. Maybe this trip would be the beginning of getting their forever back.

❖

The day had been hot and the sky a perfect blue with not a cloud in sight, and as night had fallen, the air had cooled but remained still. Elaine sat on the patio in one of the poolside lounge chairs, sipping a tropical-looking blue drink out of a tall hurricane glass. Christian placed a hand gently on the back of her chair and chuckled slightly to herself as she noticed the drink was the same color as the pool and both seemed to glow under the night lights.

"Well, that's a new one," Christian said as she leaned down and kissed Elaine's cheek. "What are you drinking?"

Elaine brushed her hand across Christian's cheek as she kissed her. "Hello, sweetheart. *This* is a Blue Hawaiian. This was Chacey's favorite drink when we would go to the beach. Can I get you one? They really are delightful."

"Sure," Christian said thoughtfully as she studied Elaine's mood. "Who is Chacey?"

Elaine appeared thoughtful for a moment as she contemplated her answer. "Chacey was my lover."

"Was?" Christian prodded.

"She's the woman I told you I was involved with at the time of my shooting." Elaine paused. "I called her today. After all this time, she still wants to see me. Can you believe that? So she's coming here tomorrow." Elaine's voice sounded fragile as she spoke of Chacey, as if she would disappear if she spoke too loudly.

Christian looked up briefly as one of the staff approached them. She recognized the young girl as one of the new staff that usually came on shift when Hannah wasn't there. "Can I get you ladies anything?" she asked.

"Yes." Elaine lifted her glass to the girl. "Two of these would be wonderful, Sam. Thank you."

Once they were alone again, Christian reached out to take Elaine's hand. "Talk to me. What's happened?"

Elaine sighed and squeezed Christian's hand, taking a deep breath and drawing out the exhale, as if she were preparing herself for a battle. "I'm scared. I ran away from the only woman I've ever loved because I was afraid. I was hurt, and I didn't know how to protect myself or anyone I loved from…"

Elaine paused as if to gather herself, then continued. "I haven't been able to remember who shot me, and knowing someone who wanted to hurt me that much is still out there terrifies me. Three years ago, I was mostly afraid they might hurt Chacey. I thought I was protecting her by sending her away. She tried to reason with me. She wanted to be there through my recovery, but I refused to see her. I tried to explain, but by that time, I was so trapped in my own fear that I couldn't see anything else. Now…I don't think I can run anymore. I'm so tired. Allowing myself to get close to you has helped me realize how lonely and lost I've been without her."

Elaine's eyes sparkled from the light flickering off the moving water. She looked so lost, and yet Christian could see hope beginning to surface in her features. "Oh my God, Elaine, I can't imagine what that must have been like for you…for either of you."

"What do I say to her?" Elaine asked, the pain thick in her voice. "How can I explain? How can I make up for shutting her out?" Elaine's last words were choked.

Christian considered the question. There was no way to change the past, but what Elaine was being offered was a second chance to get it right, a chance to stand up to her fear and be happy again. Christian thought of the day she had just spent with Alex. Maybe Elaine wasn't the only one being offered a second chance.

"You tell her everything." With a gentle hand on Elaine's cheek, she met Elaine's eyes. "You let her hear your pain and all the things you're telling me now. You let her share it with you and tell you all the things she's wanted to tell you, all the things she felt and is feeling now."

Elaine's eyes were pleading now as she gazed at Christian, as if the answers were hidden in Christian's soul. "What if it's too late for us?"

"You'll have to see for yourself. But if Chacey still loves you enough to come here to see you now, I think there's still hope. Give her a chance."

"She must be so angry with me. I feel like I'm being selfish by bringing her back into this. I don't know anything about how her life has changed. What kind of mess am I making by bringing all this up for her again? What if I was right all along, and she isn't safe with me?"

Christian could hear the fear in Elaine's voice and wished she had the answers to comfort her, but no one knew better than she did that sometimes there just weren't any answers. Sometimes, you just had to put one foot in front of the other and keep moving and see what happened. She leaned forward, placing her elbows on her knees. "You can't do this to yourself. Chacey agreed to come here to see you. If it wasn't important to her, she would have said no. There's no way to know how she feels until you ask her. I get it that you're scared. Anyone in your position would be, but what if you were wrong and there is no danger? What then? Don't you deserve to find out?"

Elaine relaxed back into her chair with a sigh. "You're right. No matter what happens, I have to do this."

Elaine shifted to stare out over the pool. When she turned back to Christian, her expression looked almost peaceful. She tilted her head to the side, her eyes moving over Christian's face. A faint smile began to quirk the corner of her mouth. "I almost forgot to ask about your date with Alex." Elaine ran her finger across Christian's cheek. "Looks like you got some nice sun today. How did it go?"

Christian smiled, feeling her cheeks grow warm. "Wonderful. It was wonderful."

❖

Elaine looked around the room, seeing it through a haze as if her vision was out of focus. She felt strangely disconnected. She heard Dr. Cook's voice coaxing her in the distance. "What do you see, Elaine?"

"I see my office," Elaine answered, her voice sounding flat to her own ears. "I see myself sitting at my desk reading a file." Elaine studied herself in the vision, finding it odd to look upon herself.

"Do you see anyone else in the room?"

It was as if Elaine could see the entire room without shifting her gaze. It reminded her of watching suspect interviews through the two-way mirror. The room was quiet, the only sound the rustling of paper as she saw herself leaf through a file. "No. No one else is here."

"What file do you see on the desk?"

"I have several closed files that are facedown. That means I'm done with them and they're ready to file. I'm looking at photographs of Missy Carlton. I'm reading the case file on Eric Flask." A cold chill ran down her spine and she shivered.

"Very good, Elaine. Now, I want you to think of your safe place. Do you remember what we talked about to keep you safe?"

Elaine thought of a garden, and the smell of roses wafted across her senses. "Yes. I remember." She kept her voice calm and steady.

"Good. When you feel calm, I want you to move forward to about twelve o'clock the same day. You're still just an observer in the room. Nothing can harm you."

Elaine sighed and took a deep breath.

"What's happening now?" Dr. Cook asked.

Elaine was silent for a moment. She could see the clock on the wall. She could hear the faint tick as the second hand moved across the clock face. There was the sound of a bell outside the door. "I hear the elevator outside ding. I look at the clock and realize that Sandy, the receptionist, is probably going to lunch."

"Very good. Keep going, Elaine. What happens next?" Dr. Cook's voice sounded gentle and Elaine wanted to answer her.

"I hear a knock at my door. I look at the clock again. It's too early for my next appointment. I get up and walk to the door." Elaine saw herself reach for the door. Her hand was on the knob. She could feel the cool metal in her hand. She froze when she heard Dr. Cook's voice in the distance.

"I want you to stop there, Elaine. I don't want you to open the door yet. I want you to think about feeling safe. I want you to think about the safe word we agreed on." A few moments passed. "How do you feel now?"

"Safe," Elaine repeated. She didn't feel anything at that moment. Time itself had frozen.

"Good. Now, remember, you're only an observer. You're watching yourself from far away. No one can hurt you here. Now I want you to open the door and tell me what you see."

Elaine felt her hand tighten around the round, smooth surface of the doorknob. "I'm opening the door." She watched the vision of herself step back as the door swung open. "I look surprised. I say something to the person outside." She saw her lips move, but the sound was garbled and she couldn't make out the words. Elaine felt confused and disconnected watching this image of herself, not knowing what was happening.

"What do you hear, Elaine?"

"Nothing. I feel confused. I don't know what she's doing here."

"Whom do you see?"

Elaine turned her head, looking in the direction of the door. She gasped sharply as if stunned. "Bright light is in my eyes. I can't see." Paralyzing fear gripped her.

"Okay. I want you to think about the roses now. You're safe. You're safe among the roses." Dr. Cook placed a finger on Elaine's wrist. "I'm going to bring you back now, Elaine. You will feel more awake as I count forward. When I get to three, you will wake up and feel safe and refreshed. One...two...three."

Elaine sat staring at Dr. Cook for a moment, in disbelief.

Dr. Cook smiled gently back at her. "Very good, Elaine."

Elaine shook her head, trying to make sense of what she had experienced. This was the first time in months she had remembered anything new about the shooting. "It was a woman! Oh my God. We should have been looking for a *woman*."

Elaine rubbed her face with numb fingers. Understanding began to dawn, and she looked to Dr. Cook, feeling the shock of what she had learned. "All this time, part of me thought it had to be Chacey's ex-husband. He was the only one who made sense." Relief and fear warred within her as the full impact of what that meant hit her. "If it wasn't Charles, then maybe Chacey was safe. But who else would do such a thing?"

Dr. Cook nodded. "I know this is a lot to take in right now, but this is amazing new information that can help us move forward."

Elaine shook her head to herself, still struggling. "It was a woman."

Dr. Cook leaned forward, drawing Elaine's attention. "Yes, but more than that, it seems we should be looking for someone you knew."

Elaine stared, realizing the implications of this revelation. "Someone I know did this to me."

CHAPTER SIXTEEN

Alex lay on the ground and studied the giant metal form looming above her. The metal was still hot from the torch, and she watched the flame dim to the smoked sheen of dull metal. She ran her gloved hand over the surface to feel for any uneven edges. Finished. She had been up since before dawn, unable to stop thinking about Christian. She had poured herself into her work, trying to ignore the slow passage of time as she waited for Christian to call. But the day was almost over now, and the call still hadn't come.

At least her work had been productive. She had received the commission for this piece two months earlier and had difficulty getting the owner's approval on the final specs. She was happy to see the form finally in place so she could begin the real work of sculpting. A piece this size had to be form-fit to be taken apart and reassembled on-site after shipping, and she had to make sure all the pieces of the skeleton were perfect. Once completed, it would be a twelve-foot statue of the man's wife in honor of their nineteenth wedding anniversary and celebrating his wife's fifth year as a survivor of breast cancer.

Alex looked to the clock and then to her phone that sat mocking her from its cradle. Christian hadn't called. Alex wanted to hear her voice, but feared Christian would feel pressured if she continued to pursue her. She wanted to make sure the past didn't drive Christian away again. Thinking about her now, Alex could feel the hot press of Christian's lips on her skin. Sighing, she tossed her helmet onto the workbench along with her leather gloves and removed her apron.

Christian hadn't been at the lake that morning when Alex ran, she hadn't been on the lake by the house in her kayak, and she hadn't called. *I pushed too fast. Maybe she doesn't want to see me again. Stupid, stupid, stupid! How did I let this happen?* Alex ran her fingers through her already mussed hair in frustration. *I knew if I let her go, she would run from me again. How much time do I give her? Maybe I've already waited too long.*

Alex exhaled and her shoulders slumped. She couldn't stop thinking of Christian. Jaw clenched, she grabbed her keys and headed for the Jeep. She pulled up to Willow Springs just before dark and sat in the Jeep, pondering what to do. She had no idea what to say to Christian. Both hands still on the wheel, she stared out the windshield, not seeing, lost in her thoughts. She jumped when someone rapped on the passenger-side window.

"Knock, knock," a familiar voice called. "Hey, Alex, what are you doing sitting out here all by yourself?"

Alex stared at Hannah perplexed. "Hi, Hannah, I guess I got lost in my thoughts there for a while."

"Well, is there something I can help you with?" Hannah's gaze appeared kind, without the coolness she'd displayed the night before.

"Honestly, I just don't know." Alex let her head slump, her chin almost resting on her chest.

Hannah smiled. "I see. Mind if I sit with you for a few minutes? My shift is over and I'm waiting for someone to pick me up."

"Sure, that would be nice."

Hannah opened the door and climbed inside. "So, did you come out here to see Christian?"

Not surprised this time by Hannah's blunt questioning, Alex responded immediately. "Something like that."

"You really like her, don't you?"

"Is it that obvious?" Alex grimaced as she flashed a glance at Hannah.

"Well, I've never known you to spend time with anyone here before this, and I've seen the way you look at her. It isn't very hard to see that you care about her."

"Do you think that's a bad thing? You didn't seem too happy with me last night."

"Yeah, sorry about that. I didn't mean to be rude or anything, but…" Hannah paused and turned in her seat to face Alex, resting her back against the door. "I just don't want to see anything hurt her."

"I don't think you have to worry about me hurting Christian. It may be more the other way around."

Hannah sighed. "I know she's important to you. Just take this slow. Be patient with her."

"So you don't think I should approach her at all?"

Hannah looked thoughtful for a moment. "She isn't here right now, but why don't you come for breakfast tomorrow? She usually eats on the patio at eight."

Alex's curiosity was piqued. "Do you know where she went?" She regretted the question the instant it was out. She knew it wasn't any of her business where Christian was. But to her surprise Hannah answered.

"She went into town today with Elaine. I shouldn't even be telling you this." Hannah placed her hand on Alex's arm just above her wrist. "She said she wouldn't be back until late. Go home, Alex. Get some rest and come back tomorrow. Think this out."

Alex searched Hannah's eyes, seeing only tenderness and honesty. "Thanks for telling me. You're right. I should think this out. I've been reacting without thinking, and I need to do better. I'll come to breakfast tomorrow."

Hannah opened the Jeep's door and smiled back at Alex. "I'll see you tomorrow, then. Have a good night."

"Good night, Hannah."

Alex started the Jeep and headed for home. Hannah was right. She needed to be smarter and start thinking about what she was doing instead of just reacting to her feelings. The last thing she wanted was to hurt Christian. She knew she would do anything for her.

Alex grew more uneasy the closer she got to home. She had only known Christian a short time, and already her emotions were all over the place. She had resigned herself to spending the rest of her life alone, with her work. How had her feelings changed so quickly? All she knew was the longer she was away from Christian, the more unsettled she became. And Hannah had been wrong about one thing. *She* was the one in danger of getting hurt, and she wasn't sure there was anything she could do about it.

❖

It had been a long drive. Even though Chacey had stopped in Asheville for a night, she hadn't been able to rest. She'd thought the extra time would help her think about what to say and how she would react to seeing Elaine again, but the day and a half since talking to Elaine had seemed like an eternity. She just wanted to see Elaine. Then she could think.

She was relieved when she finally arrived in Knoxville and located her hotel. After checking in at the front desk, she unceremoniously dumped her bags in her room. She checked the time. She still had a couple of hours before she was supposed to meet Elaine in the hotel bar. She gathered her toiletries and headed for the shower. The water was hot and she let the pressure beat against her back as she thought of the last time she saw Elaine. She could still see her lying there in the hospital bed with tubes and monitors everywhere. She'd been so afraid. Then Elaine had said words she'd never imagined she would hear. *I don't want to see you anymore. Don't come back here. I'll tell the nurses not to let you in my room.* She had cried and begged Elaine not to send her away. She had tried to understand what was happening with Elaine. She'd known Elaine was afraid of something, even if she would never admit her fear.

Chacey had sat outside the hospital room every day for a week, hoping Elaine would change her mind. And when Elaine didn't, she'd canceled her transfer with the FBI and worked with the team trying to find the shooter. She had hoped if she could show Elaine she was safe, she would stop pushing her away. But they had not found the UNSUB. It was as if the person was a ghost. The video surveillance in the office building had been turned off, no one unusual had been seen going in or out of the building, and there were no leads. Elaine hadn't been able to remember anything.

Chacey shook the memories from her mind. What would she say when she saw Elaine? It had been three years. Now she was here, and it would only be an hour or so until Elaine would be there with her. Chacey smiled as she remembered the smell of Elaine's skin, the feel of her hair brushing against her face, her body pressed against hers as they held each other. The memories soothed her. She had never felt as complete as when she held Elaine.

Her friends had tried to get her to move on with her life, but she hadn't been able to let Elaine go. She had spent months investigating her ex-husband. He'd claimed he had been on his boat getting drunk on the day Elaine was shot, but he had no alibi, and he was the one person she knew had motive to hurt Elaine. But they couldn't place him at the scene of the shooting. No one had seen him in or around the building. Hell, no one had seen him at all.

She had become obsessed, certain she had been the reason Elaine had been hurt. She couldn't be free until she knew what had happened.

There were so many unknowns. She didn't know what had happened to Elaine once she left the hospital. She had tried to keep track of her through her connections, but Elaine would simply vanish for months, and there was a limit to how far Chacey would go to trace Elaine. She realized now that Elaine must have gone to the retreat. They had planned on spending the summer there once they had their life together settled. It had seemed the perfect place to start over. Chacey had never imagined that was where Elaine would go alone.

Chacey heard her phone ringing as she stepped out of the shower. Immediately she thought of Elaine and hoped she had not changed her mind. Disappointment and relief hit her as she recognized the number. Karen. She ignored the call and pushed all thoughts of Karen out of her mind. She had more important things to think about. Elaine.

❖

"Are you ready?" Christian asked as she brought the car to a stop outside the hotel.

Elaine had been quiet on the drive and now looked as if she was about to be sick. "I don't know if I can do this."

"Of course you can. Come on. Let's get inside before you're

late." Christian walked around the car, placed her hand in Elaine's, and steered her into the hotel lobby. The bar was small but quaint, and they quickly found a fairly private table in a corner where Elaine could watch the door without being seen.

Christian moved to the bar to order a glass of wine for the two of them and tried to prepare to meet Elaine's lover. She watched Elaine while she waited. She could see Elaine's trepidation. She felt slightly out of place but had agreed to come, knowing that Elaine was too afraid to face her past alone. She tried to imagine what it must be like for Elaine to sit there, waiting to see the woman she loved after such a long time, with so much pain between them.

Elaine's eyes grew wide and she pressed a shaking hand to her lips as a woman, about forty, Christian guessed, entered the bar. She wore pressed chinos and a simple white shirt, unbuttoned and loose at the waist. Beneath the shirt, she wore a gray camisole that showed her slim, muscled chest and waist. Her hair was brown, cut just above her collar with the top shaped in long layers to one side and tucked behind her ear.

Christian had no doubt, by her movements and her body language, that she was a cop. She scanned the room methodically, noting each patron—including Christian—and the layout of the room. Christian watched, mesmerized, as Chacey's eyes finally met Elaine's. Chacey stood frozen for a moment as if she had suddenly lost the ability to move of her own accord. Slowly, her right hand moved to her chest, where she appeared to hold her beating heart. Elaine stood, her hand grasping the back of her chair for balance, as Chacey began to make her way across the room.

Christian could see why Elaine was so taken with Chacey. She was beautiful, strong, completely absorbed in Elaine and still obviously very much in love with her. She knew they'd have many things to discuss before their wounds could mend, but at least they could heal together now. The energy between the two women was palpable, and Christian's skin rippled in anticipation.

❖

Elaine felt the air rush out of her lungs when Chacey entered the room. Her legs felt like wood as she tried to stand, and she had to steady herself with her chair. Everything else in the room slid out of focus as all of her attention centered on the woman in front of her.

"Hi, baby," Chacey said when she was close enough to reach out and touch Elaine.

Elaine could feel the sting of tears brimming her eyes, and her hand trembled against her lips. "You came," she whispered.

Chacey's smile was warm. "I will come for you always and forever. I never left you." Chacey held out her hand to Elaine as if asking permission to touch her.

Elaine drew Chacey's hand to her chest. "Oh, Chacey, I'm so sorry. I've hardly been alive without you."

Chacey didn't hesitate now. She took Elaine into her arms and held her. Elaine instantly wrapped her arms around Chacey's shoulders, clinging to her back, and pressed her face against the soft skin of Chacey's neck.

Elaine felt her heart swell as she drew in the faintly masculine smell of Chacey's cologne. The sensation was beyond her imagining. She was flooded with happiness, grief, hope, and fear, all mingled together. When she pulled away, Chacey gently brushed her tears away with the stroke of her thumb and a gentle kiss.

"Shall we sit?" Chacey asked, her gaze never leaving Elaine's. Elaine nodded, and Chacey guided her back to her seat and took the chair next to her.

Elaine didn't think she could look at Chacey enough. And she wanted to do more than look. She wanted to touch her face, her hair, her lips, just to make herself believe she wasn't a dream. She looked across the room to where Christian stood at the bar and gestured for her to join them.

Christian walked over and placed a glass of red wine on the table in front of Elaine. Elaine touched Christian's arm. "Christian, this is Chacey Bristol. Chacey, I'd like you to meet my dear friend, Christian Sutter."

"It's a pleasure to finally meet you, Chacey," Christian said, extending her hand.

"Thank you. I assure you the pleasure is mine," Chacey said with a smile as they shook hands across the table.

Christian turned to Elaine. "I don't want to seem rude, but I think I'll be getting back to the lodge. I think you two have some catching up to do."

Elaine grasped Christian's hand and peered up at her. She wasn't sure she was ready for her to leave. As if sensing her roiling emotions, Christian leaned down and kissed Elaine's cheek. "You'll be fine. I'm sure you're in good hands. And you know where to find me if you need me."

Elaine took a deep breath and nodded. "Thank you."

Christian smiled. "It was nice meeting you, Chacey. I hope to see you again."

With Christian gone, Elaine turned back to Chacey. Her heart fluttered and her head felt light. She had no idea what to do next.

CHAPTER SEVENTEEN

Christian caught the smell of the river and heard the whistle of a riverboat as she left the hotel. She was only a street away from the river and felt drawn to the gentle sounds emanating from the water. She drove to the river walk, her mind clouded and her heart heavy. She stood gazing over the railing, watching the yachts and riverboats swaying in the current, tethered to the pier for the night. The wind blew her hair back from her face. The warm summer air was refreshing, and she imagined that the brush of her loose shirt across her arms was the touch of her lover gently comforting her.

Seeing Elaine and Chacey reunite after their long ordeal had left her reminiscent, and she found herself missing Cara. She tried to imagine what Elaine and Chacey would say to each other, or if there was really any need for explanations. She recalled the look of desperate hope on Chacey's face when she first saw Elaine. She had no doubt that Chacey had fought a silent battle of her own, trying to find her way back to Elaine.

Christian drew in a deep breath and wiped her hand roughly across her cheek, brushing the loose curls away from her face. She wanted to be angry. She wanted to scream at the universe that it wasn't fair. She had loved Cara, and she had been taken from her and robbed of her own life. She ran her hand through her hair and felt the scars, hollow under her touch. They were constant reminders of the violence of the crash and the void left by Cara's death. She would never have that second chance to hold Cara and tell her how much she loved her. She would never hear her voice or watch the emotions play across her face when she saw something beautiful. She would never again feel Cara's body pressed against her as she slept.

Laughter caught Christian's attention and she turned, searching the pier for the source of the unwelcome intrusive joy. A couple sat out on the deck of a boat, sipping wine as they took in the warm night.

She thought of Alex on the lake, her skin red and angry from too much sun. She shuddered slightly at the memory of Alex's eyes peering into her as she leaned in to kiss her, at the memory of their bodies pressed against each other and Alex's lips on her skin. She gasped as she remembered waking in Alex's arms.

Christian stared at the boat, her thoughts of Cara and Alex warring in her mind. She was so confused. It was times like this that she felt her heart would never mend, the pain of losing Cara so raw, she felt she could scream. Then there were moments like those with Alex when she wanted to lose herself in passion and hope.

Alex had awakened feelings in her she thought she would never know again. She craved that closeness, but what did she really have to offer anyone now? She felt broken. It was best not to encourage this connection with Alex. She would put distance there and hope Alex would forgive her. She couldn't risk losing again.

❖

Elaine stared at Chacey, not believing she was there. She could feel the brush of Chacey's fingers along the top of her hand, but she struggled to register that Chacey was real. She was afraid it was another dream, that any minute a door would open and her nightmare would begin again.

"Talk to me," Chacey said gently.

Elaine's chest tightened and she shook her head. "I'm afraid."

"I know, but I'm here now. You don't ever have to be afraid again. We can do this."

Elaine looked around the room, feeling like a wild animal trapped in a cage. She could feel her heart pounding in her chest as she fought the urge to run. She felt hot. Where had all these people come from? She gripped the edge of the table, trying to quiet her fear.

Perceptively, Chacey suggested, "Would you like to go somewhere a little less crowded? We could go to my room if you would be more comfortable there."

Elaine's shoulders eased. "I think that would help. I can't do this here." Chacey's hand slid into hers, gently tugging as she led her through the hotel lobby. Chacey's touch was tender, and Elaine was thankful for the contact, feeling more grounded now that she was away from the crowd. Then it occurred to her that she was about to be alone with Chacey. There would be no more barriers between them, and she would have to explain what she had done. Where would she start? How would Chacey feel about what she would tell her? Could she bear losing her all over again? Elaine shut her eyes briefly, trying to quell the memories of that day in the hospital when she had sent Chacey away. She wouldn't do that ever again. If she'd learned anything from her ordeal, it was that there are some things worse than dying. She squeezed Chacey's hand. "I'm glad you're here."

Chacey looked at her. "Me too. I can't believe it's real."

The elevator door dinged and they stepped out. Chacey led the way down the hall, holding tightly to Elaine's hand.

Once in the room, Chacey poured a drink and set it on the small coffee table in front of Elaine. She'd booked this junior suite so they'd have somewhere private to talk without having to sit on the bed. Slowly, she moved to sit next to Elaine on the sofa. She sat with one knee drawn up and her left arm draped casually along the sofa's back. The pain in Elaine's eyes was tearing her apart. She knew Elaine was struggling. So was she. She had feared she would never see Elaine again, and being here with her now was…all the happiness in the world all at once. She followed the faint lines around Elaine's eyes that hadn't been there before. Elaine was thinner and her skin paler than she remembered, but just as beautiful as ever. She wanted to touch her. She wanted to wrap her body around her so she would have no doubt she was real.

Chacey was afraid she would frighten Elaine and knew she had to temper her need to touch her. She clasped Elaine's hand in both of hers, turning it over to trace the lines of her palm. "I can't tell you how much I've wanted to see you. I've thought of you and waited for your call every day since that last day in the hospital. I've missed you so much."

"I'm so sorry, Chace. I know I've hurt you. I'm so sorry I sent you away. I'm sorry I didn't give us the chance to get through this."

"Can you tell me why?"

Elaine sighed. "I was so afraid. Every time I saw you, the fear grew until it was more than I could handle. I didn't feel like I had a choice."

Chacey let out a long breath. "I know you were scared. I'm sorry I couldn't protect you. I'm sorry I couldn't make you feel safe."

"What?" Elaine gasped. "Oh no, Chacey, I never thought you couldn't protect me. I thought I was protecting you. I was afraid the person who shot me would come back, and I was afraid something would happen to you. I couldn't have lived with myself if I'd let that happen."

Relief flooded Chacey's heart as she realized Elaine hadn't felt she'd failed her. But she had known what her ex-husband was capable of, and she had been naïve enough to think he would only hurt her. "If I hadn't left for Boston without you, if I had stayed or if I had insisted that you not wait until the case was over, that you leave when I did, maybe none of this would have happened."

"How could you blame yourself? You couldn't have known anything like this would happen. I was at work, Chacey, in my private office, not at the FBI working the case. You know you couldn't have been with me even if you hadn't gone to Boston."

Chacey chuckled. "Yeah, well, it seems about as rational as you trying to protect me from some unknown crazy person by cutting me out of your life." She hadn't expected her tone to be so cutting. Elaine immediately broke eye contact. Chacey's gut clenched. "I'm sorry. I know you were trying to do the right thing. I don't know what I'd have done if our roles had been reversed." She lifted Elaine's chin with a finger. "I just want us to start again. I still love you, Elaine."

"I love you too. I never stopped. I just didn't know how to stop running."

Chacey's mind raced. She couldn't think about who was to blame or what had gone wrong anymore. The most important thing was the woman sitting next to her. The shooting had already taken too much from them, and she wasn't about to waste another moment.

"I have an idea. Let's not talk about the shooting. Let's talk about what you've been doing, about the retreat, and your new friends. I want to know everything I've missed. Then maybe we'll work our way backward through the tough stuff. We can order dinner and make a night of it." Her words were playful and encouraging and she hoped she had managed to ease Elaine's worry.

Elaine glanced around the room. Chacey was afraid she would leave, but after a few moments Elaine's shoulders relaxed. "Okay. I think I'd like that."

❖

Elaine picked at her room-service pasta, her attention focused on the sound of Chacey's voice, the way she moved her hands when she talked, the curve of her lips when she smiled. She wanted to memorize every move, every line of her face, everything about her.

"Are you still with the bureau?"

Chacey nodded. "I canceled the transfer to Boston and came back to Virginia. I'm still in my old house. You should see Miss Priss, she's a mess."

"I guess she's not a kitten anymore." She'd given Chacey the tiny orange ball of fur to keep her company after she'd left Charles.

"Ha! No, fully grown and great company for me. A little territorial at times, but she keeps me entertained."

Elaine imagined Chacey at home in her favorite lounging spot on the sofa, petting the cat and reading a book. It was a picture she remembered clearly and it made her feel homesick for the life they'd had together.

Chacey pushed her food aside. "Come on, I can see you aren't really going to eat that. Come sit with me."

Elaine followed her across the room. She smiled when Chacey sat on the sofa and patted her lap. "Stretch your legs out and get comfortable."

There had been so many nights when Chacey had sat rubbing her legs as they talked about the day, made plans, watched movies. Elaine marveled at how they had fallen into this old pattern so easily after so long apart.

"So it's you and Miss Priss?" Elaine asked, needing to know if

Chacey was involved with anyone before she let herself hope too much. "Do you have someone in your life?"

"*You*. I told you. I never left you." Chacey pulled Elaine's legs onto her lap and ran her hand up her leg, massaging her calf muscles and the tender area just behind her knee.

Elaine drew in a sharp breath and felt another part of the ice around her heart melt away.

Chacey deepened the massage. "God, you're even more beautiful than I remembered."

Elaine felt her neck and face grow warm. Her heart beat wildly in her chest, and fear threatened to take over. "Chacey…"

"Don't be afraid, sweetheart. I'll never hurt you. You don't ever have to be afraid again."

Elaine froze as Chacey leaned closer, her hand gently pressing into the back of her neck, her gaze intent and hungry. Their faces only inches apart, Chacey took Elaine's hand and placed it on her cheek. "Can you feel it?"

Elaine's hand tingled as if an electric current flowed beneath Chacey's skin. She moved her fingers lightly across Chacey's face. Her breathing slowed, all her senses focused on the energy passing between them.

Elaine smiled. "I can feel it."

Before Elaine could say more, Chacey's lips met hers and flames shot through her blood. She swooned and she thought for a moment that she was floating. When they finally parted, Elaine's arms were around Chacey's neck, she sat atop Chacey's lap, and her body was pressed tightly to Chacey's. Tears streaked Chacey's face. Chacey pushed the hair back from Elaine's face, as if reluctant to stop touching her.

Elaine peered into Chacey's eyes for a moment, her breathing heavy. Her heart was simultaneously breaking and filled with joy. She had her lover in her arms, the one woman she knew she did not want to live another minute without. But she also knew she had been the one to put the pain in Chacey's eyes. She brushed Chacey's tears away with kisses, wanting to make it right, wanting to make the pain stop.

"I'm sorry, I promised myself I wouldn't cry. I just can't seem to hold it all in now that I have you here. I thought I had lost you forever." Chacey's voice was a whisper and shook with emotion. "I feel like the last three years have been a bad dream, like it wasn't real. Now I have you and I can finally breathe again."

Chacey's hold on Elaine tightened, pulling her closer. And Elaine felt love overtake her fear. Hearing the promise in Chacey's voice, Elaine knew that, this time, Chacey would never let her go.

❖

Alex sat by the lake watching the sunrise. Her voice was quiet and her body still. She had come here to talk to Sophia as she always did as the sun rose, but today she felt a new heaviness upon her heart.

She didn't understand her feelings for Christian and she didn't know what to do about them. *What do I do, Sophia? I feel like such a mess.* Her thoughts drifted to the day she'd met Sophia. They had taken an art class together and worked side by side for weeks before Alex had the nerve to ask her out. Sophia had laughed and teased her. *Took you long enough, sport. I was beginning to think I was going to have to ask you to pose for my nudes in order to get you in bed.*

Sophia had always been in charge, teaching her how to love her. No wonder she didn't have a clue what she was doing now. Then Sophia's words struck her again. *Took you long enough, sport.* Maybe she just needed to go after what she wanted. Maybe she didn't need to sit back and wait for Christian to come to her.

The memory of Christian's body pressed against her as tears streaked her face tore at Alex. She thought about how different Sophia and Christian were and realized for the first time that what she felt for Christian was love. Sophia had guided her through her fear and taught her how to take a chance on love. Now maybe it was her turn to help Christian take a chance and learn to love again.

CHAPTER EIGHTEEN

Elaine had fallen asleep sometime around four in the morning, cradled in Chacey's arms. She dreamed she was being chased through unfamiliar corridors, and she struggled to find a way out. She startled herself awake to find Chacey still holding her against her chest, stroking her hair. They lay on the sofa, still in their clothes, and the upholstery buttons pressed into Elaine's thigh, but at that moment she couldn't have felt better. Being in Chacey's arms was the most *right* feeling of her life. She wound her fingers through Chacey's hair, relishing the warmth and safety of her embrace.

But as much as she wanted to pick up where they had left off, Elaine knew that too much time had passed for that. She knew Chacey, but didn't know her. She knew the woman she had loved. She knew the life they once had. But three years left a mark, and she knew it would take time to learn to be together again.

Elaine turned to Chacey. Fatigue clouded her eyes, and she had the feeling Chacey hadn't slept at all. "You should rest, sweetheart. Have you been awake this whole time?"

"I've been enjoying watching you sleep. I feel like I've missed so much already. I'm afraid to close my eyes. I don't want you to disappear again." Chacey leaned down, kissed Elaine's forehead, and ran her fingers through her hair.

Elaine heard the vulnerability in Chacey's voice. "I promise not to disappear. Now, you need to get some rest. Let's get you to bed. This sofa is like sleeping in a pickup truck." Elaine peeled herself away from Chacey, pulling her up with her as she stood.

Chacey locked her arms around Elaine and held her tightly, and she swayed a little on her feet. "Okay, maybe I'm a little tired."

Elaine chuckled and pulled Chacey toward the bed.

They didn't bother undressing. They were too tired. Elaine pressed against Chacey's chest, urging her onto the bed. As Chacey's body relaxed into the comforter and her head lay cradled by the pillow, Elaine climbed into the bed next to her. Her head lay on Chacey's shoulder and she burrowed her face into the smooth, soft skin of her neck. As she skimmed her fingers across the taut muscles of Chacey's stomach, Chacey caught her hand, drew it up to her chest, and placed it over the spot where Elaine could feel the rhythmic thrum of Chacey's heart.

Elaine knew time hadn't changed the most important thing. "I love you," she whispered.

Chacey let out a heavy sigh and squeezed her arm tighter around Elaine's shoulder. "I love you too, sweetheart."

Chacey's lips brushed against her hair and she felt Chacey drift off to sleep.

❖

A shadow fell across Christian's face, rousing her from her slumber as she sat sunbathing on the patio. Looking up into the sun, she couldn't make out the face hidden in shadow, but as her eyes skimmed the tall, muscular body and took in the broad shoulders and short, thick hair, she knew who it was instantly. She would know Alex's shape anywhere.

Holding a hand up to shield her eyes, she saw Alex beaming down at her. She wore a tight-fitting tank top that showed off her arm muscles and hugged every contour of her body. Cargo shorts hung loosely on her hips as if the slightest tug could dislodge them. She held two drinks, one of which she extended toward Christian.

"You looked so relaxed over here, I couldn't resist joining you. I thought you might be thirsty from the sun, so I brought you a drink," Alex said, her tone casual and relaxed.

Christian studied her for a moment before reaching out and taking the drink. "Thank you." She wondered why Alex was there.

As if reading her mind, Alex launched into explanation. "I'm teaching a pottery class today down at the pavilion. You should come."

"Thanks, but no. I'm not very artistic."

Alex laughed. "That wouldn't matter today. The first day is usually a mess for everyone. Besides, pottery is one of those things anyone can do with a little practice." She shrugged. "But suit yourself, if it isn't your thing, that's okay too."

Christian watched Alex let her eyes roam down the expanse of her exposed skin. To her surprise, Alex didn't flinch when she realized she was being watched. It was as if Alex wanted her to see. "What are you doing, Alex?"

Alex looked innocent for a moment, then smiled sheepishly. "Just admiring you and imagining my hands all over your body."

Christian was caught off guard by Alex's frankness. Her jaw dropped in disbelief—had Alex just said that? It wasn't like her to be so forward. What was going on?

"What? Is there something wrong with admiring a beautiful woman? You know I want you."

Christian's face burned. "Alex. Don't do this. I can't do this."

"Do what?" Alex laughed. "You may not want to admit it, but you want me too, and I'm not going to give up."

Alex stood and stripped off her shirt, her muscles rippling with each movement as she stretched her arms over her head, then leaned down and shucked off her shorts. "I dare you not to watch me walk over there and dive into that pool." Alex smiled wickedly at Christian. Then she walked away. Her shoulders squared, Alex stalked across the patio with the grace of a jungle cat.

Christian clenched her jaw. She could not take her eyes off Alex's body even knowing Alex was purposely antagonizing her. She surged with heat and her stomach tightened as she studied each inch of muscle, Alex's thin black bathing suit only accentuating her slender hips, the curve of her butt, and her high, tight breasts. Christian's groin pulsed and she stifled a moan. Despite her attempts to bury her feelings for Alex, her body rebelled against her resolve and hungered for more.

A long minute later, Christian tried to focus on the book she was reading when Alex returned to her side dripping, her skin glistening in the sun.

"Did you watch?" Alex asked, her voice playful.

Christian surrendered and played along. "As a matter of fact, I did. Nice show."

"Good. How about a swim, then? I bet you could use a nice cool dip right now." Alex flicked her fingers, spraying Christian with cold droplets of water.

Christian flinched and giggled, despite herself. "Okay, that's enough. You win!"

"You'll stop avoiding me, then?"

"I'm not *avoiding* you. I'm just taking time to sort out…stuff."

Alex cocked her head. "Not good enough." In one smooth motion, she scooped Christian up into her arms.

Christian squealed and smacked Alex on the shoulder with the palm of her hand. She wasn't sure if she was delighted or horrified. "Alex, put me down!" Why was she doing this?

Alex carried Christian to the pool and stood on the edge, holding her over the water. Alex held her securely and Christian knew there was no real threat. But Alex seemed to be enjoying herself. And they were beginning to attract attention.

Alex said, "Admit you were avoiding me. Say you'll have dinner with me tonight."

"Alex, I don't think that is a good idea."

People were beginning to laugh. One woman cat-whistled and yelled, "Say yes!"

"Oh, great, now you have the whole resort on your side," Christian grumbled.

"Hey, I can't help it if I'm right and you're just plain stubborn."

Christian smacked Alex on the shoulder again.

"Okay, if that's how you want to play it…" Alex moved as if she would drop Christian into the water.

"No. Wait! I'll go. I'll go!"

"You'll have dinner with me?"

"Yes, I'll have dinner with you!"

Cheers erupted from the surrounding tables. Alex smiled down at Christian, a devilish look on her face. "That's better." Alex raised one eyebrow, said, "Now for that swim," and stepped off the side into the pool, Christian still cradled in her arms.

"Alex!" Christian's yell was stifled as she plunged into the water. Strong hands pulled her into an embrace and slick skin slid against her own. Their arms and legs entwined in a lovers' embrace. Christian felt the last shred of her resistance break, and desire sparked in her middle. She was laughing as her head broke the surface of the water, her arms wrapped around Alex's neck and her face only inches from Alex's lips. Water streamed down her face, and she blinked, trying to focus on the ice-blue eyes glistening back at her. "You're crazy, you know that."

Alex just smiled and leaned in and kissed her.

She couldn't resist any longer. Her fingers tangled their way through the thick, wet layers of Alex's hair. Her body wrapped around Alex like a vise. Christian pressed into the kiss, pushed Alex back under the water, and joined her there, never breaking the kiss.

CHAPTER NINETEEN

There was a knock at the door promptly at six thirty. Christian stood in front of her mirror, fussing over her hair and berating herself for agreeing to this date with Alex. She was so excited she could hardly breathe. What had happened to her resolve not to see Alex anymore? *Oh God, what am I doing?* When the second knock sounded, she sighed and turned to answer the door.

Christian stood frozen as she took in the unexpected change in Alex's appearance. Her hair was combed to the side and revealed the strong angle of her jaw. She wore tailored black dress slacks, a baby blue dress shirt, and a fitted black-on-black satin vest with an intricate pattern across the chest. Her black shoes were polished to a shine. The clothes brought out the color of her eyes, now the blue of the ocean on a clear, sunny day.

Alex smiled. "Hi. I hope I'm not early."

Christian pulled herself from her trance, finding it hard not to stare at Alex. God, she looked good. "No, you're right on time. Come in while I gather my things."

Alex stepped into the room and stood by the door. She watched Christian move about the room and marveled at how elegant she looked. Christian wore gray dress slacks, modest black heels, and a long white silk dress shirt, gathered at the waist by a silver chain that acted as a belt. The collar of her shirt was open and revealed the gentle swell of her breasts. At the hollow of her throat lay a small silver pendant that reminded Alex of a Celtic knot. Matching silver earrings glistened in the light and drew Alex's eye to Christian's delicate neck.

Alex suddenly felt like a schoolgirl going on her first date with the prom queen. Her palms began to sweat.

Christian moved toward her, a clutch purse held firmly in her hand. "Are you all right, Alex?"

The concern in Christian's voice drew Alex back to the moment. "You're beautiful," she said reverently.

"Thank you," Christian said as she leaned in and kissed Alex on the cheek. "So are you," she whispered softly.

Alex ran her hands around Christian's waist, the soft fabric a cruel barrier between her and the delicate skin she longed to touch. She licked her lips at the thought of her mouth on Christian's stomach, and on the delicate flesh below.

Christian felt her body go hot as gentle hands pressed into her back and Alex brushed against her breasts. A quiver ran through her and she shuddered. She could almost feel Alex's eyes burning a path across her skin as her gaze roamed the length of her neck, down her chest, to the supple cleft between her breasts. Breath shaky, she leaned in and whispered, "I think we'd better go."

"Yes, ma'am." Alex stared for a moment as if about to kiss Christian, then hesitantly released her hold and turned to open the door. As they made their way down the hall, Alex took Christian's hand, as if she couldn't stand a moment without her touch.

There seemed to be a change in Alex, and Christian tried to place the subtle difference. It wasn't a physical change. A thrill ran down Christian's spine when she remembered the way Alex had looked at her in her room. The look had been confident, as if she knew something Christian didn't.

Alex stopped and opened the door to the Jeep. Christian noted that the top had been put on. She smiled at all the trouble Alex had gone to just to get her to go to dinner with her. Alex waited solicitously until Christian was settled in her seat, then shut the door. Halfway down the drive, Alex reached across and took her hand again, and Christian realized she had missed her touch.

She needed to break the silence. "Where are we going?"

Alex smiled. "You'll see."

"Come on, just a hint?"

"Nope. You'll just have to wait." Alex stroked her hand with her thumb. "Let me guess, you don't like surprises."

"No. That's not it. I just wonder about the things you like." She wondered what Alex had up her sleeve. "Besides, after the stunt at the pool, who knows what you're up to?"

Alex laughed. "I promise to take you to a perfectly normal place for a perfectly normal meal. Think you can handle that?"

"Yes. I think I can handle that," Christian said, her curiosity beginning to get the better of her.

"Good, because we're almost there."

The restaurant Alex parked behind was a small, intimate place, the walls simple exposed brick hung with paintings of Spanish women dancing and bullfighters narrowly escaping a charge. The room was long and narrow with only a few small tables set to accommodate couples and romantically lit, a soft glow illuminating the room and small candle lanterns flickering on each table.

A woman led them to a table and took their drink orders. Alex ordered a carafe of white sangria and water for them both. "You have to try this sangria. It's the best I've ever had. If you don't like it, they also have wine and beer."

Christian smiled. She had been pleasantly surprised by Alex's take-charge behavior and was intrigued to see where the night would lead. When they had first met, Alex had seemed reserved and guarded, but now she was open, adventurous, playful, and when she looked at Christian, she oozed sexuality.

Dinner was served as tapas. Christian sampled the small dishes, each exquisite in its individual flavors. First she tried the churrasco, a seared skirt steak that melted in her mouth the instant it made contact with her tongue. Christian's eyes closed in bliss as she relished the charred flavor of the tender meat.

Alex smiled. "How is it?"

"Oh, it's fantastic!"

Alex looked pleased and pushed the plates around, pointing to the aïoli potatoes. "Now try these. If you like a little heat, put some of this chili paste on them." Alex prepared a bite with her fork and offered it to Christian.

Christian leaned in, allowing Alex to glide the delicate morsel into her mouth. Instant pleasure played across her taste buds. "Wow, that's wonderful," Christian said her eyes wide in pleasure. Taking a drink of the sangria, she was pleasantly soothed by the cool citrus mix of wine and fruit. Dangerous. It was like drinking fruit punch on a hot summer day, and she knew she had to be mindful of the alcohol.

"My, Alex!" a tall woman called as she approached the table. She had skin the color of caramel and a long braid of black hair draped across her shoulder and down one breast. She was dressed all in black, both slacks and snug-fitting open-neck pullover hugging the curves of her body. She came to the table, ran her hands across Alex's shoulders, and played with the hair at the base of her neck. "Alex, how good to see you. Where have you been? I've missed you." The woman looked across the table at Christian, her eyes ablaze. "And who is this beauty you bring to us tonight?"

Christian felt her body tense as the woman's hands rested on Alex's shoulders. She didn't like the way she was touching Alex. Who was this woman and what gave her the right? Was this someone Alex had dated? Christian had the sudden urge to smack the woman's hands away.

Alex took the woman's hand and kissed it gently. "Maria, this is my friend Christian Sutter. Christian, this is Maria Alvarez. Maria owns the restaurant."

Maria left Alex and came to Christian, both hands outstretched, and took Christian's face in her hands and kissed her cheek. "Welcome. I'm so pleased to meet you. I hope Alex has introduced you to some of our special flavors. Has everything been to your liking?"

"Oh yes. Everything has been wonderful, thank you." Christian felt herself relax as Maria refrained from touching Alex again. Where had this jealousy come from? She had no claim on Alex. But the thought made her palms sweat, and she really hoped Maria would go away.

A waiter called to Maria from behind the bar, and she excused herself. "I'm sorry—duty calls. It's so good to see you again, Alex. You and your friend must come again soon."

Alex smiled again. "I'm sure we will, Maria, thank you."

Christian watched Maria move around the bar and begin speaking with the staff. She admired her confidence and grace. "She's very beautiful," Christian said. "Have you known her long?"

"I come here sometimes. Maria has always been very kind."

Christian looked at Alex now, curiosity getting the better of her. "Were you two ever lovers?"

Alex laughed. "No. Maria is very beautiful and, as you saw, open with her affection, but Maria is also very married. Her partner, Sebastian, is a police officer here in town. They opened the restaurant a few years ago, and I met them here shortly after the opening. I come here about once a month, so we've become friends, I guess."

Something like relief settled over Christian. She had no right to be possessive of Alex. She hadn't wanted to feel anything for her. And now the mere thought of someone touching Alex made her stomach tighten into knots.

"Has there ever been another woman since Sophia?" Her barriers were crumbling, and she needed to know more about this beautiful woman who made her feel so alive again.

Alex took in a deep breath and closed her eyes briefly.

"I'm sorry, Alex. I shouldn't have asked."

"No, it's okay. I don't mind, really." Alex reached across the table taking Christian's hand. "There have been times when the loneliness has been too much and I needed to feel the touch of another woman. There have been brief interludes, but there has been no one I've wanted to know more about or share more with than just sex."

Christian was thoughtful for a while as she thought of Alex meeting strangers, trying to fill the ache of her loss. "And what is *this*, Alex? What do you want from me?"

"I've spent a lot of time asking myself that very same question. You're not like any other woman I've met. I want to know you. I want to breathe the air you breathe." Alex sighed and she leaned in, closing the distance between them. "The time I spent with those women, I felt like I was trying to prove to myself that I was still alive. I felt that if I didn't reach out, I'd slowly disappear. But afterward I'd feel empty, and it would make me feel even more alone."

Christian gripped Alex's hand. She knew the loneliness that Alex spoke of.

"It's different with you," Alex went on. "Every time you look at me I feel alive. Every moment with you is a treasure. And when you're not with me, I'm thankful for the time I've had with you and I long for more."

Christian felt her mouth go dry. She knew this was more than she had to offer. "What if I can't give you more, Alex?"

"Then I'll be happy to breathe the air you breathe. I'll be happy having everything you choose to share with me. I'll know that I'm alive because you've shown me that I can love again."

Christian's heart skipped and her breath caught. Alex made it all seem so simple, but it wasn't. She did feel alive with Alex, but she couldn't make that leap. She couldn't give that much of herself and survive losing all over again. "Alex, I can't…"

"I don't expect anything, Christian. Please don't run away from me again. Just be here with me right now. Be *alive* with me, right now."

Unable to say more, Christian nodded.

❖

Alex insisted upon walking Christian to her door, not wanting the night to end. She knew Christian had feelings for her, she could see it in her eyes. But she didn't know what it would take to convince Christian of that.

Alex took the key from Christian and opened the door. Before Christian could walk inside, Alex embraced her. "Thank you for spending the evening with me," Alex said before her mouth was on Christian's.

She felt Christian stiffen momentarily before her lips softened and she gave herself over to the kiss. When she felt Christian's mouth part, granting her entrance, she filled her with insistent strokes of her tongue. Her hands pressed into the soft swell of Christian's hips, holding her in the embrace. When she heard Christian whimper and felt her cleave to her, Alex guided Christian into the room. Her growing hunger overwhelmed her senses. She sucked Christian's tongue, explored her mouth. The moans of answering pleasure made Alex melt inside, and she slipped her hand up to caress Christian's breast.

Christian moaned as Alex pressed her lips to the tender flesh of her neck and her hand found Christian's firm, round breast. Alex pinched the hard erect nipple between her finger and thumb. Her own breasts were hard, and the fabric of her shirt felt rough against her tender nipples as her body slid against Christian's. She felt Christian's hips surge into her, and fire exploded in her clitoris. She had dropped all her shields, and Christian was pushing her to the edge of desire. But as much as she wanted to take Christian in that moment, she knew it wasn't enough. She wanted something deeper.

Alex pulled away and let her fingers drift down Christian's torso, coming to rest on her waist.

The sudden loss of Alex's touch on her breast left Christian clinging to the resonate pulse of her heartbeat in her groin. Breathless, she leaned her head forward and rested her forehead against Alex's chest. One hand rested on Alex's biceps and she could feel the tension in the taut muscle. Gathering herself, she drew in a calming breath. "Why did you stop? My God, Alex, you're driving me crazy."

Alex brushed a hand along her cheek, and Christian felt her grip tighten on her waist. "I stopped because I was almost beyond the point where I could. I want to make love with you again, but I want to know that when I do, it's what you want. I don't want you to have doubts about me, and I certainly don't want you to have any regrets."

Christian ran her hands down the front of Alex's shirt, feeling the tight, hard nipples brush roughly against her palms. Alex stiffened and her fingers dug into Christian's back. Christian paused, knowing her hesitation was her answer.

Alex loosened her grip and took a step back from Christian. "I should go," she whispered.

"I can't believe you're talking me out of having sex with you."

Alex chuckled. "I told you. I don't want you to have any doubts. When you're ready, you'll come to me. You won't have any more questions. And I'll be waiting."

Alex kissed her again. This time, the kiss was slow and gentle. Alex's lips were soft as they brushed against her mouth.

"Good night, Christian," Alex murmured and turned to go.

"Alex…" She wanted her to stay, but she knew Alex was right.

Alex stopped at the door, her hand resting on the latch, and looked back at Christian over her shoulder, desire still written on her face.

"Thank you."

Alex smiled and opened the door. "I'll see you tomorrow." She winked at Christian as she disappeared into the hall, closing the door.

Christian stood staring at the door until she was certain she wouldn't run after her. Her knees felt weak from the absence of Alex's touch and the desire that still throbbed in her middle. She ran a hand down her front and clutched her stomach. Her body ached for Alex and she had been ready to give in to desire. She couldn't believe Alex had stopped. She had felt the hunger in Alex's touch and knew she was close to erupting.

Alex had stopped because she didn't want this to be sex. She had wanted it to be love.

God, what was happening? She hadn't wanted this. She hadn't wanted any of this. But she had wanted Alex. She had wanted her from the first moment she'd laid eyes on her. She had sought her out, day after day, trying to get close to her. And now things had gone too far. She couldn't love Alex. Could she?

Christian's hands shook as she rubbed her face and headed to the shower to quench the fire burning through her body and the confusion clouding her mind.

CHAPTER TWENTY

Being with Chacey again was like coming home. In all her imaginings, nothing had prepared Elaine for what she was experiencing. She loved Chacey with all her soul and being with her again was like being made whole again. But after spending a night and a day with Chacey, Elaine was glad to be back at the retreat. She had to get some fresh clothes and wanted some time to process everything that had happened. She still felt the lingering fear that always haunted her, but it was different now that Chacey was back in her life. Now the fear of not having Chacey in her life was greater than her fear of harm coming to her, and she would not send her away again. She'd promised Chacey she would only be a few hours, and they would meet for dinner.

Chacey had been reluctant to let her go but had given in when Elaine had promised she would be back. Elaine knew Chacey was afraid she would run away from her again. But that wasn't going to happen. She was relieved to be back at the retreat but missed having Chacey with her. After her shower, she made her way around the grounds looking for Christian. Hannah had said she had gone for a walk early, but hadn't come back for lunch. Elaine thought she knew just where she could find her.

The roses hung heavily along the trellis as Elaine stepped into the secret garden. She found Christian sitting on a bench near the hammock where they had spent that first day in the garden together. Elaine could see that Christian was lost in thought and hadn't heard her approach.

She seemed troubled. Concern flashed over Elaine and she stepped closer. "I thought I might find you here."

Christian lifted her head and looked up at Elaine. Her skin was pale, her eyes unfocused.

"Oh, dear," Elaine said and came to Christian's side. "What is it, sweetheart?" Elaine suddenly realized that of all the time they had spent together comforting each other, Christian had never talked about the demons that haunted her. Now Elaine could see the pain as vividly as if it were alive and hovering over Christian like a menacing beast.

Christian didn't answer. She just returned to staring at her hands, lying limply in her lap.

Elaine sat down with Christian and placed her arm around her shoulders, pulling her head to her chest and rocking her gently. Elaine let the silence linger for a while longer before prodding further. "Christian. Talk to me, sweetheart."

Christian slowly raised her head and sighed. "I don't know how," she said, her voice hollow and defeated.

"Just start at the beginning. I find that is always easiest."

Christian took a deep breath and began her story. "A little over a year and a half ago, I was in a terrible car accident. My lover, Cara, was killed. Now, no matter how hard I try, I can't figure out how to go on living without her. She was so *amazing*. I thought we would grow old together. We would even talk about it and make jokes about being two old lesbians chasing each other around the old folks' home with our canes and wheelchairs. She was the life, love, laughter, and happiness of my world. She was my champion." Christian smiled weakly as she glanced at Elaine.

"I came to Willow Springs to try to figure out how to live in a world without Cara. The head injury I received in the crash left me with seizure-like spells. The fainting and the times I've seemed lost in my thoughts and almost unreachable are all the result of my injuries. I don't know how to trust myself in my work or doing most normal everyday things. Since coming here, I've been better. I've gotten stronger and the spells have receded."

"I'm so sorry. I didn't know."

"I know." Christian forced another smile. "I guess I thought if I came somewhere where no one knew my story, I could figure out how to start over and put the pain in the past."

"So, what's happened?" Elaine's voice was soft and gentle as she encouraged Christian to keep talking.

"Alex happened." Christian let out a long breath and her shoulders slumped.

"Alex?" Elaine asked, trying to put the pieces together.

"During all the years I knew Cara and even since the accident, I've never wanted another woman. Alex stirs feelings in me that I thought I'd never feel again."

Understanding began to surface as Elaine thought about the years without Chacey and her lack of connection with another woman in all that time. Although she'd felt she could not be with Chacey, she had wanted to be faithful to the love she still had for her. "But there's more, isn't there," she said knowingly.

Christian nodded. "I still love Cara. I miss her every day. I feel like I'm betraying her if I allow these feelings for Alex." Her tears fell freely. "I don't think I deserve to have someone love me. I should have died that day."

"Oh, sweetheart," Elaine whispered, taking Christian into her arms again. "You didn't leave Cara. You haven't betrayed her. And I'm sure that she would never have left you, given a choice. A love like that is a rare and special gift. If you had spent fifty years together, it wouldn't have been long enough to outlive that love."

Christian sighed. "No."

"So, what do you think Cara would say to you right now if she could tell you what to do?"

Christian was quiet for a while before answering. "I'm not sure."

"Well, maybe you should ask. Put yourself in her place, knowing how much you loved her. What would you say if it were you?"

After a long silence, Elaine spoke again. "I loved Chacey so much that I'd have sacrificed myself for her. I became so caught up in seeing the situation from my point of view that I wouldn't look at it any other way. By trying to protect her, I hurt her. My refusal to give up that control cost me precious time and almost cost me the person I love. It sounds like you're only looking at your situation from the point of losing Cara. But what was all the time you spent together about? Don't do what I did. Open your heart to the different possibilities."

Christian remained quiet for a long time. Elaine sat thinking about her own revelation. She had only been seeing her situation from one point of view. She too had to open herself to more possibilities. A thought struck her. She had created the fear that trapped her memories in her mind. She had to start seeing the problem from a different point of view. And this time she wouldn't do it alone.

❖

Chacey grabbed the phone on the first ring, her heart in her throat. "Special Agent Bristol speaking."

"Hi, Chacey," a cheerful male voice said over the line. "How's it going?"

Chacey pushed out a sigh of relief at hearing Joey's voice. "Hi, Joey. Things here are good. Is everything good with the house? Is Miss Priss giving Charley a hard time?"

Joey laughed. "No, things here have been great. I just wanted to check in and see how your trip is going. You know, you left in a bit of a hurry, and I thought maybe that special project you've been working on finally came through."

Chacey smiled. She loved Joey. He always looked out for her, and she appreciated his faithful confidence. "Something along those lines, yes." Chacey was smiling now, thinking of having Elaine back in her life. "I think some of the things I've been looking for are falling into place."

"Well hallelujah," Joey said. "I'm happy as hell to hear that. So I guess that means you'll be out of town a few more days, then?"

Chacey thought about her answer and didn't know what she expected with Elaine at this point. "I'll have to let you know, Joey. I have a lot to work out before I'll know what my plans are. I'll get back to you in a few days. Will that be okay? Seriously, is Miss Priss tormenting Charley?"

Charley was Joey's cat, a monster of a feline, weighing in at about twenty pounds. He and Miss Priss had not had a pleasant history. Upon their first meeting, Miss Priss had pounced on Charley's back, bitten a chunk out of his left ear, and taken his favorite sleep pillow. Charley had never forgiven the small intruder and had set out to ambush Miss Priss every time he found her asleep. The result was an all-out war.

"No, no. Nothing like that—they're actually getting along this time. I think Miss Priss feels a little bad about the last time they had a sleepover and has been making it up to him. But there is one thing you could do for me."

Chacey was mystified. What would Joey need her to do in Tennessee? "Okay. What is it?"

Joey was hesitant and then blurted, "Can you get that crazy bitch Karen to stop calling me? She's been hounding me ever since you left, trying to get information about why you left town. Seriously, that woman is not right in the head. You sure she's not an ex-girlfriend?"

Chacey laughed. "I'm sure. I'll see what I can do, Joey. I'm sorry she's been pestering you. I know she can be a bit…persistent."

"Persistent, hell! I thought she was going to come over here and look under the bed and make sure you weren't hiding there. I have these images of being under a bright light in an interrogation room like in the old cop movies. You know I don't like her anyway. She's like a bad rash that just won't go away. And the whining—really, I think my ears are bleeding."

Chacey was laughing so hard she was holding her side now. "Okay, okay. I'll talk to her. I wouldn't want big, burly, two-hundred-pound Joey being afraid of little, girly, one-hundred-ten-pound Karen."

"Very funny," Joey huffed. "You know you avoid her half the time too."

"Yeah. You're right. Thanks again for all your help, Joey."

"No problem. Good luck, Chacey. I've got my fingers crossed for you."

"Thanks. I'll talk to you in a couple of days."

Chacey was smiling as the call ended. She had good friends. Heaving a deep sigh, she dialed Karen's number. She suspected she'd regret it, but a promise to a friend was a promise.

"Chacey, sweetie. Oh my gosh! I'm so glad you called! I've been worried sick about you! Where are you?" Karen's voice was shrill, and Chacey wondered if she would take a break from Twenty Questions long enough for her to answer.

Hearing Karen pause for a breath, Chacey cut in, "Hello, Karen."

After ten minutes of nonstop prattle, Chacey was tired of the questions. "Look, Karen. I'm not telling you where I am. Joey doesn't know either, so you don't have to try to pull it out of him. You really don't have to worry about anything. I'm fine, the house is fine, the cat is fine, and I'll see you when I get home."

Karen's voice came back hurt and whiny. "You're upset with me."

"No. Karen, listen to me. I appreciate your concern, really. But I just need you to back off a little."

"Okay, sweetie. Just be safe out there and come back soon." Karen's voice still seemed small and wounded, making Chacey feel guilty for hurting her feelings.

"I will. Take care." Chacey ended the call and fell onto the bed. She couldn't wait to see Elaine again.

CHAPTER TWENTY-ONE

Elaine brought the wineglass to her lips and savored the sweet blend of fruit and wood. Chacey sat across from her at the small hotel bar, her fingers gently massaging the back of Elaine's hand. The touch was soothing as Elaine explained that she had been participating in therapy and was undergoing hypnotherapy to regain her memory of the shooting. She wanted Chacey to know she hadn't stopped trying, that she hadn't just run away to hide. She was trying to find out who had done this to them.

"So you still can't remember what happened?" Chacey's face seemed neutral, but Elaine could see the pain and desperation hiding in her eyes.

"No. I still can't remember who shot me. I've reached the point where I open the door, but my subconscious still won't allow me to see the face of the woman standing there."

Chacey jerked back as if stunned. "Did you just say *a woman* shot you?"

"Yes. That bit of revelation came in my last session, just before I called you. But the most disturbing part is that it had to be someone I know based on my reaction to her when I opened the door." Elaine could practically see the wheels spinning in Chacey's mind and gripped her hand. "Chacey?" Elaine was concerned. She couldn't figure out what was upsetting Chacey so. "What is it? Are you okay?"

Chacey took a deep shuddering breath. "I guess part of me always feared it had been Charles. I thought I'd brought this on you. I thought he hurt you to get to me."

Elaine understood. This was why Chacey blamed herself. "Oh, Chacey. Baby. I may not know who the shooter was, but I know in my heart and soul that you're not to blame. Honestly, I always feared it was him too, but now I'm confident it wasn't."

Chacey slumped in her chair for a moment before regaining her composure. She felt as if a toxic presence had been drawn out of her body. If Charles wasn't the shooter, then she wasn't responsible for what had happened. She was free. She could let go of her guilt. Chacey's thoughts shifted from relief to determination. If it was a woman, the FBI needed to change the focus of the investigation. Chacey was in work mode now and her thoughts were racing. "Well, that gives us more to go on. The original profile said it was likely a man. We may have overlooked details. I'll need to—"

"Chacey." Elaine's voice was soft, but Chacey immediately looked at her, stopping in midsentence. "Not now. Please, not now. I can't go through this again. I just need a little more time." Elaine's eyes were pleading, and Chacey could feel Elaine's fear radiating off her.

"I'm sorry, love. I didn't mean to get carried away. I just want to make sure that freak can never hurt you again." She needed to do something, anything, to stop this.

"I know. But I'm only just beginning to remember. I'm afraid that if I push too hard or the stress becomes too great, my subconscious will shut down and the memory will be lost. Just give me a little more time."

Chacey relented. Here was the woman she'd loved and lost and found again. She had spent the last three years searching for the person responsible for the shooting. If it meant keeping Elaine with her, she could wait a little longer to find the UNSUB. Right now, she wanted to be with Elaine—to know everything she had been through and to be there for whatever lay ahead. "Okay. We'll do this your way. Anything you need."

Elaine's long, willowy legs wrapped around Chacey's ankles under the table. "Right now, all I need is you."

Chacey felt the world melt away, and nothing else mattered but Elaine. The memory of Elaine lying naked on top of her made her skin grow hot, and she knew she was blushing.

"Hmm," Elaine muttered. "I'd like to know what that thought was all about."

Chacey raised an eyebrow and smiled at Elaine. "Fond memories and new hopes," she said, drawing Elaine's fingers to her lips.

Elaine recalled her conversation with Christian earlier in the garden. She studied Chacey's face and let her eyes roam the contours of Chacey's body. She had lost three years of loving this woman, and she wasn't going to waste another moment. "Chace, take me to your room."

"What about dinner? Are you still hungry?"

"Yes," Elaine said with a grin, "but if we want, we can have food delivered to the room. I think what I have in mind requires a little privacy."

She followed Chacey into the room and heard her stop to close the door behind them, but Elaine kept walking until she was next to the bed. She turned to face Chacey, her hand clutching her blouse tightly. She was afraid of what Chacey would think when she revealed herself.

"What is it, darling?" Chacey placed her hand over Elaine's and gently pulled her fingers free, pulling them tenderly to her face.

Elaine swallowed. "I don't look the same. The scars are…" She could hear her voice shake as she spoke. She couldn't bear the thought of Chacey rejecting her, of Chacey turning her face away in disgust.

"The scars are part of you. They tell the story of the fight you fought, the journey you have traveled. I'll hate the pain you felt, but I'll love every inch of you." Chacey stepped back from Elaine and began to unbutton her own shirt. The fabric fell from her shoulders, revealing a firmly muscled chest and arms. She pulled the straps of her bra down and deftly snapped its clasp open, allowing it to fall, freeing her breasts. Her eyes never left Elaine as she paused, as if inviting Elaine to study her body.

Elaine was transfixed by the vision standing before her. She let her eyes drift across the curve of Chacey's shoulders, the delicate protrusion of her collarbones, and the soft swell of her breasts. She knew she had never beheld anything more beautiful in her life. Slowly Elaine reached out and touched the skin just above Chacey's left breast, feeling her heartbeat against her palm. The thrill ignited a thirst deep within her.

Chacey undid the button of her jeans, hooked her thumbs in the waistband, and slowly slid them, along with her black lace panties, down the curve of her hips to her ankles, where she finally stepped out and tossed them aside. Chacey stood there naked and exposed to Elaine. She could feel Elaine's gaze on her newly exposed flesh, and she wanted her touch. She craved to have Elaine's hands on her everywhere, but she knew to go slow. They were just discovering each other again, and she wanted to enjoy every moment of the journey.

She took Elaine's free hand and placed it on her waist. Her hands then found the buttons of Elaine's slacks and tugged until they were open and hung loosely on her narrow hips. Sliding her hands beneath the fabric, she caressed Elaine's smooth thighs and firm buttocks. Slowly, she guided Elaine out of her pants and turned to place them across the back of a chair. Then she began to work on the buttons of Elaine's shirt.

Feeling Elaine stiffen slightly, she leaned close and kissed along her neck. Elaine's head fell back exposing the delicate skin in offering. Chacey felt like she was opening a precious gift, finding a lost treasure. She pushed the shirt open and guided it over Elaine's shoulders. Again, she took great care in putting the clothing aside before returning her attention to Elaine. She guided Elaine back onto the bed and slid over her like a blanket, their breasts pressing against each other, softness on softness.

Chacey's skin tingled everywhere they touched. She explored every inch of Elaine's body as she had promised. She tenderly kissed her face and chin, lingering on her lips to savor the taste of her. Her hands slid along the tender flesh of her breasts and down her sides. When her fingers found the dip in Elaine's lower abdomen, she took a long time touching the foreign landscape, learning the feel of it, the shape of it. Her heart ached, knowing it was a symbol of the pain Elaine had felt. A reminder that things were irrevocably changed. She pushed the pain away and focused on loving the strength of the woman in her arms. Her lips played along Elaine's neck and down to her chest, again finding a jagged, angry scar where a bullet had pierced her lover's skin. She kissed the puckered, gnarled mark, running her tongue along the edges and rubbing her face against the roughened skin.

Chacey raised her head and looked into Elaine's eyes as they searched hers for any hint of disgust, discomfort, or rejection. Chacey knew there was none. She knew all Elaine could see behind her eyes was love and longing.

"You're even more beautiful than I remembered," Chacey whispered, her lips brushing Elaine's with warm breath. She felt some of the tension dissolve as Elaine relaxed against her. She wanted to show Elaine the depth of her love for her. She wanted to join their bodies and chase away all the doubt and fear she had seen in Elaine's eyes.

Chacey felt the moment when Elaine opened herself to her. Pressing against Elaine, she pushed between her legs and ran a hand along the inside of her thigh as she took her breast into her mouth. Elaine's body rose and her ankle wrapped around Chacey's leg and pressed, encouraging her closer. Elaine's hands played in her hair and her nails scraped along her back, and Chacey moaned as she pulsed in time with her heartbeat. She gloried in the feel of Elaine's skin, the softness of her breasts, the subtle changes in her breathing, and the tender sounds evoked through each touch.

Making her way down the length of Elaine's body, Chacey kissed and licked the tender skin, making Elaine writhe with want. Joy filled her when Elaine moaned against her, her breathing heavy, her hands pressed into her skin. This was everything she would ever need. She kissed the length of the scar that ran the length of Elaine's stomach, bisecting her navel, where the surgeons had cut her to repair the damage from the bullet that had torn through her body. She flowered the scar with kisses and strokes of her tongue, claiming this new part of her lover. She gently made her way down Elaine's body. Her head moved to the triangle that pointed the way to the center of the universe.

Chacey's lips caressed the tender flesh, her tongue parting the lips to expose the exquisite wetness. Chacey closed her lips around the tender folds, sucking and pulling, then licking and sucking some more, relishing the scent and the taste of her. Her fingers played at the opening of Elaine's sex, waiting for the moment when Elaine would need her inside.

Just as Elaine felt she was about to explode with pleasure, she pushed Chacey's face away. "Come here, sweetheart. I need to feel you too." She wanted to see the look in Chacey's eyes as they touched.

Chacey lifted herself, kissing her way back up and supporting herself on her elbow. Elaine reached her hand between them and pressed against the mound between Chacey's legs. The heat poured into her palm, and she could tell that Chacey was ready. Pressing two fingers between the slick, wet folds, she felt her heart break with the love she held for Chacey.

"I want you inside me," Elaine said, her breath fast and heavy now as she pushed her pelvis up to meet Chacey's touch. She slid her own fingers slowly into Chacey's opening and felt the muscles tighten around her. They rocked against each other slowly, allowing the pressure to build until neither could hold any more.

Chacey's breath was ragged against her ear, sending waves of sensation through Elaine's body. Her skin thrummed with ecstasy. "Now, baby. I want…I'm right there…I want to feel you—" Her words were cut off as her body shuddered, rocking into Chacey, pushing her deeper inside her. An explosion erupted at her center and moved through her like a tidal wave, and she cried out from the intensity of her orgasm. Then Chacey clamped down on her hand, and Elaine felt muscles ripple and shudder, tightening around her fingers.

Their bodies finally still, Elaine slipped her hand out of Chacey and wrapped her arms around her. The last thing she remembered was the feel of Chacey's body blanketing her with softness, her hand still between her legs, cupping her.

Elaine pressed her cheek into Chacey's hair and breathed in the scent of her, relishing the ecstasy.

❖

Chacey woke to the sound of the shower running. She blinked, trying to clear the sleep from her eyes. As she moved, she could feel her nakedness against the sheets, and the thought of Elaine's body against hers sent new waves of want to her center. Being with Elaine had been fulfilling, exciting, healing. She threw back the covers and made her way to the bathroom. Even this short distance between them was too much. She had to see Elaine, touch her, relish just being in the same room with her.

"Good morning, sweetheart," she announced as she entered the bathroom.

"Ah…you're awake." Elaine's voice coming from the shower sounded light this morning, and Chacey's heart soared.

Chacey stepped into the shower and said, "I thought I'd join you."

Elaine turned away from her. Chacey saw her hand quickly cover the scar on her abdomen and knew Elaine was still self-conscious about her scars. Chacey slid her hands around Elaine's middle and pressed her body firmly against her. Her hand found Elaine's breasts as she placed tender kisses along her shoulder. She felt Elaine relax against her, and all protest fled, to be replaced with pleasure.

Chacey turned Elaine to face her, skimming her hands along her breasts as the water cascaded down her body and ran from her erect nipples. Chacey took in the angry red scars that marked Elaine's body and found her own anger simmering below the surface. Someone had done this to her. Someone had purposefully hurt her and left her to die. How could anyone want to hurt someone so precious?

Chacey stepped into Elaine, sliding their wet bodies together and rubbing her thigh between Elaine's legs. Her lips found Elaine and she explored her mouth thoroughly, sucking her tongue, then pulling back to lick the supple swollen lips. Her hand slipped between Elaine's legs and she stroked her with her fingers.

"Chacey. If you keep doing that I'll have to have another shower."

Chacey dropped to her knees, pushing Elaine's legs apart, and pressed her face into the folds of her sex. This time, she held Elaine in her lips, her tongue playing along the stiff shaft of her clitoris until she felt Elaine twitch and rock against her face. She slid her hand into the slick opening, her other hand braced behind Elaine to keep her upright as she worked her with her tongue and fingers.

Elaine cried out as the first wave of orgasm pulsed through her. Her legs were trembling, and she rocked against Chacey's face with each spasm of orgasm. Chacey held her firmly and continued the attention on her clitoris until the last ripples of her pleasure subsided. Chacey kissed her once more tenderly before extracting herself from the sweet folds. She stood and took Elaine in her arms again, brushing strands of wet hair from her face.

"Mmm," Chacey murmured. "That's better. How do you feel?"

"Whole," Elaine answered. "A piece of my heart has been returned to me and I'm whole again."

❖

Christian let the pen fall from her fingers. She had been staring at the blank page for an hour, trying to write. Thoughts of the night Cara died kept playing over and over in her mind. They had dined at Cara's favorite sushi restaurant and walked through the small park, viewing various sculptures that were part of a special production of Art in the Park. Christian had bought her flowers from a street vendor, and they'd stopped to watch the sun set over the river. The memory was so vivid she could almost feel her arms wrapped around Cara's body as they stood watching the water. Everything had been so perfect, another perfect evening in their perfect lives. How had it all gone so terribly wrong?

Christian had been driving. During the ride, Cara's fingers had played in Christian's hair along her ear, making Christian's skin break out in gooseflesh. Cara had told a story from her childhood that had made Christian laugh. There had been a loud boom, and sparks flew from under a truck heading straight for them. Cara's scream lingered in her ears.

Christian shook herself. *No. I won't remember you this way. Elaine was right. I'm only remembering from the point of losing you.* She knew she was holding on to something that didn't exist anymore. She had to stop trying to make sense of something that had no reasoning. It was just a freak accident. But she understood that part. The thing she couldn't get past was how she was supposed to go on. Elaine had asked her what Cara would do, what she would say if their positions were reversed. What would she say if she could answer the haunting question? Christian tried to imagine, but she just couldn't see it.

And then Christian picked up her pen and began to write. *Dearest Cara...*

CHAPTER TWENTY-TWO

Alex saw Hannah smile as she stepped into the lobby. "Wow, this must be a record—this makes three days this week I've seen you around here."

"Are you saying you're getting sick of me?"

Hannah laughed. "Oh no. Quite the contrary. You seem to have an uplifting effect on the guests. And I'll admit, I kind of like having you around. Let me guess…you're looking for Christian."

"You would be correct. Have you seen her around?"

Hannah's smile faltered. "I'm sorry, Alex. She left a couple of hours ago. She said something about needing to do something in town. She didn't say when she planned to be back."

Alex leaned her shoulder against the wood column and rapped her knuckles against her thigh to cover her disappointment. "Well, that's okay. I have some work to get done anyway. If you see her, will you tell her I stopped by?"

"Of course."

She turned to leave, but Hannah stopped her. "Alex? Would you mind if we talked for a few minutes?"

Alex frowned. Something in Hannah's voice was off. "Is there something wrong?"

"In private would be best, I think." Hannah took Alex by the arm and led her outside, where they walked among the giant oak trees. Alex waited patiently for Hannah to tell her what was going on, but she was about to demand that Hannah tell her when Hannah stopped and faced her.

"Are you serious about Christian or is this just a summer hookup?" Hannah's face was blank, but Alex could feel her eyes boring into her as if searching her soul.

"What? Hannah, I don't think I should be talking with you about this. It's between me and Christian." Alex rubbed her face with her hand and turned away from Hannah, her frustration teetering on the verge of anger.

"Please answer the question, Alex. I need you to tell me. It makes a difference."

There was something in Hannah's voice now that made Alex turn back to her and step into her personal space. "You know something about Christian, don't you? There's something you're not telling me."

Hannah held her ground. "Do you care about her?"

Alex ground her teeth and stared into Hannah's eyes. She rubbed her hands against her jeans nervously. Alex knew it was Christian she should be telling her feelings to, not Hannah. But Hannah obviously knew something, something it was critical for her to know, and she would not share until she was certain of Alex's feelings.

Something in Alex broke, and she took a deep breath and then another before meeting Hannah's gaze square on again. "Yes. Of course I care about her."

"Good. She needs you. I don't think she realizes it yet, but she needs you."

"What are you talking about, Hannah?"

"Christian came down this afternoon and asked that I keep an eye on her things for her for a couple of days. She had me call a taxi, and she made arrangements to be taken to the airport. She said she wasn't certain how long she would be gone. I could tell she had been crying. When I asked if she was okay, she said she was, but that she had some things she needed to take care of that she had been putting off. I asked where she was going. She looked at me for a few minutes as if she didn't know the answer, and then she simply said she was going home."

Alex didn't know what to think about this revelation. She didn't even know where Christian lived. Even if she could pursue her, she wouldn't know where to look.

Hannah placed a hand on Alex's shoulder. "There's something else. She wanted me to give you a message if you came looking for her."

Alex felt like shaking Hannah at this point. Hannah reached in her back pocket, pulled out a small white envelope, and handed it to Alex, who looked at it as if the paper might spontaneously combust. After a moment she took the envelope from Hannah. "Thank you."

Hannah squeezed Alex's arm, then left her alone with Christian's words.

My sweet Alex,

Forgive me for leaving so suddenly. I knew if I tried to tell you, I wouldn't be able to go through with this. I hope to only be gone a few days, but I'm uncertain what I'll find among my memories. My broken past won't allow me to be the woman you need. You said you wanted me to be sure before anything happened between us. I've thought about that and realized it's time to stop running. If I'm ever going to be able to love you the way you deserve to be loved, I have to go away for a while. I'm sorry.

You've made me feel alive in a way I never dreamed possible. Thank you. These weeks with you have meant more to me than you can ever know. Perhaps, when I return, I'll have the answers to the questions.

All my love,
Christian

Alex read the letter through three times, trying to make sense of it all. Then the realization hit her. She sighed heavily as all the air was pushed from her lungs. Christian was gone.

❖

Christian clutched her shoulder bag as the plane touched down in New Orleans. A sickening feeling gripped her stomach the closer she came to the city she used to call home. The Cities of the Dead.

Not stopping for fear of losing her resolve, she hailed a cab. "Cypress Grove Cemetery, please, City Park Avenue." Christian closed the door as the cab pulled away from the curb.

The cabbie studied her through the rearview mirror. "You're not here for the tour of the dead, are you? Your journey has been long to find this place, no?"

Christian stared out the window as the familiar buildings flashed by. She didn't answer.

"Ah well, sometimes the dead hold the answers the living cannot find. I hope you find your answers."

The driver stopped at the entrance to the cemetery. Christian gazed at the ominous gate looming above her. She had been here many times with Cara when they would visit the family tomb. She had never imagined she would be here to see Cara.

"I will wait here for you. Go find your peace."

Christian met the man's eyes for the first time, seeing his compassion for her and understanding of her pain reflected in his gaze. She nodded and stepped out of the car. The door shut with a dull thud behind her.

The path through the cemetery was lined with rows of crypts that had stood in this place for a century. Some of the plots were surrounded with iron fencing and little gates. Cara had always thought it funny to put up a fence around a tomb. *Are they trying to keep the dead in or the living out?* Cara had asked on one of their visits. Cara had always loved to visit the cemeteries and learn about the history stored among the dead.

Without realizing how long she had been standing there, Christian found herself before a modest crypt. The white marble showed stains from years of pollution exposure. An angel stood on top of the structure looking down at her with pity, its arms outstretched as if welcoming her into an embrace. She ran her hand across the newly inscribed name of the woman she loved.

"Hello, my love." Christian leaned in, kissed the name, and brushed her fingers across the letters as if she could somehow feel Cara there. The stone was cold. Christian pulled a letter from her bag and held it in her trembling hand. She opened the envelope and began to read.

Christian stood there and poured her heart and her grief out before the grave of her lover, her words stricken and hollow. When she finished the letter, she closed her eyes and pressed her hand to the cold stone. Her heart ached. Her legs felt weak and her feet heavy.

When she had no more tears to shed, she lifted her lips once more to the beloved name that rested beneath her fingertips. "I love you," she whispered, as if her words could travel beyond this cold, hard barrier into a world where Cara could feel her embrace.

❖

"Hello, this is Christian Sutter. May I speak with Joshua Pierce, please?" Christian waited on the line for the call to go through.

The sweet voice of her law partner came on the line only moments later. "Christian? Is that really you?"

"Hi, Josh. How's the practice treating you?"

"God, Christian. Where the hell have you been? Of course things are good here, no need to worry, but we've all been frantic trying to figure out where you disappeared to."

"Sorry about that, Josh. I know I've made this hard on everyone, but I need to ask a favor." Christian waited for Josh to gather himself from his shock. He had always been a little melodramatic.

"Sure thing, sugar. What can I do for you?"

"I need you to contact Howard Lewis and get the final information about Cara's estate. I'll be at the condo when the paperwork is ready."

"Uh, okay." Josh seemed hesitant. "Are you sure you're ready for this, Christian? Can I at least come by and just be there with you? I mean, you haven't been back to the house since the accident."

"Thanks, Josh, but no. This is something I need to do on my own. I can't move forward until I take care of the past." She knew it would be hard to go back to the condo, but she was here and she wasn't going to turn back now. And it was something she had to do alone.

"Okay. Consider it done. I'll get back to you with the details. And, Christian…it's really good to hear your voice. We've all missed you."

"Thanks, Josh."

❖

Elaine brushed her hand along the sharp cut of Chacey's jaw. "Are you sure you want to do this?"

Chacey glanced at Elaine, the smile quirking the corner of her mouth. "I want to do whatever I can to help you through this. The more you remember, the closer we are to figuring this out. Are you worried about me being there?"

Elaine had to admit that having Chacey come to her therapy appointment was a little unnerving. "I'm a little anxious, that's all."

Dr. Cook was waiting for them when they arrived at the office. Elaine had called and informed her the day before that Chacey was in town and might be accompanying her to the session.

"Hello, Elaine. It's good to see you again. And you must be Chacey." Dr. Cook extended her hand to her in greeting, and they shook hands. "I was wondering if I might have a few moments alone with Chacey, Elaine. Would you mind?"

Elaine was shocked. She had expected Helen to involve Chacey in the session but hadn't anticipated the separation. Elaine's shoulders tensed and her back stiffened.

"I only want to get some details about the incident without having to drag you through those particulars. If you would prefer to be present, I don't have to meet with her alone. Whatever makes you more comfortable, Elaine."

Elaine glanced from Dr. Cook to Chacey. She tried to relax, but the sudden rush of fear was not easily overcome. But she trusted them both. She took a deep breath and said, "I think I'll be okay." Chacey's hand rested on her arm in support and her eyes were dark with concern. "It's okay, Chacey, you can go. I'll wait for you here."

Elaine imagined the questions she'd be asking if this were one of her cases. She knew Dr. Cook couldn't share information with Chacey without her permission, so she figured they had to be talking about the investigation into the shooting. She knew Chacey was familiar with every detail of the case but wondered if she was ready to hear it from Elaine's point of view. She couldn't imagine what this was like for Chacey. What would she have done if Chacey had been the one harmed? The thought made her stomach churn and she shivered. She shifted uncomfortably. The lobby suddenly felt too open, too exposed, and she looked around anxiously, then she settled her attention on the entrance.

When Dr. Cook came back to get her five minutes later, Elaine relaxed in relief. Dr. Cook's expression was neutral as she held out a hand, inviting her to come inside. Elaine found her place on the sofa next to Chacey and sank into the comfort of her welcoming warmth.

"I'm sorry to have kept you waiting, Elaine. I know that must have been uncomfortable for you. I've gone over the list of names of the people that were present in the building the day of the shooting and some of the difficulties the authorities have had in identifying the shooter. I have not disclosed any information gathered through our sessions. Okay?"

Elaine nodded.

"Do you have any questions?"

Elaine shook her head. "No." Glancing at Chacey, she took her hand and cupped it in both of hers in her lap.

Dr. Cook looked to Elaine. "I'm glad to see things are working out between you. How have you been sleeping since Chacey has returned? Any more dreams?"

"No, not that I'm recalling."

Chacey squeezed her hand and looked at her. "Sometimes when you're sleeping, you seem like you're fighting or running or something. You don't say anything, just whimper, and your body tenses." Chacey turned to Dr. Cook. "Does that help?"

"Yes. It's what I expected. Thank you. Elaine, I'd like to try a different approach today. Are you okay with proceeding with the hypnosis with Chacey present?"

"Yes."

"Okay then, let's get to it. Chacey, I need you to come sit in this chair. I need you to be very quiet and just observe what's happening. I'll guide Elaine, and if I feel she is too distressed, I'll change the direction of our exploration or I'll bring her back to the present. It's important that you not interrupt, no matter what you feel or hear. Understand?"

Chacey moved to the chair Dr. Cook indicated. "I understand."

Dr. Cook went through the guided imagery that led Elaine into a state of relaxation, and Elaine described the events just before the shooting.

"I hear the elevator ding. Soft footsteps outside my door. A tentative knock, only two raps."

Chacey's heart hammered in her chest. She gripped the arms of her chair so tightly that her knuckles ached. She felt like she was there in that room with Elaine, waiting for the unimaginable to happen. Her mouth had gone dry and her throat felt like it was closing, but she sat stone still, watching Elaine with utter concentration.

"Okay, Elaine. I want you to go to the door. When you open the door, I want you to freeze the picture and describe the person you see."

Chacey marveled that Dr. Cook's voice had remained calm through the exercise but noted that her hands clutched the arms of her chair. Chacey leaned forward slightly, the anticipation like a drumbeat in her ears. She tried to hold still, and her lungs hurt from holding her breath.

Elaine's hand twitched and her brow creased.

"Focus only on the clothing for now, Elaine. The person is of no consequence. We are simply going to talk about her clothes."

"She's wearing a red dress, dark red, not the bright color of lipstick. Her shoes are black with a two-inch heel. They're shiny."

"Very good, Elaine. That is very good. Now, tell me about her jewelry. What do you see?"

"A gold watch, small and dainty. A gold chain is about her neck, with a black tear-shaped stone in the center of a pendant. Earrings dangle from her ears—gold with black stones, like the necklace. There's something silver in her hand."

Chacey tensed. She knew Elaine was seeing the gun. She was relieved when Dr. Cook quickly changed the direction of Elaine's attention.

"How about her hair, Elaine. Describe her hair to me."

"Hmm. Simple. Brown. Shoulder length, and the sides are pulled back by some sort of clasp."

"That's very good, Elaine. You've done very well. Now, I want you to look at the woman's face. Describe what you think of when you see her face."

Elaine was quiet for a while, and Chacey was afraid something was wrong. Her heart beat wildly in her chest. She wanted to scream out, *Who is it?* She bit her tongue until she was afraid blood would fill her mouth.

"I can't." Elaine's features tensed.

Dr. Cook leaned forward. "It's okay, Elaine. You're safe. You feel very relaxed."

After a moment, Elaine relaxed into her seat, but her brow remained furrowed.

"Tell me what else you're experiencing right now, Elaine. What do you smell? What do you hear?"

"She's talking to me. Her voice is angry."

"What is she saying?"

Elaine could see the woman standing in front of her, but her face seemed blurred. Every time Elaine tried to look at her, all she could see were her eyes, angry and fierce. Elaine wondered what she could have done to make the woman so angry. Her voice was harsh and she spit words at Elaine with hatred. But her voice seemed garbled, as if Elaine were watching a movie and the sound was on the wrong speed.

"She's gone, you bitch. You sent her away. Well, you can't have her! She's mine! I won't let you take her from me. You left me no choice. This is all your fault. I can't let you come between us any longer. She loves me! I'll never let you have her!"

"She thinks I sent someone away. Something about me coming between her and someone else." Elaine paused, studying, listening. She didn't like the woman. The yelling was scaring her, and she wanted the woman to leave.

The woman raised her hand, pointing the shiny object at her. Confusion and fear muddled Elaine's reflexes. She tried to raise her hand in front of her face and pushed hard on the door to close the woman out.

The shot exploded. Elaine's ears rang with the blast. Fire pierced her shoulder, and she felt herself falling. Another shot exploded, and again the fire came, this time tearing through her side.

Elaine began to shake. She wanted to escape, she *had* to get away. But the pain was too much. In the distance, she heard Dr. Cook's voice calling to her. Elaine felt herself shift, and then she was sitting in a garden, roses were everywhere. The fear and the pain slowly slipped away. She followed the sound of Dr. Cook's voice until she became aware that she was in Dr. Cook's office. When she opened her eyes, Chacey was kneeling on the floor in front of her. Tears rimmed her eyes, and her hands grasped Elaine's arms.

Dr. Cook's voice cut through the tension, and Chacey moved to settle herself next to Elaine. "What happened, Elaine? What did you remember?"

Elaine nestled into Chacey and looked to Dr. Cook. "I remembered the shooting, but her face was still foggy. I can't make out who it was. Her voice was garbled and difficult to understand." Elaine took a shuddering breath. "She was angry with me. She thought I had taken someone from her, or made them leave…I don't know. It doesn't make any sense."

Chacey's arms tightened around Elaine's shoulders and she kissed her hair. "We have a description now. We can go back and try to find someone that fits that general appearance. Someone is bound to recognize this woman."

Elaine looked into Chacey's eyes. She hesitated, the familiar resistance beginning to build. But seeing the determination in Chacey's eyes and her fierce need to find the shooter, Elaine relented. She nodded. "Okay."

CHAPTER TWENTY-THREE

Christian stood outside the door to her condo, the key hovering just before the lock. A chill ran down the length of her spine and she shivered. Taking a deep breath, she pushed the key into the lock and turned.

The room was as they had left it. Someone, the cleaning lady she presumed, had kept the room clear of dust during her absence, but otherwise nothing seemed out of place. The room seemed stale, the air telling of the lack of habitation.

Christian walked around the room, looking at the pictures that hung on the walls and sat on tables and told the story of a happy life. The memory of Cara was everywhere. Her jacket hung on the peg by the door. Her favorite running shoes, tossed haphazardly next to a chair in the living room. The book she had been reading, lying unfinished on the coffee table, the bookmark patiently holding her page. And her smiling face beaming from the pictures. Christian half expected to hear her voice down the hall, or her laughter ringing out from some silly story she had heard.

Christian made her way to the bedroom where they had made love that night before going out. Cara had teased her about making them late and then had taken her so thoroughly that they barely made their reservation. She ran her fingers along the satin coverlet that lay folded neatly at the end of the bed, drawing up the feel of Cara's skin lingering in the memory of her fingertips.

Christian was there for hours, slowly sifting through the memories of her life. She opened a bottle of wine and retreated to the balcony to watch the sunset as they always had when the weather was warm enough. She watched the play of colors dance across the sky and marveled at the beauty.

She missed Cara, but somehow she had grown used to the silence, and she didn't feel quite as alone as she'd anticipated. Another memory flashed through her mind, a memory of sitting on a porch surrounded by trees overlooking a lake, watching the same sun setting on a different view.

Christian smiled to herself. It seemed only fitting that she think of Alex here in the world she shared with Cara, when it had been Cara she was thinking of that night with Alex. She drew her knee up and laid her head back against the soft fabric of the lounge chair, thinking of how her life had turned out.

A buzzing sound penetrated Christian's thoughts, and after a moment, she realized someone was ringing the doorbell. She slowly made her way through the living room, her bare feet padding softly on the hardwood floor.

Peering through the peephole, she recognized the round face and plump form standing outside. Christian opened the door, surprised to see the gentle old man so late in the day.

"Mr. Lewis, I wasn't expecting you this evening."

"Good evening, dear." Mr. Lewis had known Cara her entire life, having worked as her family's attorney for many years. "I hope I'm not interrupting. I just…when Josh called…I thought it best that I deliver the information you requested in person."

"Thank you, Mr. Lewis. Would you please come in? I'm afraid I don't have much to offer you since I haven't had an opportunity to have any food brought in. I can offer you a glass of wine, though."

Mr. Lewis stepped into the room and shut the door gingerly. "No, thank you, dear. Tell me, how have you been?"

Christian warmed at the kindness she saw in the old eyes. She dropped her gaze a moment and then replied softly. "It hasn't been easy. Some days, I…" Christian faltered. "I guess I'm doing okay."

Sitting in the chair facing Christian, Mr. Lewis took a large manila envelope from his briefcase and handed it to her. "These are the final papers detailing the disposition of the will. Everything has been left to you, of course. The family has not contested the will, and there are no further issues to address."

Christian nodded, not surprised by the news. She and Cara had discussed their wills at length.

Mr. Lewis studied Christian for a moment before adding, "There is one final matter."

Christian looked to Mr. Lewis, confused. What else could there be?

He reached into his briefcase again and drew out a smaller envelope. As he handed it to Christian, she recognized Cara's delicate handwriting. The envelope was addressed to Christian. With it, he handed Christian a disc. "Cara came to my office about six months before the accident and gave me strict instructions that this disc and that letter were to be given to you in the event that she was to precede you in death. I'm sorry I've been unable to meet that final request until this time. I understood the delicacy of your own recovery and hope this is the proper time to fulfill my final obligation to my dear Cara."

Christian held the letter and the disc to her chest. She'd grown cold and the room seemed to dim. Mr. Lewis's soft voice seemed distant and she couldn't make out his words. Darkness fell upon her like a heavy blanket pulling her into a dream.

❖

"Christian? Chris…can you hear me, sweetheart? Come on, try to open your eyes." Rough fingers brushed at her face, and suddenly, she was warm again. Christian slowly opened her eyes. She was lying on her sofa. Mr. Lewis kneeled beside her, his suit coat draped over her. "Oh, thank you, Jesus. You're awake. Are you all right, dear? Can I get you something?"

Christian sat up. "I'm terribly sorry, Mr. Lewis. I…this just seems to happen sometimes."

"I understand. I'm glad you're okay. Damn near gave this old man a heart attack. Is there something I should do?" Mr. Lewis said, the fear evident in his voice.

"I'm okay now, Mr. Lewis. I'm sorry I startled you."

"Sweet child. I can't say I ever understood you two girls. But I can't say I've ever seen two people love each other the way you and Cara did. Her parents were fools for not seeing it." He rubbed his cheeks with his hand and sat back up in his chair. "That's what this is about, isn't it?"

Christian was surprised to hear Mr. Lewis speak so frankly. "What do you mean, Mr. Lewis?"

"I know you loved her, child. She loved you too. I've never seen a woman as happy as you made sweet Cara. I knew her since the day she was born. I was her godfather, you know. I felt like she was my own child. She would talk to me sometimes…about you. I guess she couldn't go to her parents, so I was the next best thing."

His eyes seemed to dim for a moment as if lost in a memory, and then Mr. Lewis looked at her again and sighed. "Your happiness was the most important thing in the world to Cara. She never told me what was on that disc or what was in that letter. But I hope whatever it is will help you."

"Thank you, Mr. Lewis."

He smiled warmly at Christian. "I think Howard will do now." He stood and straightened his vest and shirt sleeves.

Christian handed him back his suit coat.

"Call me if you need anything, Chris." He leaned in and kissed her forehead, his hand resting gently on her shoulder.

Christian wanted to throw her arms around him. She didn't want this wonderful man to leave. He had loved Cara too, and somehow that made her want to hold on to him as if his presence could somehow bring Cara back. She clutched his sleeve.

"I know it doesn't feel like it right now, but you're going to be fine—different, perhaps, but still okay. We have to go on." He lifted her chin as if she were a child and smiled down at her.

She could still see the pain in his eyes, but beyond that there seemed to be more. Hope, understanding, compassion? She wasn't sure, but it helped her gather her strength. She nodded and let him go.

She saw him to the door and turned to the letter and disc that lay waiting for her. Her stomach tightened into a fist, and she trembled with fear and anticipation and pain at the thought of one last connection with the woman she had lost.

❖

Alex sat by the lake on the bench where she knew Christian usually sat in the mornings to watch the sunrise. She looked for Christian every morning as she ran by the lake, and watched for her over the water from her porch as the sun set in the evenings. As long as there was no word from Christian to send her things and close her account at the lodge, Alex held hope.

Thoughts of Christian's body pressed against hers, the memory of her touch, their lips pressed hungrily together convinced Alex that Christian would return to her. She knew Christian loved her, but it was up to Christian to find her way through her grief and open herself up to that love.

Alex knew all about that. She had fought her feelings for Christian. The fear of losing someone again had seemed almost too much to bear. But then she would remember the sound of Christian's voice, her laugh, the way Christian looked at her when she thought she wasn't looking, and Alex knew everything was worth it.

She had wanted to go after Christian, find where she had gone and follow her there, but she knew this was something Christian had to do alone and no amount of talking or coaxing on her part would change anything. But she also knew how easy it was to become lost in the past. It was easy to create an illusion of what life had been. And she knew how consuming that could be. Illusions had no flaws and they made no mistakes, making it hard to see the truth.

She had loved Sophia with all her soul and had lost her. She knew Christian's pain. But she also knew that the pain was her reminder of the love she had. The pain kept Sophia's voice alive in her mind and heart. But she had let go of the illusion that Sophia was all she could ever have. She had to believe Christian would see that too and return to her. So she waited. There was nothing else she could do. Everything was up to Christian now.

Alex ran her hand along the smooth wood of the bench. What would she do if Christian didn't return? What would she do without her illusions if Christian was not there to fill the void? She shuddered at the thought. She stood and shook herself, trying to clear those unwanted thoughts. She still had hope.

CHAPTER TWENTY-FOUR

Chacey lay with her back propped on pillows against the headboard. Elaine was cradled between her legs, her head resting on Chacey's chest. Chacey held her phone in her right hand but had not yet dialed the number. "Are you ready for this?"

They had talked about this, but she wanted to be sure Elaine was ready before she contacted her partner. She had wanted to make the call as soon as they left Dr. Cook's office the day before, but Elaine had asked her to wait. They had spent the night talking about the investigation, and Elaine had insisted that Chacey not disclose that she was with her. Chacey would have felt more secure with full disclosure, but she knew how far Elaine had come and thought it unwise to push. She gave Elaine's shoulder a gentle squeeze. Elaine sighed and nodded her agreement.

Chacey dialed the number.

"Peterson here," a rough voice spat into the phone.

"Mike, it's Chacey. I need you to do me a favor."

"Chacey?" Mike's voice now held concern. "Where the hell are you? What's gotten up your skirt all of a sudden? It's not like you to just run off and not leave any indication where you're going or what the hell is going on."

"I'm sorry, Mike. Something came up. I took some personal time. I should've let you know, my bad, you can give me hell the next time you see me."

"Yeah, yeah, all right. What's up?"

"I need you to do something for me."

"All right." Mike sounded more amiable now. "What is it this time?"

Chacey tightened her arms around Elaine. "I need you to go back over the witness reports and descriptions from the Elaine Barber shooting."

"What for? You and I both have the damn things memorized. What do you think I'm going to find that we haven't already dug up? What am I looking for?"

"I have new information about the shooter. I can't explain in detail right now, but we have to change our direction. The shooter was a woman. All this time we concentrated on a male profile, but we were wrong."

"What the hell?"

Chacey went on to give Mike the information she had.

"I don't like this, Chacey. Where did you get this information?"

"I can't tell you that right now, but the source is reliable. I'm still working on a few things. I'll let you know more as soon as I can. Trust me, Mike."

Mike grumbled, and Chacey could imagine him running his hand over his bald head like he always did when he didn't like something. "All right, I'll do some checking and I'll get back to you as soon as I know anything. And, Chacey, try to be careful. I don't like this. You should at least tell me where the hell you are."

"I'll do the best I can, Mike. I'm sorry I can't give you more," Chacey said sincerely. "If you get anything, call my cell."

"Okay then. I'm on it."

Chacey was relieved to finally be doing something. Watching the fear wrack Elaine during her hypnosis had been almost too much to handle, and Chacey felt like breaking things. She wanted someone to answer for what had been done to Elaine. She trusted Mike. He would come through. She just hoped Elaine's recollection was enough to change the course of the investigation and finally get some real answers.

She closed her eyes when Elaine turned and pressed her face against her chest, wrapping her arms around her. Elaine pressed a kiss just above her breast and said, "Thank you."

Chacey kissed the top of her head.

❖

Christian sat in her apartment staring at the television screen. She couldn't believe the image she saw there. Cara sat in the very same room looking back at her, smiling. Her voice was happy.

Hello, love. I know this must seem a little weird, but I know you, and I need to know you're okay. Since you're viewing this, it means I am no longer with you. I'm sorry for that. I wanted us to grow old together. I was looking forward to seeing you change and grow throughout a lifetime. But it looks like that wasn't to be.

I hope I've always shown you and told you how very much I love you. More than that, I need you to know how very loved you've made me feel. I'm thankful for every day I've had with you. I never knew happiness like I've known with you. I couldn't have asked for a better life.

Now, baby, it's time for you to get to work. I can't imagine what I'd have done if you had gone before me, but I know it would have been hard to live without you. But you have to, sweetheart. You have so much to give. The love you have in your heart is too precious to waste.

The message continued. True to form, Cara made her laugh despite her grief. She brought back the memories of the joy of their lives together, and somehow, Christian was able to say good-bye.

It was as if Cara had known. As if in answer to a prayer, she had gotten her one last moment with her love after all. She had come home to face the past and find truth, and Cara had shown her the way. Christian felt something settle inside her. All the guilt she had carried began to melt away when she accepted that Cara wanted her to go on with her life.

Christian shook her head. Cara was right. She was wasting precious time, and she knew exactly what to do now.

❖

Chacey opened the door to the restaurant and placed her hand gently on Elaine's back, following her inside. A waiter led them to a balcony overlooking the Tennessee River. It was nice to be outside for a change. They had spent most of their time since Chacey's arrival inside the hotel, and Chacey was eager for the fresh air and sunshine.

Elaine sat looking out over the water, her face peaceful and serene. The city lay along the shore framed by the majestic mountains towering in the background.

"What?" Elaine asked playfully.

Chacey chuckled. "It's nice to see you so relaxed. I'd say you even look happy."

Elaine turned to face Chacey squarely and reached across the table to take her hand. Leaning in slightly, holding Chacey's gaze, she said, "I am happy." Smiling broadly, she squeezed Chacey's fingers.

The waiter returned with two tall glasses filled with an icy blue mixture.

Chacey laughed. "Oh my goodness! I haven't had one of these in years. Remember that trip we took to the beach and you entered that karaoke contest…"

Elaine laughed. A faint buzzing noise caught Chacey's attention and she pulled her phone from her pocket. It was Mike. She hated the intrusion and knew it would dampen Elaine's joy. "Do you mind if I take this call? It's my partner. He may have some new information."

Elaine's smile disappeared. "Okay. Go ahead. I'll be waiting here."

Flipping her phone open as she moved away from the table, Chacey said, "Bristol speaking."

"I think we may have found something." Mike's voice sounded stern and urgent.

"What have you got, Mike?" Chacey's heart pounded and her skin tingled with anticipation.

"We went back over the list of people known to be in the building the day Elaine Barber was shot. Based on the description you gave us, we came up with a woman by the name of Katherine Marie Waters. I read through her interview and it seems clean enough, nothing stands out. There wasn't any connection between her and Ms. Barber other than working in the same building. She was a new employee, working as a security analyst for a company on the third floor. They were doing some restructuring of the security system, and that's why the cameras were turned off. Most people in the building didn't even know her since she had only been there for less than a week."

Chacey could hardly control her excitement. They had a name. "That's great, Mike. Where is she now?"

"That's just the thing, Chacey, we're tracking her down now, but it could take a while. She's no longer in the area and didn't give a forwarding address. But she'll be in the system somewhere. We'll find her."

"Then she could be anywhere. Damn it!" Chacey cursed and began to pace the hallway outside the restroom.

"Chacey, I don't like this. You really need to tell me where you are. If you're in the middle of this, let me help you." When Chacey didn't answer, he said, "It's me, Chace. Trust me."

Chacey thought about her promise to Elaine. She didn't want to do anything to pressure her or make her pull away. But now that she had Elaine back, her first priority was to keep her safe, and that meant doing her job and finding the shooter. "All right, Mike. But I want this low profile. Understand? I can't afford to have anyone blow this."

"I understand. I'll see to it myself."

❖

Elaine studied Chacey as she worked her way through the crowd on her way back to the table. Her shoulders were tense and she had the look of a warrior about to go into battle—or one who carried bad news. Chacey sat in her chair and heaved a sigh.

"What is it?" Elaine asked, mentally preparing herself for the worst.

"Mike found the name of someone in the building matching the description you gave us. They're tracking her down now, but we don't have a current location."

Elaine's brow creased in frustration as she took in the information. "Well, that just leaves us at the same dead end we were at three years ago. I'll just have to keep working and hope the hypnosis continues to give us more." Elaine felt a little sick to her stomach, but seeing the look of frustration and despair on Chacey's face made her want to treat everything as if it was no big deal. She had let the shooting come between them once, and she was determined not to let that happen again.

"What was the name they found?" Elaine asked suddenly. "It's supposed to be someone I know. Perhaps I will recognize the name and be able to give you more information."

Chacey looked hopeful. "Katherine Marie Waters."

Elaine searched her memory for anyone in her life by that name. It definitely wasn't one of her friends or anyone she knew from work. "I don't know, Chacey. The name isn't familiar to me. I know it isn't a friend or colleague, but there's no way I could know if she was somehow connected to one of my private clients. There could be any number of people related to clients that wouldn't be listed in any of my files."

"But that tells me you must have known her by some other name. Like you said, this is supposed to be someone you know. You said you were surprised to see them at your office, remember? That tells me it's someone from your personal life or connected to your work for the FBI."

Elaine sighed. "I'm sorry, Chacey. I want to remember. I just can't."

Chacey took Elaine's hand in both of hers. "Listen to me. We're going to figure this out. Together. Okay?"

"I know, sweetheart. I know." Elaine pulled her hand free, taking Chacey's hand and giving it a little squeeze. "I guess that leaves us no choice now but to enjoy our dinner. This place is so beautiful, and the day is too perfect to let this thing ruin it for us."

Chacey smiled. "You're right. Okay. Change of subject. You know, I'm dying to see what Willow Springs is like. I can't believe you still haven't taken me there."

Elaine averted her gaze from Chacey, who chuckled at her obvious hesitation.

"It's okay, sweetheart. I understand you want to take things slow. I get it. Willow Springs has been your safe place, and I don't want to intrude."

Elaine shook her head. "It isn't that you would be intruding, Chace. I'm just not ready to let go of that small bit of anonymity I have. You're right. Willow Springs has been my safe place. It has been the only place where I've felt sheltered from all the fears that haunt me. It isn't that I don't want to share it with you, it's just that I'm not ready to let go of the one place on earth where I can go and the world doesn't follow."

"It's okay. Really, Elaine, just having you back in my life is enough. But I can't help but be curious. We once planned to experience Willow Springs together. I haven't forgotten."

Elaine took in a deep breath. "What did I ever do without you?"

"You never have to figure that one out. I'm never leaving you again."

Elaine smiled. "Well. Come to think of it, I suppose I will be needing a date for the dance."

Chacey frowned. "What dance?"

"Oh, they have a ball every summer. I've always gone alone and no one will expect you. I can't wait to see the looks on everyone's faces when they see us together. I will be the queen of the ball."

Chacey laughed. "That's my girl."

CHAPTER TWENTY-FIVE

Karen sat on a park bench on the river walk, peering onto the deck of the restaurant. She'd followed Chacey from the hotel when she saw her leave with Elaine Barber. At first, she'd thought about trying to follow them inside but spotted this view from the landing and knew she would be able to observe without risking being seen.

This wasn't the first time she had followed Chacey, but this was the first time she had seen her with Elaine since the shooting. A pain began to throb in her temple. Elaine always got in the way of Chacey's happiness. Why couldn't she just go away and leave Chacey alone?

Chacey looked troubled. Karen watched her brief exchange with Elaine and saw Chacey leave the table. Elaine must have said something to upset her. Karen watched the door, but Chacey didn't leave the building. Karen seethed as she sat staring at Elaine. Why was she back? What if Elaine had remembered?

Karen glanced around her and nervously pulled the hat she was wearing down a little lower over her eyes. No one was watching her. But why would they be? No one knew she was here, and it wasn't like she didn't know how to change her appearance when she didn't want to be noticed.

She had to put a stop to this. She had to set Chacey free once and for all. And this time, she would make sure Elaine Barber didn't come back.

❖

Elaine strode into the parlor at Willow Springs at eight o'clock with the intent of gathering clothes and other things she needed to refresh. She had agreed to meet Chacey back at the hotel for breakfast in the morning.

"Good evening, Ms. Barber. It's good to see you," Hannah said as she climbed down from a ladder where she had been hanging decorations.

"Thank you. How are the plans for the ball going? Looks like you have everything well under way."

Hannah grimaced. "I just don't know how we'll manage to get everything done by Friday. Every year I go through this, and just when I think there's no way we'll be ready, it's like everything just magically happens."

"Well, I think you do a wonderful job. You always pull through." Elaine was smiling at the unusually disheveled look about Hannah. Her ponytail had fallen at some point and hung limp against her back, and she had a smudge of dust on her left cheek. She looked positively delightful.

"You aren't trying to do all the work yourself, are you?" Elaine asked skeptically.

"Oh no, Alex has been helping as much as she can, and the rest of the staff are doing their parts as well. I just get a little carried away sometimes."

Elaine became thoughtful at the mention of Alex. She hadn't heard anything from Christian since her sudden departure. She wondered now how her friend was doing and how Alex was dealing with her sudden absence. She'd been so wrapped up in the changes going on in her own life that she hadn't thought about anything else. The realization made her feel a little guilty—and concerned for Christian.

"Has there been any word from Christian?" Elaine asked.

Hannah sighed. "No. To be honest, I'm a little worried about her. She said she'd be returning, but we haven't received any word at all from her."

"How is Alex?"

Hannah glanced over her shoulder toward the ballroom. She shrugged one shoulder slightly and drew in a heavy breath. As she exhaled her shoulders seemed to slump a little. "She tries to put up a good front, but I can tell she misses her. She's been spending a lot of time around here lately. I think she just wants to be here in case Christian returns or calls or *something*."

Elaine thought of the talk she'd had with Christian before she'd left. Christian seemed in such turmoil about her feelings for Alex and her unresolved loss of her lover. Elaine knew these were complicated issues that wouldn't be solved easily, and she hoped her friend was okay.

"Well, perhaps we will hear something soon." Elaine looked about the familiar room, searching for the familiar face she knew she wouldn't see. She had the odd feeling someone else had entered while they were chatting, that they were being watched. Seeing no one around, she dismissed the thought, but decided it was time to head to her room.

She loved being with Chacey at the hotel, but they'd both needed an evening apart. Chacey had some things to catch up on with work, and Elaine knew the call from the FBI earlier had her distracted. Elaine herself had been more rattled by the call than she had admitted and had wanted to retreat to the safety of Willow Springs. Now here, though, she felt a little lonely and missed the comfort of having her lover with her.

"Have I missed anything exciting while I've been away?"

"Nothing much. We did have a new guest arrive while you were out. She's a little different from our usual guests, not really the outdoorsy type. She seems pretty intense. I don't know much about her yet, and she's mostly kept to herself so far."

Elaine paused. "That's odd. You usually win everyone over immediately with your sweet charm."

Hannah stepped away from the work she was doing. "I don't think she's here to make friends. She made me a little nervous, to tell the truth."

Elaine studied Hannah's expressions as she talked. Her body language was unusually tense. Something had definitely put Hannah on edge, and that made Elaine uneasy.

"Well, I'm sure she has her reasons for being here. Just like the rest of us." Elaine forced a smile. "I think I'll turn in for the evening. Good luck with the decorations."

"Oh, there was one more thing," Hannah said, stopping Elaine as she turned to leave. "I got a weird phone call earlier."

Elaine's hands clenched into fists at her sides. "What kind of call?"

"Well, a woman called, asking if you were a guest here. I didn't give her any information, of course, and explained that all client information was confidential. But then she got really upset with me and became a little confrontational. Something about the tone in her voice and her evasiveness made me uneasy."

"Evasiveness, what do you mean?"

"Well, when I asked her name, she wouldn't tell me who she was despite her claim that she was a friend of yours. Anyway, I thought it was something you should know about."

A cold chill settled over Elaine, and she felt the desperate instinct to run. She drew a ragged breath and searched her mind for a plan. Trying to hide her panic, she turned to Hannah. "Thank you for letting me know about this, Hannah. I don't know what it means, but I think it's important. Please let me know if anything else unusual happens, anyone asking questions about me in any way. Okay?"

"Yes, ma'am."

❖

Karen relaxed in a vanilla-scented bubble bath, contemplating her evening. She had watched Elaine leaving the hotel and been pleasantly surprised that Chacey wasn't with her. Maybe Elaine wasn't getting inside Chacey's head so easily, after all. Chacey only thought she loved Elaine, but Karen knew Chacey really wanted *her*. She'd had the sudden urge to run Elaine down with her car. But it would have been too risky. There were too many cars around, and she might have missed. There could be no more mistakes.

She'd watched Elaine get into a black sedan with a round logo on the side. It looked like a rental. She'd been about to follow Elaine when, as luck would have it, the car turned and headed straight toward her. As the car passed she'd read the logo on the door. Willow Springs Resort. She smiled, remembering the moment with satisfaction. She wouldn't need to follow Elaine. She already knew where to go. She could stay put and focus on her real interest, Chacey.

❖

This new information had shaken Elaine. She didn't know what to think about the call. Since the shooting, she always took extra precautions to protect her privacy, especially when she was at Willow Springs. She had no friends. Christian was the only person she could think of besides Chacey who would have called her, and they both knew how to reach her. No. This didn't feel right.

Once in her room, Elaine bolted the door and called Chacey. She couldn't risk either of them being in danger. It was time for Chacey to come to Willow Springs.

As the phone rang, her sense of unease continued to grow and she began to pace back and forth across the floor by her bed. When Chacey answered on the third ring, Elaine was almost in a panic. "Oh, thank God, Chacey, you're there."

"What's happened? Are you okay?"

"Yes, darling. I'm okay, but there's been someone calling Willow Springs asking if I'm a guest here. Chacey, no one knows I'm here. No one should be calling for me. What does this mean?"

Chacey's voice was hard when she answered. "I don't know, sweetheart, but I don't want you alone. I need to be with you. I need to keep you safe."

"I know. I feel the same way. I don't want to be alone. And I don't want you to be alone. Are you ready to come to Willow Springs?"

"Of course. I'll come tonight."

Elaine gave Chacey the directions to Willow Springs and then called down to let Hannah know to be expecting her. Then Elaine paced some more, anxiously waiting for Chacey to be safe in her arms.

❖

Chacey made good time getting herself cleared out of the hotel and finding Willow Springs. She arrived only two hours after Elaine had called. When she entered the room, she breathlessly grabbed Elaine and squeezed her tight, needing the reassurance of touch. She stroked Elaine's back and fought back the bile that had been seething in her stomach since Elaine's call.

After a few moments, Chacey pulled away reluctantly and peered into Elaine's eyes, searching for any sign of the demons that had separated them for so long. She saw only love. Chacey chuckled in relief. "Look at us. I feel like my legs are rubber. I've been freaked out since receiving your call. God, Elaine, I'm so glad you called. I don't ever want to be separated from you again. Not ever."

Elaine brushed her hand along Chacey's jaw. "I know, sweetheart. At least we're safe here. You can stay with me, I've already made the arrangements. You don't have to worry."

Chacey led Elaine to the small sofa, and as they sat close, their bodies cleaving to one another, Chacey wondered how she had ever existed without Elaine and how she would keep her safe.

"How could someone have traced me here?" Elaine whispered, as if afraid to express the thoughts aloud. "The arrangements for my stay at Willow Springs are extremely confidential, and I have it worked out that no one ever knows where I am. In three years no one has ever found me here."

"I know," Chacey said emphatically. "I kept up with you myself for a while, and it was as if you would vanish for months at a time." Chacey broke eye contact with Elaine as she realized she had just confessed to following her. She wondered how Elaine would take this information.

Elaine reached out a hand and grasped her arm, drawing her gaze. "Thank you for never giving up on me."

Chacey smiled and shook her head, deeply relieved. "You are my love. I will never stop fighting for you as long as I draw breath and my heart continues to beat. And I don't know how, but it seems someone is trying very hard to find you. I don't like it."

"There's something else. Hannah told me about a new guest that arrived while I was at the hotel with you. Something about the woman troubles Hannah. It might not mean anything, but I don't like it."

"I'll look into it. And I know you aren't going to like *this*, but I'm going to have to call Mike. I have to let them know what's happening here."

Elaine nodded.

"Good. Now let's get started."

CHAPTER TWENTY-SIX

Christian checked her watch again as she gathered up her bags. She took a final sweep of the condo, making sure all appliances had been turned off and all windows were locked. Pausing at the bookcase, she ran a finger across a picture of Cara smiling from the still photo. *I love you, Cara. Thank you for knowing how to love me.*

Heaving a heavy sigh, Christian picked up her messenger bag and her keys. Closing and locking the door behind her, she knew she was not running away from her life this time, but was walking straight ahead into her future. She still didn't know what was in store for her, but for the first time since Cara's death, she felt ready to live again.

The cab sat at the curb waiting for her. When she'd settled into the seat, she was surprised by the voice greeting her.

"Hello. We meet again."

Christian looked up into the gentle eyes of the cabbie who had driven her to the cemetery and then home, over a week before. He sat with his arm thrown over the back of the seat so that he could face her, instead of looking at her in the rearview mirror's reflection. Christian smiled at the man warmly, feeling comforted that he should be the one to send her out on the next leg of her journey.

"I see you found your answers," he said jovially. "The light has returned to your eyes. You no longer carry your burden."

Christian looked back up at the stone steps and the big wood-and-glass door that led to her apartment. "Yes. I suppose I have."

"Very good. Where can I take you today?"

"The airport, please."

"The airport it is," he said with a hearty laugh. "It's a good day for an adventure."

Christian sat back and watched the city flash by her window, a smile edging the corners of her mouth. She was returning to Alex. "Yes, it is."

❖

Christian felt strong and confident as she stepped through the doors of Willow Springs. Unlike her first arrival, when she'd come looking for answers about her past, now she was seeking her future. She hadn't notified anyone she was returning and was surprised when Hannah ran to her, threw her arms around her, and exclaimed, "You're back!" The welcome only solidified Christian's belief that she had been right to come back. She smiled when Hannah released her and gave her a quick appraisal.

"Oh my goodness, Christian, you look great. We've been so worried about you!"

Christian laughed. "It's good to be back. I'm sorry I worried you."

"Oh, Alex is going to be so relieved that you're back. Bless her heart, she's been here every day since you left, and—"

"Wait, Hannah. I don't want you to tell Alex I'm back just yet. I have something else in mind."

Hannah looked at Christian questioningly, her brow furrowed in confusion.

"Trust me on this, Hannah. Just give me a little more time. Is Alex here now?"

Hannah looked over her shoulder toward the ballroom. "I think she left a couple of hours ago. She's been helping with the decorations for the ball tomorrow."

"Good." Christian loved Hannah for worrying about Alex and for her generous heart. She was always trying to protect others. "Is Alex planning to come to the dance?"

"Yes."

"Very good. Is Elaine here?"

"Yes, she's here. She has a new friend staying with her. I believe they're out on the patio by the pool."

So Chacey was here. An interesting development. Christian couldn't wait to catch up with her friend. But not tonight. "If you don't mind, can I have some food brought up to my room? I think I'd like to have the evening alone, and I still haven't had dinner."

Hannah nodded.

"And will you keep my secret just a little while? It will only be until tomorrow. I promise."

Hannah took in a deep breath, "Of course. Whatever you need."

Christian leaned in and kissed Hannah's cheek. "Thank you."

❖

Chacey escorted Elaine down the elegant staircase, her arm held formally at an angle with Elaine's hand resting lightly at her elbow. Chacey thought her heart would burst with pride when they entered the ballroom and all the guests turned to look at them. She knew they still had much to overcome in rebuilding their relationship, but the weight of Elaine's hand on her arm and the sway of her body with each step reminded her that they were moving forward into their future together. Chacey could hear the hushed whispers of surprise as Elaine strode into the room, her hair pulled up at the back with loose auburn curls framing her porcelain skin. Her dress was a formfitting black silk that cut sharply across her chest, revealing the delicate skin and bold prominence of her collarbones. Over the dress, she wore an equally elegant long black silk Asian dress coat that matched the delicate cut of her dress, embroidered with red poppies down the right sleeve and, at an angle, down the length of the garment.

Chacey leaned in and whispered, "You really are the belle of the ball."

Elaine smiled broadly and squeezed Chacey's arm. She was simply beaming.

Chacey scanned the room, letting her eyes drift across the many faces looking back at them. She noted the various doors leading to different parts of the building and exits leading out to the courtyard. There was no way for her to keep an eye on all of them.

They paused when Hannah stepped forward and greeted them warmly and escorted them to their table. "You look beautiful tonight, Ms. Barber," Hannah said as she pushed in Elaine's chair and nodded across at Chacey.

"Thank you," Elaine said.

Elaine looked around the room, scanning the faces she knew from Willow Springs and those who were strangers. She felt she was among family as she took in the smiles and warmth of the women around her. The room was beautifully decorated with tables covered in silver tablecloths adorned with fishbowls of floating candles surrounded with magnolia blooms. Elaine drew in the fragrance of the flowers, and her skin tingled. But there was nothing more beautiful than the woman beside her. Chacey wore a black velvet tuxedo jacket with satin lapels over a bright red camisole that matched the embroidery on Elaine's dress. Her black cotton crepe pants showed off her slim, athletic figure. The image was so perfect Elaine couldn't stop touching her, wanting to feel the promise flowing between them. They were together at last.

Continuing her survey of the room, Elaine saw Alex standing alone at the bar, and she wondered where her dear friend Christian was on this night. She owed so much to Christian and her friendship, and she felt a little sad that she wasn't there with them. She wished Christian and Alex had been able to find happiness together the way she had found hers with Chacey.

The room seemed alive with the gentle murmur of voices. A band was set up at the opposite end of the room, and the center was clear of chairs and tables to allow for a dance floor. As the band changed songs, Chacey leaned in and asked, "Would you like to dance with me?"

Elaine met her gaze and her heart skipped a beat. She had barely been able to make herself leave their room once she had seen Chacey in the black tuxedo, and now all she could think about was methodically undressing her. Desire coursed through her, and she felt the telltale heat of arousal and need.

Chacey smiled knowingly and held out her hand to Elaine as she stood.

Elaine took the offered hand and followed Chacey to the dance floor. She leaned into Chacey's arms and allowed the familiar embrace to flood her with teasing anticipation of the hours to come when they would be alone and she could show Chacey the depth of her need for her. In that moment she felt like the princess in a fairy tale, holding her happily-ever-after in her arms.

Chacey guided Elaine across the floor with ease, relishing the feel of her body pressed against her own. She felt drunk on love, her heart breaking with the joy of being with the most beautiful woman in the world.

Elaine brushed her hand across Chacey's chest, sending a burst of pleasure racing down her spine. Chacey growled her excitement and leaned in to nip at Elaine's lip.

"Okay, tiger. I think I need a drink to cool this down before I forget myself," Elaine said, pulling away gently.

"Sure, whatever you want. But don't think you're not mine at the end of the night," Chacey said.

"Looking forward to it."

Chacey instantly felt the change in her lover when Elaine stopped abruptly. "What is it?" she said, peering at Elaine. When she didn't answer, Chacey followed her gaze to the front of the room as she tightened her grip protectively around Elaine's waist.

❖

Alex leaned against the bar and watched the crowd of women, all smiling and enjoying the evening. But the one woman she sought was not there among the smiling faces. She had hoped that Christian would return for the dance, and as the night lingered, she felt the last vestiges of her hope begin to fade. Christian wasn't coming back.

Alex saw Hannah coming her way. Hannah stepped close to her and bumped her playfully with her shoulder. "Hey, sport. How are you doing?"

Alex chuckled as she glanced at Hannah. "I'm not exactly the life of the party, but hey, the night is young."

"Yeah. Think you might want to dance? Andi can't come till later because of work, and I thought we could liven this party up a little."

Alex looked at Hannah and smiled, knowing that Hannah was trying to cheer her up. "Thanks, maybe later. You did an amazing job this year. Everything is perfect."

Hannah smiled. "Thanks."

Alex was about to comment on the pink tennis shoes Hannah was wearing with her tux when Hannah's face changed suddenly as she looked over Alex's shoulder. Alex turned to see what had distracted Hannah, and her breath caught and her heart seemed to stop.

A tall, slight figure stepped into the entrance, looked around, and began making her way across the room toward her. Alex took in the short curls tucked behind a delicate ear, the slim frame draped with ripples of black fabric that showed off strong, bare shoulders and a delicate curve of breast. Her stride was purposeful and strong, and her gaze was fixed on her target.

❖

Christian took a deep breath as she straightened her dress one last time. She could feel the pounding of her heart in her chest and thought she might hyperventilate. *Here goes*, she thought as she stepped into the room. She let her eyes roam the room of familiar faces. She met Elaine's gaze briefly and smiled. Elaine smiled back, nodding slightly. Then she found the one woman she was hoping to see.

Taking another deep breath, she made her way across the room to where Alex stood next to the bar. Hannah was with Alex, but she could tell by the look on Alex's face that Hannah had kept her promise. She soaked up every inch of Alex's exquisite form. Alex wore a black tuxedo that hugged her muscular shoulders and tapered at the waist to show her slim hips. Her hair was brushed back with the tips curling around her nape, framing her beautiful face.

She caught her breath, and the familiar sting of tears pricked her eyes as she saw how Alex had changed in her absence. Alex was paler than she remembered and she had lost weight. Her usually strong features were now sharply angular at her cheeks and jaw. Christian held her resolve and focused her gaze on the woman now staring back at her.

The music in the room barely penetrated her senses as she made her way through the throng of women gliding around the dance floor. Stepping up to Alex, she smiled, cocking her head slightly to the right.

"Hello, Alex. I'm sorry I'm late, but I was hoping I might have this dance."

Alex stared at her blankly. When she spoke, her voice sounded hoarse, as if it hadn't been used in a long time. "Christian?"

"I know I've got a lot of explaining to do, and I promise to tell you everything. But right now, I just want to dance with you."

Christian reached out to Alex, took the glass of wine from her hand, and set it gently on the bar beside her. She took Alex's hand in hers like a delicate flower, suddenly afraid Alex might pull away from her. When she felt no resistance, she pulled Alex closer to her. When they reached the dance floor, the music changed, and the band began to play Patty Griffin's "Burgundy Shoes." Christian slid her arm along Alex's shoulder and guided Alex's hand to her waist. She pressed her face to the soft skin of Alex's neck and breathed in the clean scent of pine and soap.

Christian sighed in relief when Alex began to move, slowly guiding her across the floor. It was as if all her senses were heightened with the new awareness of her feelings for Alex, and she marveled at the feel of Alex's hands brushing across the fabric of her dress to press against the bare skin of her back. As the music rose and fell, Christian was led across the floor with such flourish that she felt like she was floating. And then, suddenly, Alex lifted her into her arms as they turned. Christian laughed and held tightly to her shoulders. Alex peered up at her with such intensity that Christian felt as if her heart could burst.

As the song slowly faded, Christian placed her hands on Alex's face and drew their faces together until their lips met. Christian took Alex into her with abandon and poured her heart into the kiss as she swept her tongue into Alex's mouth.

The sound of clapping reminded Christian they were not alone to pursue their abandon. As she pulled away gently, Alex slowly lowered her to the floor. Christian gazed at Alex, overwhelmed with love for her.

As the clapping continued, Christian found herself unexpectedly shy. She laughed out loud and buried her face against Alex's neck.

❖

Elaine's smile broadened as she watched Christian make her way to the table. She had never been happier. She had the woman she loved beside her, and her dear friend had returned to share this magical night with her. She was also pleased to see the subtle change in Christian that told her she had released some of the past that had haunted her so deeply. The dark circles were gone from beneath her eyes, her shoulders were squared and her head held high. Christian looked radiant.

Elaine stood as Christian reached out to her. She wrapped Christian in a hug and allowed yet another connection to solidify in her life. The two women stood for a moment, as a current of understanding passed between them through their embrace.

"I'm so happy you returned," Elaine said.

"Me too. You look beautiful, Elaine."

"As do you, sweetheart."

Chacey cleared her throat and moved Elaine's chair. "Would you two ladies like to join us at the table, or do you plan to stand admiring each other for the rest of the evening?"

Elaine and Christian laughed simultaneously and glanced sheepishly at Chacey and Alex who stood waiting.

Elaine looked at the three beautiful women around her and knew they would become a family. Chacey was her love, Christian was her friend, and she knew that Alex too would find her special place. In one magical night, Elaine felt like she had discovered the world and was now part of something beautiful.

❖

Karen brushed her hand across the gun to make sure it couldn't be seen under her apron. She had watched Chacey and Elaine make their entrance, and her blood boiled seeing Elaine's hands on Chacey. And Chacey had smiled like she was enjoying it. She knew things had gone too far. Elaine was taking Chacey away again.

Karen set a glass of water on the table and moved closer to better see what was happening. She needed to understand why Chacey was doing this to her. Two other women were sitting at the table now, obviously friends of Elaine's by the way they embraced. But they were inconsequential. She didn't care about them. She knew this was just an act. Chacey wasn't happy. She couldn't be happy with anyone but her.

She walked across the room, pushing a chair in at a table where someone had left it askew, probably on their way to the dance floor. Exactly what a waitress should do. She smiled to herself for her cleverness. No one even noticed her as she'd made her way through the crowd. But they would notice her soon enough. She knew what she had to do. The decision excited her. She was going to show them who Chacey really loved. She was going to save her from Elaine once and for all, and Chacey would belong to her.

She was getting close now. Her anticipation grew with every step. It would only be a few more minutes, and then it would all be over.

CHAPTER TWENTY-SEVEN

Elaine traced a finger across Chacey's hand as Chacey told a story about Elaine's fondness for karaoke and her interpretation of blues classics. Elaine relaxed as she listened to the sound of Chacey's voice. Darkness had fallen, and the lights around the pool glowed, inviting the guests to extend their festivities outdoors to the patio. Dinner was being served, and bottles of champagne had been brought out to each table. The sudden pop of a cork at the table behind them made Elaine jump. Instantly, Chacey took her hand as she leaned in and whispered softly, "You're all right, darling, it's just the champagne."

Elaine was embarrassed by her overreaction and felt the heat spreading through her cheeks, but she recovered her composure without drawing additional attention to herself. And as Chacey whispered into her ear, Elaine brushed close and made contact. Chacey's lips skimmed her neck, and she shivered with arousal.

Laughter broke out at the table behind them, and the women cheered as the champagne bubbled from the bottle. Everyone turned to watch the celebration and laughed as the Haverty sisters scrambled to fill their glasses with the effervescent wine. The shrill shriek of a woman nearby and the sound of shattering glass brought everyone's startled gazes back to the center of the room.

Elaine blinked and couldn't quite process what she saw. Standing before their table was one of the waitstaff, a slight woman with jet-black hair pulled back at the neck and fierce, glaring brown eyes. Black teardrop earrings dangled lightly from her ears. Some of the guests had scattered to the sides of the room, staring in shock, while others were leaving as quickly as they could. Elaine thought someone might have yelled, "Gun!" She registered the gleaming silver pistol pointed directly at her.

Chacey moved to put her body between Elaine and the gun, only partially succeeding since the chairs and table left little room to maneuver. Alex and Christian both stood abruptly, knocking chairs over with their sudden movement, and Alex grabbed Christian's arm, pulling her back away from the table.

"Stop," the woman ordered flatly, her voice indicating she was in complete control.

Alex and Christian froze as the gun moved slightly to point at them momentarily before the woman returned her focus to Elaine.

"I knew it had to be you," the woman snarled. "I told you she was mine. You can't have her. I warned you. You knew I wouldn't let you have her." The woman spoke through gritted teeth, rage blazing in her eyes. "You should have died the first time."

"Karen?" Chacey's voice was uncertain, as if she couldn't believe what she was seeing.

The woman shot her gaze to Chacey. "Of course, sweetheart. Who else?"

Elaine stared, frozen in place as a roaring flooded her ears. People seemed to be moving quickly around her, but the sound was muffled and seemed in slow motion. She found the contrast of her senses disorienting, and she blinked, trying to register the information before her. The shimmering glint of silver metal shook her memory. A gun. She felt the sudden jolt of Chacey's body pressing into her, trying to shield her. A sharp pain pierced her side as Chacey's elbow caught her old scar. Suddenly, Elaine's focus returned, and she realized her fears had finally risen from her past and demanded an end.

The sound of the woman's voice suddenly came into crisp focus, and Elaine could hear the anger directed at her. "I guess you forgot my little promise to you, so I'm here to remind you. Chacey is mine!" The woman had become more hysterical as she spoke.

"What the hell?" Chacey yelled. "Don't do this, Karen."

Elaine sat motionless for a moment as memories flashed before her eyes, culminating in the shooting at her office. The image of the face was clear now, the memory solidifying in Elaine's mind as all the fragments came together to make sense of her nightmares. It had been Chacey the woman wanted. And she'd made it clear she would stop at nothing to have her. Elaine had pushed Chacey away to protect her because this woman had promised to kill them both if Elaine stayed. After three years of living in fear and confusion, the sudden flood of memories instantly erased the uncertainty that had paralyzed her since the shooting.

"Chace. Trust me. Move away, sweetheart." Elaine's voice was barely a whisper as she spoke. She felt Chacey stiffen and knew she would not want to move away, her instincts telling her to protect her lover. But she had to give Chacey time to figure a way out of this. If she could keep Karen's attention on her, maybe Chacey could do something.

"Trust me. Now move, sweetheart." Elaine pressed her hand into Chacey's back, encouraging her to move away.

Speaking in a calm voice, Elaine responded to the woman's tirade. "I gave you three years. If you couldn't win her in that time, she will never be yours." Elaine gently pushed a shocked Chacey aside and stood to face the woman.

"Shut up, bitch!" The woman glanced nervously at Chacey.

"So, tell me, how did you find me? I thought I had been quite clever hiding here." Elaine's voice was deceptively calm as she tried to keep the woman talking. "How did you know Chacey had returned to me?"

"You always thought you were so smart," the woman snarled. "Who's the smart one now, bitch? I put a tracker on Chacey's car. I always know where she is. When she wouldn't tell me where she was going, I knew it had to be because of you." The almost childlike voice seemed oddly bubbly as she reveled in her feeling of superiority.

Elaine felt Chacey shift. She'd turned her body so that she was facing Elaine, her legs spread slightly apart. Elaine could barely make out the movement of her hand sliding along her hip and up behind her jacket. She knew Chacey was focused on something she couldn't see. She had to buy them more time.

"So, Karen, tell me, how has your relationship been going? I mean, with me out of the way, you must have had no trouble sweeping Chacey off her feet."

Karen's eyes flared with hatred as she looked at Elaine. "I've been there for Chacey. Not like you, always so wrapped up in your self-righteous work. You aren't good enough for her." Karen's eyes flashed like flames as she glared at Elaine. "Even after I got rid of you, you never left. I knew I should have finished you. I thought you were dead for sure, but no…you just won't…go…away!"

"So you failed?" Elaine said petulantly. "I mean…it sounds like you're telling me you couldn't win Chacey, even with me out of the picture." Elaine knew she was pushing too hard and hoped Karen wouldn't overreact. Elaine was careful not to move her eyes from Karen's face as she watched a woman with a gun drawn approach Karen from behind.

Karen's face had turned blood-red, and her hands shook violently now. "Chacey loves me. She would have been happy with me if you had just stayed out of it. But no. She wouldn't come to me. Not as long as you were alive." Karen's eyes shifted, "I did everything, Chacey. I did everything to make you love me."

"Please, Karen, don't do this. You were my friend. This has to stop now," Chacey pleaded.

"FBI," a strong voice announced, making Karen jerk slightly as if she had forgotten anyone else had been in the room. "Drop your weapon."

Elaine could feel the moment when Karen broke. She saw her eyes close briefly and then focus longingly on Chacey. "I just wanted you to love me," she said. Her face hardened, and her body tensed, and she looked back at Elaine. Elaine knew there was nothing she could do. All the time she had spent running had caught up with her. She had Chacey back and it had been so beautiful. She didn't want to let that go again.

"No!" Christian screamed.

No. Not Christian. Oh God, let her be safe. She looked so happy with Alex. She deserved a chance to be happy.

"Down!" someone yelled, and Chacey dove into Elaine as Karen pulled the trigger.

❖

Christian fell. A searing pain burned through her left arm. Chaos broke out around her as people converged on her. Strong hands gripped her around the waist and slid her across the floor until she was behind the bar. The faint smell of pine tickled her senses, and she clutched the hand grasping her waist. *Alex?*

More shots rang out around the room, and Christian felt her heart pounding in her chest as the adrenaline poured through her veins urging her to fight for safety. She clutched at the arms that moved around her and pulled her across the floor.

When the movement stopped, Alex was lying on top of her, her eyes wild with fear. She felt Alex's strong hands rough on her skin as she searched her body. The weight of Alex's body made it difficult for her to move. Christian screamed as pain shot through her arm, and Alex grabbed her. Alex drew her hand away, and Christian watched all the blood drain from her face as she lifted a crimson hand.

"Oh God, sweetheart, you're hurt." Alex's words sounded rough and painful as if she was choking on them.

She saw pain wrack Alex's face, and a new fear gripped her heart. Something was wrong with Alex. "Alex, are you hurt?" Her fear grew when Alex didn't respond. "Baby, look at me. Are you hurt?" She held her breath searching Alex's face for an answer. She couldn't bear to lose Alex now.

Alex shook her head, and Christian relaxed in relief. "Oh, thank God."

Then a new fear swelled. "Where is Elaine?" Christian asked.

Alex frowned and turned toward the space where they had last seen Chacey diving into Elaine. "I don't know," Alex answered. "I can't see her. I think Chacey grabbed her just as the shots were fired."

Christian thought her heart might stop.

There was shouting, and Alex shielded Christian with her body again. When Alex lifted some of her weight off Christian, she drew Christian to her chest as she rolled and sat up.

Christian realized that Alex was crying. The words she heard seemed out of place until she realized Alex was rocking her and stroking her hair. The words slowly began to make sense.

"Please don't go. No. No. No. Please…"

Christian pressed her hands against Alex's chest, forcing her head up so that she could see Alex's face.

"Alex, sweetheart. It's me. It's Christian. Alex, I'm okay." Christian grasped Alex's hands, stilling them, and sat up so she was looking directly into Alex's eyes. "Alex, honey, look at me." She continued to talk to Alex until the focus returned to her eyes and she became aware of Christian sitting in her lap.

"Oh God, Christian. I'm so sorry. I thought I'd lost you. I thought…" Alex's voice trailed off.

"It's okay, sweetheart. I'm here. Everything is okay. I won't leave you. Are you hurt?"

"I don't think so." Alex looked at her hands and then looked back toward the room.

Christian followed her gaze, desperately hoping her friend was okay.

CHAPTER TWENTY-EIGHT

Fire seared through Chacey's head and she felt a hot trickle on her face as she pressed her palms to the floor and attempted to sit up. She hissed as the pain sent a shock wave down her spine.

"Special Agent Bristol, are you all right?" a woman's voice called out.

Chacey blinked and tried to focus her eyes on the woman standing before her. She held a gun trained on the prone figure of a woman lying on the floor at her feet as she surveyed the room for any sign of threat.

Chacey moaned when she saw Elaine lying on the floor beside her and she felt the world tilt. "Elaine. Sweetheart!" Hands shaking, Chacey placed her fingers along Elaine's neck, checking for a pulse. She felt the strong rhythmic beat of Elaine's heart and began to relax. As she checked for further signs of injury, Elaine's eyes fluttered and then opened.

"Oh, thank God," Chacey whispered. "Thank God you're okay." She took off her jacket, folded it into a pillow, and placed it under Elaine's head, brushing her fingers lightly across her cheek.

"Special Agent Bristol, are you all right?" The unfamiliar voice was more insistent this time, and Chacey turned and answered.

"I'm all right. Are we clear?" Chacey had no idea who this woman was but recognized a colleague by her manner, even though she was dressed as a guest.

"Clear," the woman answered sharply. "My name is Special Agent Sandra Evens. Mike sent me to give you a hand."

The mystery guest everyone was so anxious about. Chacey was very glad she was there.

Special Agent Evens flashed her badge. "FBI. Is anyone hurt?"

"Over here!" Alex called. Chacey could see her sitting with her back against a column, holding Christian in her arms. She had torn the sleeve out of her shirt and tied it around Christian's arm where a red stain spread as blood seeped into the fabric.

Chacey lifted her head as she heard the wail of sirens. "Good. Someone called an ambulance." She glanced around the room. Women sat holding each other, some crying, some staring blankly, others moving from one group to the next checking on friends and helping others.

She observed the woman lying on the floor. Karen stared blankly, eyes glazed in death, and Chacey felt a wash of relief as she realized their nightmare was over.

❖

Elaine sat next to Christian as the paramedics wrapped a bandage around her left arm. Alex stood watch, keeping an eye on Christian as if she were afraid she might vanish if she stopped looking at her.

The enormity of what had happened hadn't set in yet, and Elaine knew it would only get worse later. She could still see the gun pointed at her. She had been so afraid, but not for herself. She had been afraid for Chacey and her friends. She trembled slightly at the thought of what might have happened. The horror of her shooting was beyond words, but the thought of losing Chacey after all they had been through made her knees weak, and she thought she might be sick. And poor Christian was an innocent in all this mess. Her heart ached to think of how hard it must have been for her to face losing another lover. Yes, they would all have their own traumas from what had happened here.

A second paramedic came up to Elaine to check her out. "Ouch," she said and winced as gloved fingers probed her forehead. She frowned, trying not to flinch when she saw Christian's frightened eyes flash to her when she heard the cry. "How is your arm, dear?" Elaine said, trying to sound calm.

"I'm fine." Christian smiled at Elaine halfheartedly. "Burns like a bitch, though."

Elaine chuckled. She remembered the searing pain of her own shooting. She had felt like her body was on fire, as if she had been run through with a hot iron.

Elaine felt some of the weight of her worry lift as Christian took her hand. "It's all right. It's over now."

Elaine smiled faintly. "I guess you're right. This nightmare has been going on far too long. It's hard to believe it's over."

"Who was that woman?" Christian asked, glancing toward the white sheet that had been draped over the body.

"I met her a few times at gatherings with some of Chacey's friends. We talked mostly about her interest in forensic profiling. I remember her as a very bright and tenacious young woman."

"We're ready to go here," the paramedic announced, interrupting Elaine's story.

They were getting ready to load Christian into the ambulance for transport. "Wait." When they stopped she looked past the paramedic. "Alex."

Alex jumped as if startled. "I'm here," she said, her voice dry and rough.

"Will you go with me?"

"Of course I will," Alex said with obvious relief. She leaned in and pressed her lips to Christian's mouth.

Christian stroked her face with her fingertips, and then grasped her hand as she was lifted into the ambulance.

"You'll need to come in to the hospital and have that looked at," the paramedic said to Elaine. "You took a pretty good hit to the head, and they said you were unconscious for several seconds. They'll need to keep an eye on you and check you for a concussion."

"Thank you," Elaine said, meeting his eyes. "I'll be fine."

"I'm sure you will be," he persisted, "but you still need to come in with us."

"Not a problem," Chacey said, stepping up to the little group.

The paramedic nodded to Chacey and stepped aside to check on one of the other guests.

Chacey sat down on the other side of Elaine and let out a heavy sigh. She rubbed her face with her hands and moaned. She was still trying to put together all the pieces of what had happened when she looked up and saw Elaine watching her. "Her name was Karen Wilson. I met her when she worked as an intern at the bureau, years ago. She was assigned to my team for a few months back then, and I thought we were friends." Chacey closed her eyes hard, trying to shut out the realization that she had been so close to Elaine's shooter and hadn't known it. Even worse, she was the reason Elaine had been shot. "All that time I blamed myself when I thought Charles was the shooter. I never imagined this. It really was my fault."

"No, sweetheart. This was not your fault. You couldn't have known. She made sure we wouldn't make the connection. She used her relationship with you and her contact with the bureau to stay one step ahead. She was obsessed with you. It wasn't anything you did."

Chacey winced. "Sure. Can we talk about this later?"

"Of course," Elaine said as she leaned in and kissed Chacey gently. "And thank you." Elaine reached up and gingerly ran her fingers along the skin below the bandage that covered the place where Chacey had been cut by a piece of broken glass. "You saved my life."

Chacey looked up then and met Elaine's gaze. Tears threatened as her eyes dimmed with the overwhelming relief that Elaine was alive. "I love you," Chacey said, her voice rough with emotion. "I was so afraid I'd lose you again."

"I love you too, sweetheart. Forever and always. The nightmare is over."

Chacey wrapped her arms around Elaine and pulled her head to her chest, vowing to herself to never let anything come between them again.

CHAPTER TWENTY-NINE

Ready to go?" Alex said, pushing the wheelchair into the room and grinning broadly at Christian. The wound to Christian's arm had required some minor surgery, and she'd had to stay in the hospital for a couple of days for observation. Alex had stayed with her and was anxious to be leaving the sterile hospital.

Christian laughed at the sight of her. "You don't really expect me to trust you to drive that thing, do you?" She knew the last couple of days had been hard on Alex despite her attempts to hide her discomfort. Alex had shared a lot about her past since they'd had so much time alone to talk. In Alex's experience, hospitals were just a reminder of how fragile life was, and she didn't like to remember how close they had come to losing each other.

"Suit yourself, but I hear the nurses are taking dibs on who gets to give you a sponge bath later. My money is on Mona." Alex was smiling mischievously as she held her hands up, showing Christian her palms. "She has really big hands," Alex mouthed, eyes wide.

Christian laughed and held her hand across her chest, protectively holding the sling that supported her injured arm. "Stop that. Don't make me laugh. It hurts when I laugh."

Alex stepped up to Christian and kissed her hair.

Once outside, Christian noticed the long black limousine waiting at the curb. She gave Alex a questioning look as the door opened and Chacey stepped out of the car.

"Hello, ladies, can I offer you a ride?" Chacey bowed dramatically and motioned for Christian and Alex to get into the car.

Christian laughed—gently—as she slid onto the soft leather seat and found Elaine waiting with an open bottle of champagne. "I should have expected you to do something like this."

"What? You didn't expect me to allow Alex to pick you up in her Jeep, did you? That old thing would have you beaten half to death and have your arm screaming with pain by the time you got halfway across town."

"Hey. No picking on the Jeep," Alex said with mock hurt.

Elaine winked at Christian. "Besides, you gave me a good excuse. I love these things," Elaine said, handing out the champagne.

Christian took her glass and settled in next to Alex, relishing the warmth that seeped into her body as Alex put an arm around her and pulled her closer, being careful of her arm. She looked around at Elaine and Chacey and thought of what they had been through together and wondered what they would do now that the mystery had been solved and the terror was behind them. She thought about how much her life had changed during the weeks she had been at Willow Springs and realized she didn't know where she was going from this point either.

She leaned her head back so that she could look up at Alex, who smiled down at her and kissed her nose. She didn't know what would happen next, but right now she was very, very happy.

❖

Christian stood on the open deck of Alex's cabin and watched the limousine drive away. It seemed odd to see such an elegant thing moving through the trees down the old dirt road. Her friends had seen to it that she was safe and comfortable and then taken their leave.

It seemed forever ago when she had watched the sunset in New Orleans and thought about Alex. It had been a difficult road, but she had realized where she belonged. Things had not gone as she had planned, but she was here now.

A warm hand touched her arm, drawing her back from her thoughts. "How are you doing?" Alex asked tentatively.

"I'm okay," Christian said, turning to face her. She placed her hand on Alex's chest and ran her hand across her broad shoulder. They were finally alone. Her fingers brushed against Alex's neck, and she worked her hand inside the collar of her shirt, feeling Alex's pulse thrum against her fingertips. Her skin tingled as heat flooded her middle.

"The last time I was alone with you like this, you told me that you didn't want to be with me until I was certain of what I wanted."

Christian felt Alex still, but she didn't move away.

"I'm sorry I had to leave the way I did, but you were right. And I had something I needed to do in order to figure out my feelings for you."

"Okay." Alex's voice rasped as if she was holding back a great weight.

"And I found what I was looking for. I had to come back so I could tell you that I love you, Alex. I love you and I want you. I want you in my life."

The sigh that escaped Alex was so deep, Christian thought she was going to melt.

Alex slid her left hand around Christian's waist, her fingers playing lightly across her back. With one step Alex pressed her body against Christian's and tangled her right hand in her hair. "And I love you. I can't tell you how happy I am to hear you say those words."

Christian moaned as Alex's mouth melted into hers. She drew in a sharp breath, inhaling the scents of pine and soap. Her stomach clenched and her body cried out to be touched. Her lips parted and a moan barely escaped her before Alex's mouth claimed her again.

A flood of sensation pulsed through Christian's body like ocean waves caressing the sand as she opened herself to Alex. She drew Alex deeper into her mouth, tasting her, guiding her, encouraging more. Christian shifted her weight so that Alex's thigh slid between her legs. Her body twitched at the sudden rush of blood as her excitement grew.

Alex moaned as she grew hot and her body shuddered pleasurably at the pressure of Christian's body against hers. Their thighs rubbed rhythmically against each other and Alex savored the sweeping, gentle caresses of Christian's tongue inside her mouth. She felt like she had been waiting a lifetime for this moment. Christian loved her.

"Will you stay with me tonight?" Alex asked, drawing away just enough to catch her breath.

"Yes," Christian said, her voice heavy with desire. "I want you to take me to bed, Alex. I want you to make love with me."

Alex swayed a little on her feet as her legs threatened to give way. She could hardly believe Christian was in her arms. She pressed into Christian again, her kiss promising more as she brushed her tongue teasingly over Christian's lips.

"Are you sure?" Alex asked.

"Yes. I found all the answers I needed. All I want right now is you."

Alex smiled and kissed her again, allowing her lips to savor the taste of her. Taking Christian's hand, she led the way to the bedroom.

Alex paused to turn on the bedside lamp and turn down the sheets. "Let me do that," she said when Christian reached to remove the sling that cradled her arm. Alex lifted the straps over Christian's head gently and one by one undid the buttons of her shirt. She could hear Christian's breath, ragged against her ear, as her fingers brushed lightly against the silky skin of her abdomen. Alex removed the shirt, then undid the clasp to Christian's slacks and slid them gently over her hips and to the floor. Alex knelt and brushed her lips against Christian's belly and felt her tremble beneath her touch.

"I want to watch you undress," Christian said. Alex took a step back and slowly worked the buttons of her shirt, sliding it off her shoulders and her arms and allowing it to fall to the floor. She took her time undressing, wanting to please Christian and enjoying having her watch her. She could feel the rhythm of her heart pounding against her chest until she thought it could be seen pulsing beneath her skin. Her body ached for Christian's touch.

She watched Christian's eyes roam her body, her eyes meeting Alex's skin like a caress. Alex felt her nipples harden under the want she saw in Christian's gaze.

Christian sat back on the bed and watched, captivated by the beauty. Alex's body was hard with muscle, draped with skin as smooth as silk. Her breasts were firm and round with pink nipples that stiffened beneath her gaze. Finally, Alex let her jeans fall to the floor and stepped toward the bed. Christian couldn't look away.

Christian moved in unison with Alex and allowed Alex to guide her back against the pillow. Alex placed one hand under Christian at the small of her back and lifted, shifting her farther into the bed. Their breasts touched and Christian almost came. She gasped and lifted her hips, sliding her thigh between Alex's legs and pressing into her.

Tender hands stroked her hair and wet lips played along her neck and down her chest to find her breasts. She moaned and pressed Alex's head down until she took the offered breast into her mouth. Christian's body sang with pleasure as Alex sucked and bit and played her tongue over her skin.

"I want to touch you, Alex."

"Your arm…" Alex let out a groan as Christian slid her right hand between her thighs and cupped her sex in her palm.

"This one seems to be working just fine, and I can use…other things," Christian teased, feeling Alex stiffen in her hand.

Together they moved, sliding against one another, their hands stroking and exploring as Christian learned just the right places to send Alex over the edge.

Christian felt the muscles around her hand tense and heard the catch in Alex's breath. She was close. She stroked her, following the rhythm of Alex's hips and the rapid, shallow pace of her breathing. Her fingers stroked the length of Alex's sex and slid into her with even strokes as Alex moved against her. With a moan of pleasure, Alex pressed down on her hand, taking her into her, each thrust going deeper. With a final push, Alex threw her head back and groaned as her orgasm pulsed through her body.

Christian watched Alex as she rode her hand and wave after wave of her orgasm rippled through her muscles making her jerk in pleasure. Christian couldn't believe how beautiful Alex was, and her body ached to have Alex inside her. She felt Alex shudder just before her head slumped against her shoulder. But moments later, she was sliding down Christian's body, her mouth devouring as she went.

Christian gasped as Alex slid away from her and again as Alex's mouth closed around her. Muffled cries escaped her as she ran her fingers into Alex's hair, pressing her mouth firmly against her, guiding her into her. Christian writhed beneath Alex's touch, her body surging as the pressure grew until she couldn't hold it any longer.

"Oh God, Alex."

At the first sign of climax, Alex slid into her, her hand matching the rhythm of her tongue as she stroked her. Christian screamed as her orgasm claimed her and she felt her body burst into a million pieces.

Sometime later, Christian woke to find Alex still lying half across her body, her head resting on Christian's stomach. She chuckled, realizing they had both fallen asleep, overcome by their passion.

Alex stirred and kissed Christian's belly. She looked at Christian and smiled. "You aren't going to leave again, are you?"

Christian returned the smile. "No." *Not now. Not ever.* "Rest now, sweetheart." Christian ran her fingers through Alex's hair. "Now sleep."

Alex sighed and laid her head back down against Christian's stomach. Christian marveled at how simple it all seemed now. She loved this woman, and this was the only place she would ever want to be.

❖

After a week at Alex's cabin, Christian walked out onto the patio at the lodge in search of Elaine. The sun was already getting hot despite the breeze from the water. The lake was a burst of light as the sun reflected from the surface like diamonds scattered among the ripples. The sky was a brilliant blue without a cloud in sight, a sign of endless possibilities. Christian saw Elaine sitting at the edge of the patio, her head thrown back and eyes closed as she absorbed the heat. Christian moved across the patio to stand in front of Elaine so that her shadow would block the sun and interrupt her reverie.

"Hello, do you mind if I join you?" Christian said, smiling mischievously as Elaine opened her eyes and peered at her. "I'm sorry to startle you. You just looked so alone over here, I felt compelled to thrust my company upon you."

Elaine chuckled. "Please join me, then."

Christian laughed. "I've missed you. How have you been?"

A smiled creased the corners of Elaine's mouth as she considered her answer. "Happy," she said sincerely.

"Hmm. I hoped it was like that. Where's Chacey?"

A fleeting frown marred the perfect skin of Elaine's brow. "She had to go home for a few days. She's clearing out the house and settling things at the office. She should be back later this evening."

Christian considered this information before asking her next question. "What do you plan to do now?"

Elaine sighed. "I can't go back there. The pain is still too raw. I want to begin again. I want us to build a new life together. For a while, we'll stay here. We'd always planned a summer here. What about you? Will you stay here with Alex?"

"I know I don't want to be without her, but there are a lot of details to be sorted out."

Elaine studied Christian thoughtfully. "Oh, I think there are many ways to reinvent your life. I know you love Alex."

Christian smiled. "I do. I do love her. I just want to give us both time for the relationship to develop. I have no doubt we'll figure out the rest in due course."

"So stay here for the rest of the summer. That was your plan anyway. That way, we'll all be here together, with the people who understand us most." Elaine brushed her fingers across the top of Christian's hand.

Christian felt eternally grateful for the tenderness and understanding she had found in her friendship with Elaine. "That sounds wonderful." She smiled. "You know, I don't know if I'd have been able to get through all this if it hadn't been for you. You're a good friend. I think I'd be happy if we were all here together."

"Thank you for that," Elaine said softly. "It seems we both came to the right place at the right time. You've been a great comfort to me. You're a treasure."

Christian sat back in her chair, her heart secure in the knowledge that the friendship that had been forged between them would carry far beyond the summer.

"Who would have thought we would all end up like this?"

"I know," Christian said. "I will be forever grateful for the tenderness you shared with me. You made all the difference in helping me heal my broken heart."

"It was you who showed me tenderness, remember? I was so lost and alone before you came into my life and taught me how to trust again."

"I love you so, Elaine. I'm so pleased you're happy and you have Chacey back."

Elaine drew in a deep breath and sighed, then leaned in and kissed Christian's cheek. "It seems we have all healed our broken hearts."

"Yes," Christian said. "It seems we have."

❖

Elaine worried as she waited for the plane to land. Every day Chacey had been away had felt like a heavy weight sitting on her chest, and she wondered how she had ever lived without the strength she drew from her. Elaine caught a glimpse of a familiar figure moving through the crowd, and her heart beat wildly as she anticipated Chacey's return.

She saw Chacey step out from the crowd, her gaze fixed and determined. She moved swiftly to Elaine and threw her arms around her. "There you are." Elaine felt herself being lifted off the ground and felt her breasts being pressed against Chacey's.

Elaine let out a sigh of relief, laced her arms around Chacey's neck, and kissed her deeply. She didn't care about the many people moving around them or the stares they were getting. She didn't care about anything in that moment except having Chacey back in her arms.

Chacey pulled back again and looked into Elaine's eyes. "I missed you."

"I missed you too, darling. I don't ever want to have to let you go again."

Chacey chuckled. "It's all done, sweetheart. We can do anything we want now."

"Good," Elaine said, fixing Chacey with a lustful gaze. "Let's go. I can't wait to get my hands on you."

Chacey laughed. "Looking forward to it."

In the car Elaine realized just how tense she had been while Chacey was away. She closed her eyes and reassured herself that this was real. She finally had her life back. There was nothing more important to her than the woman beside her.

"So you're sure you're okay with this?" Elaine asked. She never wanted to take anything from Chacey, and she knew it had been a huge sacrifice for her to leave her career at the bureau. "I don't want you to have to give anything up—"

"Shh. I haven't. I've gained everything. You're my everything."

❖

Christian watched the sunset from the porch of Alex's cabin, leaning against one of the large wooden posts. They had spent the day on the lake, and the sun had bathed them in serenity. Christian heard Cara's sweet voice in her memory. *Look, Chris, the light show is starting.* She smiled warmly at the memory and felt grateful to have so much love within her. She looked around and watched Alex, who sat with her head thrown back and her eyes closed, as if catching the final rays even as the sun set. Christian trailed her gaze along the length of her, feeling happiness wash over her.

She took a sip from her glass of wine and thought back on her arrival at Willow Springs and the hope she'd had for learning to live without Cara. She couldn't have imagined her life would have taken such a dramatic turn. What had started as an attempt to survive had brought her this wonderful new love.

Christian stepped forward and sat gingerly across Alex's lap, hugging her and pressing cheek to cheek. She felt Alex wrap her strong arms lovingly around her. "Have I told you today how much I love you?" Christian asked.

She felt Alex shift beneath her and Christian sat up. The look on Alex's face was pure tenderness.

"I do, you know." Christian caressed Alex's cheek. She couldn't stop touching her. "I can't believe how happy I am."

The smile that crossed Alex's face echoed Christian's happiness. "Christian, you're the reason for all my joy. You make the sun brighter, the air sweeter, and you make my world complete. There is nothing in this life more important to me than your happiness."

Christian kissed Alex then, pouring all her love into her touch. It was the perfect end to the perfect day and the beginning of a lifetime.

About the Author

Donna K. Ford is a licensed professional counselor who spends her professional time assisting people in their recovery from substance addictions. She holds an associate degree in criminal justice, a BS in psychology, and an MS in community agency counseling. When not trying to save the world, she spends her time in the mountains of east Tennessee enjoying the lakes, rivers, and hiking trails near her home. Reading, writing, and enjoying conversation with good friends are the gifts that keep her grounded. *Healing Hearts* is her debut into the world of writing lesbian fiction.

Books Available From Bold Strokes Books

Battle Axe by Carsen Taite. How close is too close? Bounty hunter Luca Bennett will soon find out. (978-1-60282-871-1)

Improvisation by Karis Walsh. High school geometry teacher Jan Carroll thinks she's figured out the shape of her life and her future, until graphic artist and fiddle player Tina Nelson comes along and teaches her to improvise. (978-1-60282-872-8)

For Want of a Fiend by Barbara Ann Wright. Without her Fiendish power, can Princess Katya and her consort Starbride stop a magic-wielding madman from sparking an uprising in the kingdom of Farraday? (978-1-60282-873-5)

Swans & Clons by Nora Olsen. In a future world where there are no males, sixteen-year-old Rubric and her girlfriend Salmon Jo must fight to survive when everything they believed in turns out to be a lie. (978-1-60282-874-2)

Broken in Soft Places by Fiona Zedde. The instant Sara Chambers meets the seductive and sinful Merille Thompson, she falls hard, but knowing the difference between love and a dangerous, all-consuming desire is just one of the lessons Sara must learn before it's too late. (978-1-60282-876-6)

Healing Hearts by Donna K. Ford. Running from tragedy, the women of Willow Springs find that with friendship, there is hope, and with love, there is everything. (978-1-60282-877-3)

Desolation Point by Cari Hunter. When a storm strands Sarah Kent in the North Cascades, Alex Pascal is determined to find her. Neither imagines the dangers they will face when a ruthless criminal begins to hunt them down. (978-1-60282-865-0)

I Remember by Julie Cannon. What happens when you can never forget the first kiss, the first touch, the first taste of lips on skin? What happens when you know you will remember every single detail of a mysterious woman? (978-1-60282-866-7)

The Gemini Deception by Kim Baldwin and Xenia Alexiou. The truth, the whole truth, and nothing but lies. Book six in the Elite Operatives series. (978-1-60282-867-4)

Scarlet Revenge by Sheri Lewis Wohl. When faith alone isn't enough, will the love of one woman be strong enough to save a vampire from damnation? (978-1-60282-868-1)

Ghost Trio by Lillian Q. Irwin. When Lee Howe hears the voice of her dead lover singing to her, is it a hallucination, a ghost, or something more sinister? (978-1-60282-869-8)

The Princess Affair by Nell Stark. Rhodes Scholar Kerry Donovan arrives at Oxford ready to focus on her studies, but her life and her priorities are thrown into chaos when she catches the eye of Her Royal Highness Princess Sasha. (978-1-60282-858-2)

The Chase by Jesse J. Thoma. When Isabelle Rochat's life is threatened, she receives the unwelcome protection and attention of bounty hunter Holt Lasher who vows to keep Isabelle safe at all costs. (978-1-60282-859-9)

The Lone Hunt by L.L. Raand. In a world where humans and Praeterns conspire for the ultimate power, violence is a way of life… and death. A Midnight Hunters novel. (978-1-60282-860-5)

The Supernatural Detective by Crin Claxton. Tony Carson sees dead people. With a drag queen for a spirit guide and a devastatingly attractive herbalist for a client, she's about to discover the spirit world can be a very dangerous world indeed. (978-1-60282-861-2)

Beloved Gomorrah by Justine Saracen. Undersea artists creating their own City on the Plain uncover the truth about Sodom and Gomorrah, whose "one righteous man" is a murderer, rapist, and conspirator in genocide. (978-1-60282-862-9)

The Left Hand of Justice by Jess Faraday. A kidnapped heiress, a heretical cult, a corrupt police chief, and an accused witch. Paris is burning, and the only one who can put out the fire is Detective Inspector Elise Corbeau...whose boss wants her dead. (978-1-60282-863-6)

Cut to the Chase by Lisa Girolami. Careful and methodical author Paige Cornish falls for brash and wild Hollywood actress Avalon Randolph, but can these opposites find a happy middle ground in a town that never lives in the middle? (978-1-60282-783-7)

Every Second Counts by D. Jackson Leigh. Every second counts in Bridgette LeRoy's desperate mission to protect her heart and stop Marc Ryder's suicidal return to riding rodeo bulls. (978-1-60282-785-1)

More Than Friends by Erin Dutton. Evelyn Fisher thinks she has the perfect role model for a long-term relationship, until her best friends, Kendall and Melanie, split up and all three women must reevaluate their lives and their relationships. (978-1-60282-784-4)

Dirty Money by Ashley Bartlett. Vivian Cooper and Reese DiGiovanni just found out that falling in love is hard. It's even harder when you're running for your life. (978-1-60282-786-8)

Sea Glass Inn by Karis Walsh. When Melinda Andrews commissions a series of mosaics by Pamela Whitford for her new inn, she doesn't expect to be more captivated by the artist than by the paintings. (978-1-60282-771-4)

The Awakening: A Sisterhood of Spirits novel by Yvonne Heidt. Sunny Skye has interacted with spirits her entire life, but when she runs into Officer Jordan Lawson during a ghost investigation, she discovers more than just facts in a missing girl's cold case file. (978-1-60282-772-1)

Blacker Than Blue by Rebekah Weatherspoon. Threatened with losing her first love to a powerful demon, vampire Cleo Jones is willing to break the ultimate law of the undead to rebuild the family she has lost. (978-1-60282-774-5)

Murphy's Law by Yolanda Wallace. No matter how high you climb, you can't escape your past. (978-1-60282-773-8)

Silver Collar by Gill McKnight. Werewolf Luc Garoul is outlawed and out of control, but can her family track her down before a sinister predator gets there first? Fourth in the Garoul series. (978-1-60282-764-6)

The Dragon Tree Legacy by Ali Vali. For Aubrey Tarver time hasn't dulled the pain of losing her first love Wiley Gremillion, but she has to set that aside when her choices put her life and her family's lives in real danger. (978-1-60282-765-3)

The Midnight Room by Ronica Black. After a chance encounter with the mysterious and brooding Lillian Gray in the "midnight room" of The Griffin, a local lesbian bar, confident and gorgeous Audrey McCarthy learns that her bad-girl behavior isn't bulletproof. (978-1-60282-766-0)

Dirty Sex by Ashley Bartlett. Vivian Cooper and twins Reese and Ryan DiGiovanni stole a lot of money and the guy they took it from wants it back. Like now. (978-1-60282-767-7)

The Storm by Shelley Thrasher. Rural East Texas. 1918. War-weary Jaq Bergeron and marriage-scarred musician Molly Russell try to salvage love from the devastation of the war abroad and natural disasters at home. (978-1-60282-780-6)

Crossroads by Radclyffe. Dr. Hollis Monroe specializes in short-term relationships but when she meets pregnant mother-to-be Annie Colfax, fate brings them together at a crossroads that will change their lives forever. (978-1-60282-756-1)

Beyond Innocence by Carsen Taite. When a life is on the line, love has to wait. Doesn't it? (978-1-60282-757-8)

Pride and Joy by M.L. Rice. Perfect Bryce Montgomery is her parents' pride and joy, but when they discover that their daughter is a lesbian, her world changes forever. (978-1-60282-759-2)

Heart Block by Melissa Brayden. Socialite Emory Owen and struggling single mom Sarah Matamoros are perfectly suited for each other but face a difficult time when trying to merge their contrasting worlds and the people in them. If love truly exists, can it find a way? (978-1-60282-758-5)

Ladyfish by Andrea Bramhall. Finn's escape to the Florida Keys leads her straight into the arms of scuba diving instructor Oz as she fights for her freedom, their blossoming love…and her life! (978-1-60282-747-9)

Spanish Heart by Rachel Spangler. While on a mission to find herself in Spain, Ren Molson runs the risk of losing her heart to her tour guide, Lina Montero. (978-1-60282-748-6)

Love Match by Ali Vali. When Parker "Kong" King, the number one tennis player in the world, meets commercial pilot Captain Sydney Parish, sparks fly—but not from attraction. They have the summer to see if they have a love match. (978-1-60282-749-3)

One Touch by L.T. Marie. A romance writer and a travel agent come together at their high school reunion, only to find out that the memory of that one touch never fades. (978-1-60282-750-9)